MADGE'S

MOBILE HOME PARK

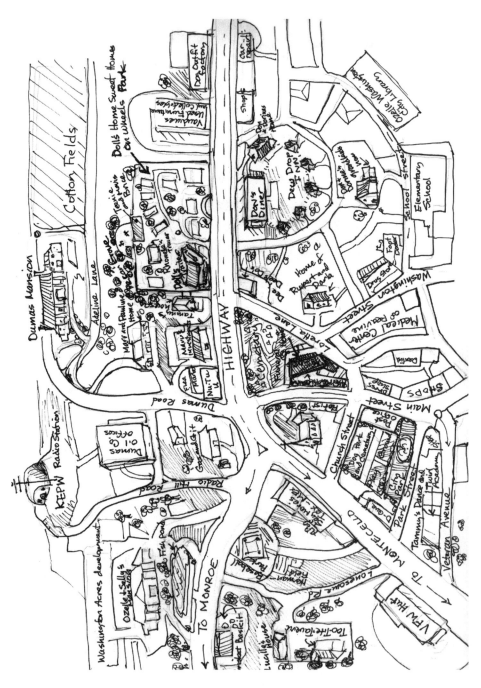

Map of Peavine, Arkansas

MADGE'S
MOBILE HOME PARK

Volume One of the Peavine Chronicles

A NOVEL BY

JANE F. HANKINS

Parkhurst Brothers, Inc., Publishers

LITTLE ROCK

www.parkhurstbrothers.com

Parkhurst Brothers books are distributed to the trade through the Chicago Distribution Center, and may be ordered through Ingram Book Company, Baker & Taylor, Follett Library Resources and other book industry wholesalers. To order from the University of Chicago's Chicago Distribution Center, phone 1-800-621-2736 or send a fax to 800-621-8476. Copies of this and other Parkhurst Brothers Inc., Publishers titles are available to organizations and corporations for purchase in quantity by contacting Special Sales Department at our home office location, listed on our web site.

This is a work of the author's imagination, a work of fiction.

Original Trade Paperback

Printed in the United States of America

First Edition, 2012
This First Edition is printed on archival quality paper.

2012 2013 2014 2015 2016 2017 2018
12 11 10 9 8 7 6 5 4 3 2 1

Library of Congress Cataloging-in-Publication Data

Hankins, Jane F., 1950-
 Madge's mobile home park : a novel / Jane F. Hankins.
    p. cm. -- (The Peavine chronicles ; v. 1)
 ISBN 978-1-935166-61-0 (pbk.)
 1. Mobile home parks--Fiction. 2. City and town life--Arkansas--Fiction.
 3. Arkansas--Fiction. I. Title.
 PS3608.A71485M33 2012
 813'.6--dc23
                                    2012005608

ISBN: Trade Paperback: 978-1-935166-61-0   [10 digit: 1-935166-61-1]
ISBN: e-book: 978-1-935166-62-7   [10-digit: 1-935166-62-X]
Design Director and Dustjacket/ cover design: Harvill Ross Studios Ltd.
Acquired for Parkhurst Brothers Inc. and edited by: Ted Parkhurst
Editor: Sandie Williams
052012

This novel is dedicated
To
My beloved husband of 40 years and counting,
Randy M. Hankins (often known as Craig O'Neill)
Who has Listened,
Encouraged,
And Loved me
All the way to Peavine and Back.

ACKNOWLEDGEMENTS

Thank you, Randy for your patience and good humor when I chatter on and on about all my imaginary friends from Peavine . . . even when you are sleepy!

Thank you Abby and Thomas for being game enough to help bring these characters to life during the reader's theater production of this book. Your voices and expert comic timing were wonderful, and made writing dialogue so much easier and fun over the years that followed.

Bob Hupp, thank goodness you said, "let's do a reading here at the Rep," after Randy blurted out, "Jane's writing a novel," at that New Years Eve Party! I may not have kept on writing without the goal of having a script ready in seven months. I know it still took eight years to finish the book, but that was the jumpstart I needed!

Thanks to my friends Susan and Jim Buckner, I was able to figure out where to put Peavine on the map, and glean such wonderful quotes and phrases that helped build characters typical of southern Arkansas; little gems like – "he's so deaf, he couldn't hear himself fart in a jug!"

I am forever grateful to the "little birdie" who told Ted Parkhurst I needed a publisher. I couldn't ask for a kinder, more understanding publisher than you, Ted. Approaching the re-write phase from the visual arts angle was spot on for a sculptor/painter turned novelist! Then pairing me up with Sandie as my editor made for a perfect match! Sandie, your literary cheerleading has sped me through the final sprint of an eight year journey, and your enthusiasm has made it so much fun, I want to write more novels!

I have so many friends and family who have encouraged me to keep on writing this story. Nothing is ever accomplished alone.

Thanks and hugs to you Dickeys; Robyn, Mary Jane and especially Helen, who was my first editor when I put some chapters up on Facebook for the world to see! Thank you to all the people who read those drafts and sent me such positive feedback. Patti, thanks for being such a sweet supportive friend. Look for your name in the book!

PROLOGUE

We are all traveling upon different roads as we move through a lifetime.

On each road, we become someone different.

We can become a blur along the highway as seen from the corner of an oncoming passenger's eye.

In one city a stranger, yet in another town, one becomes a long lost friend.

Time passes and we grow older, yet we can feel young again as we travel to new places or familiar favorite destinations.

Sometimes . . . we are merely running away.

Each turn along the way has the potential to completely change us.

Or, are we really changing on the inside, and that's why we make the turn in the first place?

*"God alone knows the secret plan of the things
He will do for the world using my hand."*
– Toyohiko Kagawa

*"Help them to take failure,
not as a measure of their worth,
but as a chance for a new start"*
– Book of Common Prayer

CHAPTER ONE

Crossing Over

Home-Sweet-Homes-On-Wheels Mobile Home Park,
Peavine, Arkansas
Just Before Midnight on December 25, 1983

White twinkle lights outlined the roofline of the largest trailer in the park. A pink spotlight aimed at an aluminum Christmas tree glowed through the picture window by the front door.

The lavender double wide was the home of Loretta Lepanto Dumas, nicknamed "Doll" by her late husband and her many friends and admirers. Much to the chagrin of the local Garden Club members, this humble mobile home park manager also happened to be the wealthiest and most beloved benefactor in the community of Peavine.

Her four year battle with lung cancer and emphysema was about over. She was well prepared to let go of this life in order to move on to the next one. Her psychic friend, Rhonelle, was constantly in contact with her own deceased granny and reassured Doll she had nothing to fear on the Other Side.

Elvis crooning "A Blue Christmas" played softly over the radio in the living room and could be heard through the open door to Doll's bedroom. Her oxygen machine was swishing and humming along. Christabelle Tingleberry, her faithful nurse and care-taker, snored gently as she dozed in the recliner chair beside the bed. A fox terrier trotted into the bedroom and hopped lightly onto Christabelle's ample lap without disturbing her. He cocked his head to one side and pricked his ears as he watched the gravely ill woman on the rented hospital bed struggle to breathe.

Doll lay with her eyes closed recalling the happy memories of the day. She was grateful to have been able to find the strength to join her friends and family once more around the Christmas tree. Her beautiful granddaughter, Tammy, decorated it for her just as she had for the past twelve years; with tiny pink poodles and silver baubles.

Doll began her nightly routine of counting her blessings in alphabetical order. When she got to the letter "M" a pesky niggling regret forced its way into her consciousness, just as it had for the past five nights. "I wonder what ever happened to Madge. I wish I could have had a chance to make my peace with her. There was so much I wanted to explain, and I've always wondered what could have happened to her. " She sighed and nudged the thoughts aside. "Ah well, I guess it's too late for that now."

Suddenly she noticed that everything around her had mysteriously gone quiet. She couldn't hear Elvis or the oxygen machine and wondered if the power had gone off. Then she realized she didn't hear a single thing, not even the sound of her own raspy breath or the beating of her heart. "Uh oh, I guess this is it," she realized in amazement. Doll was correct. At that very moment she began her journey from this life over to the next on the Other Side!

Doll Dumas Crosses Over to the Other Side

She was a little girl again, naked as a jaybird. Her long black hair streamed out behind her as she ran across green grass on a summer afternoon. All around her cicadas buzzed and sawed into a noisy crescendo. Laughing in delight she dove into the most beautiful clear blue pool she'd ever seen. Deeper and deeper she swam through the cold water like an otter until bursting out on the Other Side surrounded by a beautiful clear bright song. The voices faded to a gentle humming, wrapping around her like a soft white blanket. She felt as warm and safe as a baby in a mother's arms.

Doll's eyes fluttered open. She shut them tightly again then opened them one at a time. She felt like herself yet not herself. She was standing at the foot of her own sick bed. Surely the thin frail body she saw lying there couldn't be hers, could it?

Sensing another presence nearby, she slowly turned to her right and saw an odd apparition waiting next to her by the foot of the bed. A short, olive skinned woman wearing a long full black skirt and white blouse with a red kerchief tied around her head was standing there watching Doll with arms folded, impatiently tapping her bare toes.

"*Are you Rhonelle's Granny Laurite?*" Doll asked tentatively.

The little Creole woman nodded curtly.

"*Then I guess I must be dead, because I know you're dead. That's what Rhonelle told me. She said that I would be able to see you like she does just soon as I died!*

Of course she sees you all the time because she's a psychic. She said as soon as I saw you; I could quit worryin' about dying because that part would be over with." Doll glanced around expectantly. "*Okay, so what do I do now that I'm dead?*"

Granny Laurite rolled her eyes before answering in a low growl of a voice, *"We doan say 'dead' ovah heah. Ya did the Crossing Ovah. Ya just be changed is all."*

It took a few seconds for Doll to translate Granny Laurite's thick accent. When she realized her situation she clapped her hands in excitement, causing her to float a few inches off the floor. Granny Laurite reached up and gently brought Doll back into a standing position.

They both studied the pitiful, unrecognizable husk of a body lying in the rented hospital bed still hooked up to the oxygen machine.

*"Whew! I sure am glad to be out of **that** old body,"* Doll sighed as she took a last look around her room. There sat dear devoted Christabelle snoring away in the recliner completely unaware of the momentous change that had just taken place. The terrier, on the other hand, was sitting up with his head cocked to one side looking curiously in their direction.

Doll blew her friend a kiss and waved. *"Bye Christabelle. Thank you so much for all you did for me. Hope you like the surprise I put in my will for you."* Christabelle snorted and brushed at her nose, but kept right on sleeping. *"So long Cutie Boy, I'll say hello to Rufus and Pitty Toodles for ya!"* The terrier wagged his tail and lay back down with his head between his paws. Doll assumed all dogs went to heaven.

"It's a good thing my husband Herman Junior never saw me lookin' so puny and pitiful." Doll gave one more unconcerned glance at the shell of her former self. *"I doubt he could have stood it. Thank goodness I still had some of my looks when he passed away."*

Suddenly curious about her appearance in this altered state of being, she reached up and touched her head. To her delight, her signature fifteen inch "waitress black" beehive hairdo was back in place. She looked down and discovered she was wearing pink and purple toreador pants with a matching halter top and two inch wedged sandals decorated with big pink flowers. *"Herman Junior used to love how I looked in this outfit. Am I about to see him? I've been waiting so long!"* Doll bounced up and down as she tried to look past Granny Laurite, but could see nothing but darkness behind her.

"Where is he?" She was getting a bit annoyed by the little woman who just slowly shook her head before speaking for the second time.

"You gotta come to terms wid a few tings first, den you will see your husband, but not till time for you to 'Move On' like he already done."

A tinge of uneasiness crept up in Doll. *"What does that mean? Come to terms with what?"*

"Ya got three days to deal wid all dis . . . stuff," Granny Laurite said as she turned towards the darkness and motioned for Doll to follow.

"What stuff?" Doll stepped forward into the darkness. She was surrounded by twinkling stars. *"What stuff?"* she called out urgently as she began to fall slowly through the night sky.

"First, you gotta deal wid that stuff about Madge."

Granny Laurite's answer came from beside Doll as they began to descend into huge thunderhead clouds. Lightning flashed and snaked below their feet.

For the first time since Crossing Over, Doll felt a little afraid. Then the storm clouds parted and she could see a road below with a familiar large old black sedan. The car was driving along at a snail's pace through a heavy downpour. She wasn't sure how this could be, but she knew this was a scene from someone else's past.

CHAPTER TWO

A Dark and Stormy Night

April 1948, South Arkansas

The rain was coming down in sheets now. The only car on the road was a large luxury sedan, creeping along at twenty miles an hour, with the windshield wipers going at top speed.

A tall, powerfully-built black man hunkered over the steering wheel, squinting through his thick eyeglasses at the solid wall of rain ahead of him. Ozelle Washington, called "Mo" by all the white folks, couldn't see too well even on a good night. With this heavy rain, and the way the car windshield kept fogging up, he could barely make out the pitch dark road ahead of him. He glanced up in the rearview mirror, checking on his passenger huddled in the corner of the back seat of his boss's big black Cadillac.

She looked like a scared and pathetic child sitting there with her eyes tightly shut. Most of her heavy makeup had washed off in the rain. She was shivering. Her dungarees, the man's plaid shirt, even the bobby sox and loafers she had on were all soaking wet. Her platinum blonde hair hung in damp wavelets that clung to her face. Her only possession, a large red leather handbag, was clutched tightly to her chest. A lightning bolt struck nearby. The immediate clap of thunder caused her to jump and let out a screech.

"Miz Madge, I'm sorry but I'm gonna have to pull over soon and let this storm pass. I cain't hardly see where I'm goin." This pronouncement seemed to frighten the young woman as she clutched the purse more tightly and drew her knees up to her chest.

"Wha . . . What're you gonna to do with me?" she asked, her voice trembling.

"I just' goin to take you to the train station in Monticello, like Mr. Dumas Senior asked me to do."

Ozelle was tired of doing the old man's dirty work. As soon as he got shed of this troublesome young woman, he was going to go back and fetch his wife, Sally. The both of them could tell the Dumas family they were leaving.

Their secret marriage wasn't going to be a secret much longer, not with a baby on the way. Sally was already beginning to show a little. The thought of this made him smile. His own place and a sweet little family of his own, what more could a man want? His smile faded when he heard Madge whimpering so pitifully in the back seat.

He couldn't understand why on earth these ignorant white women were always so wary of him. It had never occurred to Ozelle that his six feet four inch two hundred fifty pound frame might seem a tad overwhelming to just about anybody. The truth was that he was quite the bookworm and gentle as a lamb.

"No you're not!" screeched Madge hysterically. "You're gonna kill me and dump my body in the river!" Then she collapsed into melodramatic tears.

"Now hold on Miz Madge, I ain't bout to harm a hair on your head. Jus' calm down now." Ozelle was wiping at the fogged up windshield, trying to see if he could pull over to the side of the road. He knew he'd better calm this crazy girl down or she'd bolt as soon as he stopped the car.

"I don' know what the Old Lady tol' you, but you don't need be afraid of me, she jus' likes to scare people. Don't you go on believin' anythin' old Miz or Mista Dumas Senior told you." He glanced back in the mirror and saw this must have gotten through to Madge as she had let up on her wailing and seemed to be considering something.

Ozelle kept up his one sided conversation to keep her distracted while he searched for a safe place to pull over. He was mighty thankful that no other cars were out on the road at this hour. "Those two folks are nuthin but a pair of mean spirited, shriveled up old crackers!" He said with uncharacteristic vehemence. "Always worryin' bout what other folks be saying about 'em."

He was amazed at himself for being frankly truthful about his employers. To be telling it to this young white woman who had been nothing but rude to him and Sally from the moment she had walked through the Dumas Mansion's front door amazed him even more.

"Sounds like you don't like 'em any more than I do." Madge said as she wiped her nose on the sleeve of her shirt. "I hate both of em! Junior ain't so bad, for a drunk, but I hate his momma and daddy!" She began cry again and wiped her nose on the other sleeve.

"Here ya go Miz Madge." Ozelle fished a clean linen hanky from his pocket and handed it to her over his shoulder. He had just glimpsed a somewhat sheltered spot by the road. Praying they wouldn't end up stuck in the mud; he slowly eased to a halt under a large oak tree.

He continued talking in as calm a voice as he could manage. "Naw, I don't hate those folks but I do have a real problem with how they behave themselves. It's just like my mamma says, 'They wasn't brung up right is all'!"

The young woman carefully inspected Ozelle's hanky for a moment before reluctantly using it to blow her nose. When she heard him quote his mamma, she gave a snort of laughter before she could stop herself. However, when she realized the car had stopped, she began to panic.

"Where are we? Why are you stopping the car here?"

"Like I told ya, Miz Madge, I gotta wait till this rain let up a little so I can see where I'm going. Jus' as soon as this storm passes I'll take you directly to the train station like I was told to do. Now jus' settle down. Nobody goin to hurt you as long as I'm here looking after you."

This had the desired reassuring effect on Madge. As she took some comfort in those words, she began to realize that she had no one to depend on now. This caused her to feel even sorrier for herself. She couldn't trust anybody anymore. Then she thought she was getting no more than she deserved after all the lies and deceptions she had come up with over the past two years. If God were to strike her dead right then, she wouldn't have been a bit surprised.

With perfect cosmic timing, a bolt of lightning struck the tree they were parked under, followed by a thunderous explosion. Madge screamed in terror as a shower of blue sparks ran down the huge tree trunk. Both she and Ozelle felt their hair stand on end and their teeth vibrate.

"Oh Good Lord Ah-mighty!" Ozelle yelled. He could hear an ominous creaking. "This ole tree is about to fall on us!"

Not only had the tree split down the middle, it was also on fire. Ozelle slammed his foot on the accelerator. The motor was still running but the back tires only spun deeper into the mud. They were stuck!

Madge was wailing and screaming, "The **Devil's** come to git me! Oh, I've been so bad the **Devil** is takin me straight to **HELL!**"

"Not if I can help it!" Ozelle shouted as he sprang into action. Practically leaping over the car seat, he grabbed Madge by the shoulders and gave her a good shake. "Now git a'hold of yourself, young Miss! You gotta help me git dis car outta heah *quick!*" He let her go, jumped out of the car into the rain then dragged her out too. She was so shocked she did everything he told her to do.

He shoved her into the driver's seat, then stuck his head back in through the open window. "When I tell you GO," he shouted, "you step on the gas real slow. You understand? It's that pedal right there. Okay now wait till I tell you . . ."

The wind was picking up. The lightning-struck tree made sounds like gunshots as fire engulfed it further. Despite this, Madge stayed focused on her hands as they gripped the steering wheel. She had never driven a car in her life, but Ozelle didn't know that.

This was one of those times when being a large strong man in the prime of life, turned out to Ozelle's advantage. He ran around to the back of the car, slipping and falling twice in the mud, and grabbed the back fender of the Cadillac. He braced his feet best as he could in a patch of gravel, and yelled over the wind and fire, **"Okay now, go easy! Whoa! EASY!!!"**

On her first try, Madge had gunned the accelerator and covered Ozelle with mud. After pausing to wipe off his glasses, he gave an enormous shove and the car shot forward onto the road . . . and kept going!

At that moment, a fireball exploded and the tree split in half and coming down with a **crash!** Ozelle slipped down in the mud and blindly rolled towards the roadside. The car jerked and swerved along the road until it finally sputtered to a halt. The car door flung opened. Madge jumped out and started running back down the road towards the flaming tree. The wind had died down and the steady rain was beginning to slack a little.

"Hey, Mo! Where are you?! Oh sweet Jesus! I've **kilt** him!" Madge was crying and screaming his name when she saw him lying on his back beside the road. The huge tree branch had fallen several feet away, and the flames were beginning to die down a bit. She fell to her knees beside Ozelle lying in the gravel and mud. "Oooooh me!"

she sobbed. "Mo, I'm so sorry, I didn't never drive a car all by myself before. What have I done to you? Speak to me! You just gotta be alive!" She grabbed his overall suspenders and began to shake him, in hopes of reviving him.

Ozelle's hands slowly rose to his mud spattered eyeglasses. He took them off and smiled up at Madge. "I'm alright, I'm alright." He began to chuckle. "I was just lyin here bein grateful to be alive and wondering how I was gonna explain to Ole Man Dumas how I let you go and run off with his favorite car!" He sat up and guffawed in a deep throated, rich laughter. Raising his face up to the cleansing rain, he began to bellow, ***"Praise the Lord, Sweet Jesus, Praise the Lord!"***

Madge was so amazed that she fell right back into the mud on her behind, and began to giggle uncontrollably. There they both sat in the pouring rain, a huge black man and a skinny young white woman laughing and shouting , ***"Praise the Lord!"*** beside a burning tree.

CHAPTER THREE

The Moving Theater

Back to the Afterlife

W*ell I'll be! I always wondered what really happened the night Madge skedaddled out of Peavine. To think it was Ozelle who took her. So why didn't he ever tell me anything? My goodness, all those years as one of my closest friends and he never said a word to me about Madge. Don't recall I ever brought up the subject though. Wait a minute! What's this place?"*

Doll became aware that she was sitting in a row of comfortable blue velvet covered seats in what appeared to be a darkened movie theater. Laurite seemed to have evaporated at some point after they descended into the storm clouds. While puzzling over how she could have arrived in these new surroundings, the aroma of fresh popcorn and a tantalizing whiff of Pall Mall Menthols drifted her way.

"Care for a smoke?" asked a voice beside her.

"Sweet Jesus, you gave me a start!"

A handsome young man with a pack of her favorite brand of cigarettes was grinning at her from the next seat. Doll couldn't help but smile back. *"Why, ah don't mind if I do. It sure can't kill me at this point. Now who might you be?"* she asked as she pulled a cigarette from the pack he was holding out to her.

"I'm not Jesus, if that's what you're thinking." He chuckled and offered her a light from his engraved silver cigarette lighter.

"As long as you aren't the Devil, then I'm pleased to make your

acquaintance." She put the cigarette in one corner of her mouth and looked up at him.

"*I'm Loretta Lepanto Dumas, but all my friends call me Doll,*" she said from the other corner of her mouth. She hesitated before continuing. With her penciled eyebrows raised and her head cocked to one side, she said, "*You're not him, I mean, the Devil, are you?*"

"*My name's Jonathan Rutherford Steele, Lieutenant, United States Air Force, at your service.*" He sat up straight, saluted and beamed a smile full of perfect white teeth at Doll. "*All my friends call me Johnny.*" He leaned back, thumped out a cigarette for himself and lit it. Doll noticed his name engraved on his silver lighter and below that was added in fancy curlicues:

With all my love – Mary Lynn

Johnny glanced down and rubbed his thumb over the inscription then quickly stowed it in his shirt pocket. "*I may have been called 'a devil' more than once but I'm just as harmless as you are, Doll . . . if I may call you that.*"

"*Sure, sure call me Doll, Johnny. You're the first friendly person I've met since Crossing Over. Can't say I would call Granny Laurite chummy. She's more like an official guide or something,*" Doll added confidentially. "*By the way, where'd she get off to?*" Doll looked all around but only saw empty rows of blue velvet theater seats surrounded by darkness.

Johnny blew out a stream of smoke as he laughed. "*Laurite has likely gone to let her granddaughter, Rhonelle know that you're doing just fine Over Here.*"

"*So that's how Rhonelle does it! I didn't quite believe her when she told me she was hearing from her dead Granny all this time. She was always right about things though. So that's how she did all her psychic readings.*

Heavens to Betsy! There are a lot of strange things to this world. Laurite was right next to me when I sort of fell into the sky. Just what is that thing there, a movie screen?" She pointed to where she thought she'd seen a dot of light disappear. Now there was only a black rectangle surrounded by tiny twinkling stars.

Johnny leaned back and stared at the same spot. *"It's my understanding that from over on This Side, we get to experience all the different points in time, Past, Present and sometimes the Future. We are the ones moving. All of Time has already happened. I call this my own private Moving Theater."*

He could tell by Doll's blank expression that none of this made a lick of sense to her. *"It's one of the advantages of Crossing Over; it allows us to play a part in their destiny."*

"Their destiny?" Doll was taken aback by that. *"And all my life I thought we had free will."*

"Oh you better believe we do! We always have a choice in whether or not to go along with the Plan." Johnny's voice rose in excitement. *"On This Side we still have a choice about how and when we Move On. We can even go back and start over if that's what we feel like doing. Or we can hang around close to the living and once in a while give them a nudge towards the right direction."*

"My stars!" Doll's jaw dropped. *"You mean we can be like a Guardian Angel or something?"* She was embarrassed to sound so presumptuous as to have thought such a thing. *"I've never considered myself as the angelic type, though."*

"That's where you're mistaken, Doll." He smiled kindly at her. *"I've been watching you, and you've no idea how much you already have done to help people."*

"She gonna find that out soon enuf." Granny Laurite had appeared, sitting in the other seat next to Doll, stuffing fresh popcorn into her

mouth. *"We need to git started on this assignment de Boss got for ya. He gave us three Live Days to get Mary Lynn to Peavine to hear de story of Madge and all de good works Miz Doll has done."*

"I'm ready," said Johnny happily. *"How about you, Doll?"*

Doll had no idea what they were talking about. She wondered what her "Moving On" had to do with Madge and somebody named Mary Lynn, but decided to go along with it. *"I'm game for anything at this point. Just tell me what to do and who is Mary Lynn?"*

The dark rectangle surrounded by stars began to waver and light up again. They were watching a middle aged woman driving along a crowded interstate as she turned onto an exit ramp . . .

Present day Mary Lynn

CHAPTER FOUR

Flashbacks and Hot Flashes

Present day December 28, 1983
A gas station just north of Blytheville, Arkansas

Mary Lynn had been traveling for about two hours now. This was her first stop since she had left Cape Girardeau, Missouri early that morning. The cold drizzle had ended, and the glow of a clear sunrise tinted the southern horizon. It looked like clear weather ahead. That was a hopeful sign for Mary Lynn, and she could use something to cheer her up about now. She got out of the car and let the southerly breeze cool her face. She closed her eyes and took a deep steadying breath.

"Kin I help ya, ma'am?" The gas station attendant asked as he came up behind her.

"Whaaat? Oh!" Mary Lynn gave such a start, she almost dropped her handbag.

"I'm sorry. I didn't mean to startle you ma'am," he said, almost bowing in an attempt to appear harmless. "You want me to fill that up fer ya?"

"Yes, please. I just didn't see you coming. Please fill it up with regular and check the tires and under the hood. Sorry about being so jumpy. I'm just not used to traveling alone. My husband usually does all the driving for me and . . . (why do I keep on talking! This man doesn't care whether or not I even *have* a husband!). I'll just go in there and get something to eat." Blushing slightly, Mary Lynn quickly dodged into the stuffy Quick Shop for a restroom visit, and to buy a breakfast of Coke and peanuts.

"I've got to calm down." She said to herself for the third time in the last thirty minutes. "Nothing bad is about to happen and it's just silly for me to be thinking that way. Come on, *cheer up*. This is supposed to be a fun adventure, isn't it?"

Despite her attempt at a pep talk, there was no denying of the feelings of dread and foreboding. Those feelings were growing stronger the closer she got to the Blytheville exit on I-55. At age fifty-seven Mary Lynn was not so energetic anymore. She could not remember the last time she had driven such a long distance from home by herself. She wondered what had possessed her to go tearing off on such an ambitious road trip all alone. It would be nice to see Lizzie again, but still . . .

Her husband, Leroy, had left the day after Christmas for his annual reunion with his hunting buddies at their duck club down in Stuttgart, Arkansas. For five testosterone-filled days they would indulge in typical male bonding by blasting poor little ducks out of the sky and watching football bowl games on TV.

Her daughter had to leave on Christmas Eve morning with her family because both of her little girls had come down with the flu. Her son had not been there at all as he was spending the holidays with his new girlfriend's family in Memphis. Yesterday at lunch Mary Lynn had sat alone over a plate of leftovers, feeling sad and abandoned. There ought to be more to her Christmas holidays than this. Without warning, a wave of unwelcome memories from her youth began to circle her mind. Determined not to indulge in melancholy she decided to call to her cousin Lizzie down in Monroe, Louisiana.

Lizzie was the only relative she had left. She had been more like a younger sister than a cousin to Mary Lynn since childhood. Their mothers were sisters and both claimed to be widows. Actually

Mary Lynn's father had disappeared during the height of the Great Depression and was presumed dead, out of convenience. Lizzie's father was quite a bit older than her mother and had died when Lizzie was only five. The two cousins had been close all their lives, and whenever Mary Lynn was feeling down or troubled she knew she could turn to Lizzie.

Out of the blue, an idea struck her, and with it a long lost feeling of exhilaration. "Why not just treat myself to a road trip down to Monroe? Lizzie and I could go to New Orleans for a couple of days. Maybe I could even convince Leroy to meet me down there to celebrate New Year's Eve," thought Mary Lynn. She got all excited and pushed aside any threat of sadness and started making plans about what she would pack to wear.

Lizzie was delighted to hear from Mary Lynn and said to come on down. They would figure out some way to drag their husbands off to the "Big Easy" to ring in the New Year. Leroy had ridden down to Stuttgart with a friend. Lizzie's husband was at a camp nearby and he could bring Leroy back to Monroe with him.

All Mary Lynn had to do was drive her car down so she and Leroy could ride back together. She would be able to use this as an excuse for her husband to buy some much needed new clothes, since all he had with him were hunting duds. How wonderful and glorious this all sounded to Mary Lynn yesterday, up in dark, gloomy Cape Girardeau. She threw the leftovers into the freezer and packed her bag. The perils of such a long lonely drive had not even occurred to her.

"What was I thinking?" Mary Lynn asked herself for the umpteenth time in alarm. Without realizing it she'd spoken out loud.

"Beg yer pardon?" The woman behind the checkout counter asked. Mary Lynn turned and jerked open the door to the drink cooler to exchange a liter bottle of Coke for a smaller one.

"I . . . uh, I sure don't need one this large, do I!" Mary Lynn covered nicely in a more cheerful friendly tone of voice. "If I drank that much Coke I'd have to stop every few miles to, uh . . . How much do I owe for these and the gas?" She grabbed two small bags of salted peanuts and laid them on top of the counter beside the half liter bottle of Coke.

Back in her car, Mary Lynn pulled out her maps of Arkansas and Louisiana. Once more she retraced her highlighted route to Monroe. She had always avoided Arkansas on her way south by staying on I-55, and crossing over to Tallulah on the way to Monroe. For a change of scenery on this trip she had decided to avoid all the big trucks and construction on the interstate by taking an earlier exit and going down Arkansas highway 65 from Pine Bluff. She hadn't planned on going through Blytheville. That would be too upsetting too many miles out of her way and too many memories.

She opened her cola and dumped the contents of a bag of peanuts down into the neck of the bottle, something she hadn't done since she was a teenager. She took a swig, smacked her lips and sighed as she turned the key in the ignition. "Nope, Blytheville is definitely not an option." As her foot touched the gas pedal she had an odd sensation as if someone was sitting there beside her.

"Come on Mary Lynn, you can do this for me can't you. It'll only take a little while."

"Johnny?"

Back at the Moving Theater in the Afterlife

"HEY, How did you do that?" Doll turned to stare at Johnny.

He shrugged innocently and glanced over at Laurite. *"I'm bound to pick up a few tips with the company I keep."*

Laurite let out an uncharacteristic giggle and covered her mouth.

"Good Lord, the poor woman already looked to be jumpy as a cat in a room full of rocking chairs, without you spooking her like that," Doll quipped as she blew a stream of smoke out of the side of her mouth and adjusted her glasses. *"Why is it so important to get her to Peavine? Is something wrong with her?"*

"All will be revealed soon." Laurite answered mysteriously as she got up from her seat. She gave a nod to Johnny before turning and disappearing into the darkness again.

"I wonder where she's off to now?" Doll was blinking and squinting in the direction where Laurite had vanished. Then she paused and looked back at the screen. *"Do I know this Mary Lynn? She seems a might familiar for some reason."*

"No, you've never had the pleasure of meeting this Mary Lynn," Johnny said as he stared at the movie of the middle aged woman glancing fearfully around her automobile. *"It's my fault she's the way she is."* He wasn't smiling now.

The images on the screen began to blur and reform themselves in a way that made Doll feel a bit dizzy. She was about to experience another scene from someone's past.

Blytheville, Arkansas 1946, Harry's Side Car Café

Johnny snuck up behind Mary Lynn and grabbed her around the waist.

"You can slip away with me a little early," he whispered in her ear. "The war's over, and we got some celebrating to do." He nuzzled her neck and planted a loud smacking kiss on her cheek.

All of the airmen at the table Mary Lynn was attempting to take

Young Mary Lynn

an order from whooped and whistled their approval of Johnny's moves. After all she was the main attraction down there at the Side Car Café.

"Stop it Johnny!" Mary Lynn giggled and blushed. "I can't leave now. I'm supposed to be working till eight thirty. You know that."

Mary Lynn was only sixteen but took great pains to appear sophisticated. In many ways she had the maturity of a much older girl. Her mother who died a year ago after a short bout with pneumonia was only thirty eight. Mary Lynn decided to drop out of high school and take her mother's job full time in order to support herself.

She had no family left in town since her Aunt Carol (her legal guardian) had remarried and moved to Monroe with her new husband and Lizzie. They had begged Mary Lynn to move to Monroe with them and at least finish school. She refused. Aunt Carol's new husband gave Mary Lynn the heebie-jeebies. She was on her own living in a trailer at the same place she and her mother had rented for several years.

Harry, the owner of the café, and his niece Patti watched over her. If a customer got out of line with Mary Lynn they had to deal with Harry. Sixteen year old girls could get themselves into all kinds of predicaments, especially with so many young airmen stationed there. Harry had promised Mary Lynn's mother that he'd make sure the girl stayed out of trouble.

A natural beauty, Mary Lynn wore her wavy auburn hair down around her shoulders. She didn't need a drop of makeup with her peaches and cream complexion and only wore a little lipstick to appear older and worldlier. Most men assumed she was at least eighteen and she never corrected them.

"Come on, Mary Lynn, you can do this for me." Johnny pleaded as he pulled her towards the back door of the diner. The table full of his pals cheered him on.

Hearing the commotion, Harry looked up from the grill. A crease formed between his eyebrows as he watched Johnny, but he didn't say anything.

"We could go to your place. I have a bottle of champagne just for you and me," Johnny whispered in her ear. The tickle of his warm breath caused Mary Lynn's hair to stand up on her neck. Champagne was something she'd only seen in the movies. She liked the thought of elegantly sipping the golden bubbly drink from a fancy crystal glass. Would it really tickle her nose? She took off her apron and giggled nervously as she hung it up and slipped out into the night, gripping his hand. She forgot there was no such thing as fancy crystal at her trailer, only cheap dime store glasses.

Outskirts of Blytheville December 1983

Mary Lynn stopped her car and stared at the parking lot of a discount store. This is where she used to live. What had happened to Harry's Side Car Cafe and the desolate place where she'd lived so long ago? She couldn't see anything remotely familiar, except for the street signs. She knew this was the right location, but it had all changed since that tragic night so long ago.

"Oh Johnny, how could you have done that to me? You managed to survive a whole big world war with nothing worse than a slight limp. Why did you have to go and get yourself killed in a car wreck? You were coming to whisk me away to be your bride." Mary Lynn pounded the steering wheel in anger. "It' just not fair!" She angrily blew her nose before turning the car around and heading back to the highway.

Time passed and scenery flashed by as Mary Lynn kept driving south. She was so immersed in her memories that she was hardly aware of where she was going. To young Mary Lynn, Johnny could have stepped right down out of a movie screen. With his handsome face and brilliant smile, he was hero and leading man all rolled into one. She had fallen in love with him quickly and completely. Nothing mattered except being with him as much as possible. It was the first time in her young life she had ever felt so excited and happy.

Getting by had always been hard for Mary Lynn and her mother. With no father around her mother had supported them by working full time as a waitress. Going to the movies and making up their own fantasies of being rescued by a handsome hero were the only escapes Mary Lynn and her mother had from their drab lives. They were more like pals than mother and daughter. Mary Lynn possessed a form of innocence that left her vulnerable to a charmer like Johnny. For a lonely sixteen year old girl all the attention from a handsome young officer was irresistible. He could cajole her into just about anything.

She knew better than to let Johnny talk her into bringing him over to her place alone. Her mother warned her of the perils of illicit romance- whatever that was!

But there he was so charming and handsome. How could she ever say no to anything he wanted from her? All too soon now his tour of duty with the Air Force would end and he would be leaving Blytheville and be out of her life forever. She had to stop him from leaving. Whatever it took to keep Johnny in her life Mary Lynn would do it.

On that fateful night, Johnny parked the car down the road by the field. They had run through the darkness the rest of the way to her trailer. Secrecy only added to the excitement.

A few months later on a warm blustery spring evening . . .

Mary Lynn was waiting for Johnny to come pick her up. They were going to Memphis that night to be married and have a short honeymoon. She felt like the star of her own romantic movie. She was happier than she had ever been in her life.

An old friend of Johnny's was the night manager at the Peabody Hotel. He was also a Justice of the Peace and was going to meet them at the hotel for a quiet little ceremony. Afterwards they planned to spend two glorious nights there, dancing and dining at the Star Dust Room. Then they were going on to Johnny's parent's home in Knoxville.

Johnny had a job waiting for him in his father's engineering firm. His family didn't have any idea he'd be arriving with a new bride but he assured Mary Lynn that everything would turn out okay. Finally she would have what she had always wanted, to be a part of a big happy family. It all sounded too wonderful to be true.

Mary Lynn sat waiting beside the small window, watching for Johnny's automobile. She was dressed in her navy blue traveling suit with the borrowed suitcase beside her. The gardenia corsage Harry had sent over that afternoon was pinned to her lapel. Its sweet exotic perfume filled the cramped little trailer.

She had counted the fat roll of bills six times. Johnny's buddies and her friends from the diner had taken up a collection for their honeymoon. To top it off, Patti had put a "wedding tip jar" out on the lunch counter and most customers had been quite generous.

Inside Mary Lynn's purse was $886.25 in cash and the blank marriage certificate Johnny had picked up from city hall that afternoon. She smiled as she remembered how pleased he was with the silver lighter she'd bought for him as a wedding gift. She had wanted to give it to him early because she was so excited. Never before had she spent that much money on a present, a whole paycheck. He didn't have a gift for her yet, but she was sure he had something special in mind to buy once they got to Memphis. She hoped he would take her to Goldsmiths Department store.

She watched as a fierce thunderstorm built up and heavy rains swept across the field. A bolt of lightning flashed nearby, followed by a clap of thunder that rattled the windows. Sirens wailed off in the distance and grew louder as a fire engine and police car roared down the road nearby. A shiver of dread slithered into her mind but she quickly banished it. She had been fearful during thunderstorms all her life. It was high time she out grew that.

Two hours went by and still Johnny wasn't there. She knew he had planned to stop by the officer's club for a few drinks with his buddies before coming to pick her up. That was probably why he was late. She waited all through the night and was still sitting by the window as the sun began to rise. That was when she saw a car pull up, but it wasn't Johnny. It was Harry and her friend Patti who was crying as she ran towards the trailer. That was the beginning of the darkest period of Mary Lynn's life.

"Okay! Now that's enough of that!" Mary Lynn snapped herself back into the present with an involuntary shiver. "I haven't dwelt on all that stuff about Johnny in years, and I'm not about to start up again now. I just can't think about that awful time. It's not an option."

Those were brave words but a sudden uncontrollable flood of tears broke loose and she was helpless to stop them. "Oh, I *hate* this! I never know when I'm gonna fall apart since I quit taking my hormones," she sobbed loudly. "I don't have anything to be so sad about now. I've got Leroy and he is a fine wonderful family man and I have children and grandkids. Why did I have to think about Johnny and all that terrible stuff now?"

This only made her feel worse. More tears began to run down her cheeks and fall on her bosom. She reached for the box of Kleenex in the back seat and fumbled out more tissue. As she angrily wiped her eyes and nose she kept repeating to herself things like "everything is fine now" and "I've got to stop this pity party!"

That didn't work very well. On and on she drove, barely aware of the towns she was passing through. At a crucial intersection the glare of the low winter sun reflecting off something shiny blinded her for an instant, causing her to miss her turn. Totally unaware she drove on in the wrong direction.

Eventually, she noticed that the highway had narrowed and the landscape didn't look right. Nothing looked right at all. Shouldn't she have gotten to Tallulah, LA by now? Then she saw the billboard:

Welcome to Peavine, Arkansas

The Little Town that "Grows" on You.

"Oh, my God!" Mary Lynn gasped. "How did I end up here?"

Back to the Afterlife in the Moving Theater

"Well now that we've got the poor woman to Peavine, what do we do

next?" Doll asked Johnny. She had several questions she wanted to ask him about his relationship with Mary Lynn.

He sensed her disapproval and changed the subject before she could say anything more. He grinned at Doll and stood up. *"Time for you to go watch your funeral."*

"And just how the heck am I supposed to do that?" When she considered the opportunity, it sounded pretty good. *"Do I really get to be there and see who showed up, and listen in and all?"* In her eagerness, Doll stood up so fast she floated up a little.

Johnny grabbed hold of her hand. *"You get to actually be there and nobody can see you. You just hang around soaking up all the Love Energy."* He smiled up at her and guided her gently back down to stand facing him. *"From what I've heard, you're going to get a whole lot of it today, more than enough to manifest yourself later on."*

"Do what?" Doll wasn't sure she had understood what Johnny had just said. *"Hey when did you get back?"*

Laurite had reappeared behind Doll. *"C'mon, you doan want to be late for your own funeral! Follow me this way"* An EXIT sign towards the back of the theater lit up over a door that was slowly opening up to bright sunlight.

Doll shielded her eyes and turned back to Johnny who was still watching Mary Lynn on the screen. *"You gonna come along with us Hon?"*

"No, I'll stay here and watch what happens when Mary Lynn meets Dorine." He waved cheerfully. *"Go on and enjoy yourselves."*

"Yeah, meeting Dorine will be a real treat." Doll chuckled. *"What a talker she is! That woman can tell you something about just about everybody in Peavine."* Doll started off towards the exit, stopped abruptly and looked incredulously at Laurite who smiled smugly back at her.

"Is that why Rhonelle told me I ought to put that bit about Dorine staying at the Diner during the funeral into my Last Wishes?"

Laurite nodded happily and pulled Doll towards the brightly lit door.

"Well, I'll be," said Doll in wonderment as she followed her.

Dorine and Dolly

CHAPTER FIVE

A Lunch Stop with Dorine

Mary Lynn's heart began to pound as she looked around wildly. "I must have made one hell of a wrong turn back there!" She was nowhere near her planned route. To have ended up here in Peavine was unbelievably stupid of her! She hadn't been through here in years, not since her terrible long dark journey after Johnny died. Back then this town was hardly more than a wide place in the road. It sure looked different now!

To her right, in the middle of a grove of pecan trees, where there used to be a bunch of old trailers for rent was now a tidy mobile home and RV park. She slowed down to read the magnetic sign by the entrance.

DOLL'S
HOME-SWEET-HOMES-ON-WHEELS
DEC 28th
DOLL'S DAY OF MEMORIALS

A wreath of white carnations hung on the corner of the sign, and various flower arrangements were placed at its base. Across the highway was a small restaurant with "Don's Diner and Dew Drop Inn" painted in pink letters across the large plate-glass window. Mary Lynn was sure that place hadn't been here back in those days either. A wreath of pink and white carnations tied with a black bow hung on the door.

Mary Lynn's hands were sweaty and shaking. As uneasy a situation as it was, she had would have to pull in there immediately for some sustenance. If she didn't stop to eat she just might pass out and end up in a ditch somewhere. Also, she noted with a growing urgency, she was in need of a restroom and cafes were usually far more sanitary than gas stations.

She turned her car into the gravel parking lot of the diner and came to a jerking halt. She wondered if the place was open because it looked deserted. Come to think of it Mary Lynn couldn't see anybody across the highway either. Where on earth could everybody be at two in the afternoon? She realized she had not passed any traffic along the highway for a while which also was a bit odd.

Hands trembling, she opened her purse, pulled out a compact and lipstick and attempted to repair her puffy, tear stained face. After a deep shuddering breath, she peered through the windshield at Don's Diner. The cardboard sign on the door was turned to OPEN. A woman was inside, standing at the window, staring back out at her.

Mary Lynn emerged from her Oldsmobile, stretching the stiffness out in her hips and knees. "I'll just go use their facilities, eat something that has protein in it and have a cup of coffee. Once I can think clearly I'll decide whether to go on toward Lizzie's from here or turn around and go back the way I came. Maybe somebody can give me directions on how to get back to Lake Providence, or was it Lake Village? Oh dear, I can't even remember which Lake it is I'm supposed to find!"

Mary Lynn opened the door to the diner making a loud **claaaang!** The bells hanging on the door handle had caught on her acrylic candy cane sweater as she tried to get in the door a little too quickly.

"Oh, I'm sorry!" She apologized as she hung the bells back on the door and readjusted her shoulder pads. There wasn't a soul in the place except for the woman standing behind the counter. She was watching in silence with eyes magnified by thick eyeglasses.

Mary Lynn self-consciously cleared her throat before speaking. "I'm planning to order something to eat, but could you please show me which way to the Ladies Room, please?"

"Down that way, on your right," the woman said as she indicated the directions with a jerk of her head while staring curiously at Mary Lynn.

Once locked in the sanctuary of the ladies restroom, Mary Lynn barely had time to put toilet paper on the seat before relieving herself. How long had it been since her last stop? Must have been that tiny gas station outside of Pine Bluff, the only one she could find with full service. She refused to fill up her own tank like those big places were making their customers do now.

After washing her hands, she patted some cold water on her face and the back of her neck. Looking up at her reflection in the mirror over the sink, she could see no trace of the pretty young girl she had been in her teens and 20's. What had she become? Who was she now? All she could see was an aging frightened face looking back at her. Her chin was going jowly. Her auburn hair kept so carefully colored was still frizzy from that spiral-wrapped perm she'd gotten last month. She straightened up and took a deep breath, exhaling through pursed lips. She had not been to Peavine since those "tragic years" after Johnny died. There was no way anyone here could possibly recognize her.

Johnny's handsome face came to mind as clearly as if she'd seen him only yesterday. This was a welcome memory. How he had laughed when she showed some spunk by demanding respect from a table full of rowdy fly-boys. *"That's my brave girl!"* he had told her proudly.

"What would he think of me if he saw me now, acting like a silly fliberty-jibbit," she asked herself. "I haven't got a thing to be afraid of. Nobody knows me here just like in Blytheville. I am a stranger among strangers. That waitress out there is definitely harmless even though she seems a little weird. Maybe I can find out something interesting about the town while I'm here. There sure have been a lot of changes, changes for the better."

Mary Lynn emerged from the restroom feeling refreshed and a bit calmer. The woman was still standing behind the counter as Mary Lynn walked across the dining room and slid into a booth beside the window. Obviously she was the only waitress. With a little starched cap perched off kilter on top of her frizzy gray hair, she was wearing a pink uniform with a white apron. Sighing loudly, she filled a glass with ice water and shuffled out from behind the lunch counter bringing along a fork and spoon wrapped in a paper napkin.

Mary Lynn noticed the woman's plastic name tag said "Dorine". It was always nice to know your waitress's name so you could seem much friendlier and get better service. Mary Lynn was real big on getting people's names right. Her eyes fell to the big fuzzy pink bedroom slippers that Dorine had on her feet. Trying to not stare, she quickly began looking for a menu. "Is it too late to order some lunch?"

"As long as it's either a chicken salad sandwich or a ham salad sandwich," Dorine drawled in a tired voice. "I'm here all by myself today, and that's all I know how to make."

"Uhmm . . . the chicken salad will be fine." Mary Lynn had been eating ham for four days now, so she decided to risk the chicken salad sandwich, praying that she wouldn't get salmonella from it. She had always avoided chicken salad from strange eating establishments for fear of getting food poisoning, but this place seemed clean enough.

Still . . . you never know.

"Do you want chips with that, or a fruit cup?"

"Oh, I think I'll splurge on the potato chips for a change. Thank you, Dorine. We girls gottta cheat on our diets sometimes. Heh, heh."

"You want a drink with that?" Dorine wasn't laughing, or even smiling. In fact she seemed downright depressed.

"I'll have some hot coffee with cream please," chirped Mary Lynn in her most cheery voice. Usually, that would bring a smile to most people. Dorine just sighed dramatically and tucked her pad and pencil away as she shuffled back to the kitchen.

Mary Lynn turned her attention to the deserted scene outside the window. She was particularly curious about the tidy, well kept trailer park across the highway. It looked like such a nice place, not at all trashy. She didn't see any people or cars and wondered what kind of residents stayed there.

The fact that there didn't seem to be anybody around except this tired old waitress was unnerving. Most things were unnerving to Mary Lynn today. She began to wonder again how she could have gotten this far off of her route. How did she lose her way in the first place? "I should have been paying better attention. Driving this far alone was a terrible idea. I can't believe I let myself get so upset. I've always heard that suppressing unpleasant memories can cause a nervous breakdown!" Panic began to rise up in her chest with that thought.

"Or I could just have low blood sugar. I just don't have enough of that blood sugar getting into my brain. That's why I was stupid enough to end up in Peavine of all places!" Her stomach gave a twinge and a gurgle of hunger.

"Maybe they have some good pie here." Mary Lynn craned her neck around to see if there was any homemade pie up in the glass shelves over behind the counter. "I just need to eat and get out of here as soon as I finish my pie." Music was playing softly over a radio beside the cash register. Mary Lynn had not been aware of it until the song ended and she heard the announcer speaking.

"That was 'Misty' by Nat King Cole, tune number 27 in honor of Doll. Next up we have her favorite dance tune 'Blue Suede Shoes' sung by her favorite singing heart-throb, Elvis, of course."

Dorine the waitress blew her nose with a loud honk and then poured Mary Lynn's coffee. She shuffled out from behind the counter with the coffee and Kleenex wad in one hand, a red plastic basket filled with a paper wrapped sandwich, bag of Zapp's potato chips and a pickle in the other. After depositing the food in front of Mary Lynn she shoved her glasses up to her forehead in order to dab at her eyes with the tissue. Dorine's glasses were so thick that Mary Lynn hadn't seen until now how red and puffy her eyes were.

"Oh dear, is this woman having a nervous breakdown, too? Or even worse, she could be coming down with the flu!" Mary Lynn wondered in alarm. "There must be a flu epidemic here, and that's why I don't see anybody out. Oh Lord! The entire town could be sick, and here I've ended up right in among them! What will I do if I come down with the flu and I'm stuck here?" One dire scenario after another flashed through Mary Lynn's mind.

"Doll never could sit still when she heard this tune." Dorine said as she smiled for the first time since Mary Lynn had entered the diner.

"Do what?" asked Mary Lynn. She was still trying to calculate how many hours she had left before either incubating flu germs or food poisoning would burst into a full blown disease throughout her entire body.

"That tune, 'Blue Suede Shoes,' Doll loved to do the bop to it and she was such a loyal fan of Elvis." Dorine's smile grew bigger as she moved her feet slightly to the beat.

"Beg your pardon?"

"*Doll!*" said Dorine, as if she thought Mary Lynn was hard of hearing.

"Who is Doll?" Mary Lynn was a bit confused, having been so involved in imagining that she was already experiencing a few flu symptoms.

"You've got to be from pretty far away to not to know who Doll is," Dorine quipped, bristling at Mary Lynn's ignorance. Then she thought better of it. "Sorry to snap at you like that, but I figured anybody who was in town today knew Doll. Her funeral is this afternoon and just about everybody in the county will be there, except for me."

Dorine's face softened a bit and she began to smile again. "I'm here at the Diner because she wrote in her 'Last Wishes' that I was to stay here and keep the place open, in case some stranger might come along and need a bite to eat. Besides she knew that I can't stand to go to funerals."

Dorine blew another big honk into her ever-increasing wad of Kleenex. "That woman thought of everybody but herself!" Dorine sat down heavily in a nearby chair and propped her pink slippers and swollen ankles up on the booth seat across from Mary Lynn.

"Forgive me, but I'm from way up in Cape Girardeau, Missouri and I haven't been down to this part of Arkansas in ages, that is if I've ever even been here in Peavine at all." Mary Lynn babbled on nervously. "So that's the only reason I wouldn't know about your friend, Miss Doll. I sure am sorry to hear she's dead. Did she run that pretty little trailer park across the street? Is that why I don't see anybody around? They're all at the funeral, are they? (Why am I asking so many questions? I sound like a blithering idiot! I just need to eat and leave this place. Maybe there is a gas station nearby with somebody to give me directions.)"

"Doll has touched just about every life in this town one way or another." Dorine sniffed wetly and then proclaimed reverently, "Why Peavine would've probably died out to a ghost town if it hadn't been for her!" She stared at Mary Lynn through the bottoms of her bifocals. "In the past forty years or so, I don't think I ever come across anybody who didn't know who Loretta Lepanto or Doll Dumas is!"

Mary Lynn could feel another one her hot flashes coming on. "Did you say Dumas as in the Dumas Oil Company?" She began to fan her face with a spare menu. When that didn't help she put the glass of ice water up to her cheek.

"Doll was Herman Junior's second wife and widow for many a year now." Dorine couldn't help but notice Mary Lynn's distress. "Are you all right, Miss?"

This embarrassed Mary Lynn further. "I'm just having a heck of a time getting off my hormone pills. I should have known better than to wear this hot sweater on such a warm day!"

"It looks to me like you should have kept on taking them pills. The Change ain't for a sissy that's for sure." She quickly added, "Not that I think you're a sissy."

Mary Lynn sighed. "It's just that my husband is a pharmacist and once he told me what those pills were made of I stopped taking them. I think it's horrible what they do to those pregnant horses." Her napkin was soggy now and she felt like she would explode if she didn't get up and cool down. "I'm sorry, I'll be right back." Once more she got up and headed back to the restroom. "I'll be okay if I put a cool paper towel on my neck," she explained.

"I'll turn the heat down. I probably shouldn't have gotten it so warm in here," Dorine called out as Mary Lynn quickly shut the door to the ladies room. Grateful for the cold tap water and privacy, Mary Lynn put a compress on her neck, wiped her damp face and then daubed under her sweater. "Calm down, calm down, I'm safe, calm down!" She repeated this mantra until the hot flash subsided.

"Dorine is harmless, and I'll bet I can find out from her a lot about what's been happening around this town since I last laid eyes on it. Besides that she seems to be taking this death very hard. I might even be able to lend a sympathetic ear." A newly cooled and composed Mary Lynn peeked out of the restroom. She watched Dorine at the counter, pouring herself a cup of coffee and dabbing at her eyes.

"Honnnk!" Dorine blew long and loud as Mary Lynn slipped back into the booth.

Another tune had started playing on the radio. "Are you lonesome tonight . . ."

"Oh Dorine, I'd enjoy having some company while I eat and I sure would like to know more about your friend. She must've been a wonderful person." Mary Lynn was trying her best to sound amiable.

Dorine eagerly scuffed over with the pot of coffee and her own cup. She plopped down in the seat across from Mary Lynn, topped off both their cups, and set the pot on the table.

After her first bite Mary Lynn discovered that the chicken salad sandwich she was eating was about the best she ever had tasted. She ripped open the package of Zapp's potato chips and popped one into her mouth. She must've been starving and not realized it until now. How else could all this taste so good?

"Well, let's see where should I start?" Dorine began as she smoothed open a paper napkin and stirred her coffee.

Madge's Mobile Home Park: A Brief History

During the early 1960's a charming little trailer park named "Doll's Home-Sweet-Homes on Wheels" opened in Peavine Arkansas.

Madge DuClaire

However due to the notorious history of the place, it was still referred to among the people of Peavine as "Madge's Mobile Home Park." To understand why it was so notorious we travel back in time to the end of World War II and 1946.

The entire courtship, marriage and honeymoon of Herman Daniel Dumas Junior to a young hussy named Madge DuClaire took place during one of his forty-eight hour benders. Herman Junior had decided to treat himself to few nights at the Peabody Hotel on his way back to Peavine after the war. His attempt to fortify himself before facing his parents and their inevitable attempts to get him married off to the latest acceptable young lady from New Orleans backfired badly.

Twenty-four hours after his first highball a very hung over and a very startled Herman Junior awoke to discover he was also very married to Madge. She was a young blonde cigarette girl he could barely recall meeting. There was a vague memory of the beguiling way she came sashaying up to his table in the Starlight Room saying, "Cigars, Cigarettes, Mi-hunts [mints]?" Unfortunately that was about all he could remember.

Herman Junior had carefully maintained his bachelorhood to the age of thirty-six only to find himself ensnared by an eighteen year old girl. However Herman Junior wasn't anything if he wasn't honorable so he decided he might as well give this marriage a try. Madge was a real dish. She looked older and acted wiser than her eighteen years so he was hoping that the age difference wouldn't present too much of a problem.

Breaking the news to his parents would be a whole nuther matter. Junior decided he and Madge should stay in Memphis for a day or two. They needed to grow accustomed to each other and their situation before he took his bride home to the Dumas Plantation and Adeline and Herman Senior. Thanks to the generous discount on cocktails (courtesy of Madge's former boss) Herman Junior was pretty fuzzy on the details of their brief honeymoon.

Who would have thought that the sole heir to the Dumas family fortune would have finally gotten hitched in such an inglorious fashion? It certainly was not what his mamma wanted and that made the whole situation easier for Herman Junior to bear .

Herman Senior had struck it rich when some oil reserves were discovered on his extensive cotton farmland in south central Arkansas. He founded the Dumas Oil Co. and Great Cotton Country Farm Corporation. The Dumas' had tripled their wealth during the war, and were one the wealthiest families in the mid-south at the time.

Herman Senior and Adeline were both born and reared middle class in Peavine, but they wanted more than anything to be accepted as high society. Ever since Herman Junior's graduation from college; Adeline had been going to New Orleans debutante parties in search of the perfect future daughter-in-law. Herman Junior had stayed in law school as long as possible to just to hold off Adeline and her bevy of respectable bridal candidates.

Horrified upon meeting Herman Junior's hardly-blushing new bride Madge, Adeline secluded herself in her room for a week. Herman Senior threatened to cut the young couple off without a dime but he couldn't bear to do it. They considered Madge trashy ill-mannered and an unfit wife for their darling only son.

After a tumultuous first few months in the Dumas Mansion Madge returned from a visit to the doctor and announced to everybody that she was pregnant. Nobody had better even think of trying to throw her out of there or she would definitely cause a ruckus! The thought of an heir seemed to soften Adeline up a little but Madge became even more cantankerous. Herman Junior began to spend more time than usual down at the local tavern.

One evening Madge decided to get all gussied up and go fetch Herman Junior home from the Tavern. Unfortunately she tripped in her red high heels as she turned to shout a parting insult at her mother in law and fell down a whole flight of stairs. Madge lost her baby that night, and spent a month recovering in the hospital over in Monticello.

When Herman Junior finally got her back home Madge wouldn't let him near her. She claimed Peavine to be the most boring place on the face of the earth. She had thought being married to such a rich man would be a lot more interesting and exciting than this.

That's when poor Herman Junior got the idea of starting up a project for Madge. He hoped he could cheer her up by giving her something to make her feel useful. He decided to fix up a little trailer park in the Dumas family pecan grove down by the highway and let Madge run it. She would get out more, meet new people and stay well out of earshot of Adeline and Herman Senior's friends. To everyone's amazement, this arrangement worked wonders on Madge's disposition. Things seemed to settle down to something close to normal for about a year.

Then one stormy night in April Madge just disappeared. Some folks assumed she had run off with one of the young men that had been staying at the trailer park. A handsome young fellow from Texas was renting there while he worked at the oil company and had just left the day before. Rumors flew that he and Madge might have run off together.

Three months went by, and nobody knew where Madge had gone. It was whispered all over Peavine that perhaps Adeline had paid that man to get rid of Madge. It was no secret how much Adeline disliked Madge. Whatever happened, Madge was never seen or heard from again!

Within three years Adeline and Herman Senior had passed away and Herman Junior took over the family business. He decided that after countless bottles of Jim Beam and numerous nights of being consoled compassionately by the tenderhearted Loretta Lepanto (called Doll by Herman and all her friends) that he knew a really good woman when he saw one.

In a completely sober moment Herman asked Doll if she would marry him. She was delighted to accept. They eloped that night and spent a week of glorious honeymoon bliss in Biloxi, Mississippi. Herman never wanted another drop of bourbon or any other liquor from that day on.

They were very happy for many years. Herman even adopted Doll's daughter, Lucille. Unfortunately the ungrateful child ran off with a motorcycle gang at the age of sixteen. While this was heartbreaking for Doll, she still had her beloved Herman Junior. She had hope that one day her daughter would return fully repentant of her wild ways.

One hot summer day Herman collapsed while out checking on his cotton. He died before they could get him back to town. Doll was left all alone in the old Dumas Mansion, sole heir to all the Dumas family oil leases, cotton farms and that old run down trailer park of Madge's.

So with Herman Junior gone to that "Great Cotton Field in the Sky," Doll liquidated the Dumas Family assets. She put most of the money into a special trust fund, keeping only enough money to pay for her expenses. Then she ordered a double-wide trailer with custom lavender siding, and moved it into Madge's Mobile Home Park. After fixing up the property, she re-named it 'Doll's Home-Sweet-Homes on Wheels' and became the new manager.

In the months and years that followed Doll looked for opportunities to help other people get a fresh start in life just like Herman Junior had helped her.

CHAPTER SIX

Curl Up and Dye Beauty Spot

The song starting up on the radio was performed by one of Mary Lynn's favorite country music singers. The announcer broke in to talk over the music: "Of course we all know who sent in this dedication, none other than Shirleen Naither. Here it is, Doll's favorite number 29, Dolly Parton singing 'Nine to Five'."

Dorine swigged down the last of her coffee, and chuckled. "Shirleen Naither was Doll's first and most famous success project, and she is quite a story."

"What happened to her?" Mary Lynn egged Dorine on with very little effort.

"Well, let me start from the beginning." Dorine cleared her throat and collected her thoughts.

Shirleen Naither

Shirleen was best friends with Doll's daughter Lucille Lepanto from the time they were youngsters and on up into their teens. That's when they began getting into some serious trouble. Both were expelled from high school repeatedly by the time they were sixteen.

Fortunately, Shirleen heeded her mother's advice somewhat more often than Lucille did. When they both decided to drop out of high school for good, at least Shirleen had the gumption to enroll in some courses at the Beauty School over in El Dorado where she could stay with her grandmother. The plan was to keep Shirleen busy and far away from Lucille's bad influence.

That arrangement didn't last more than a month or two. One weekend Shirleen returned home to Peavine for a visit and snuck over to meet up with Lucille at the Dairy Q. Unfortunately, before anyone realized what was going on, Shirleen and Lucille had high-tailed it out of town with a rough-looking bunch of characters on motorcycles.

All that is publicly known about Shirleen's "Lost Years" is she acquired plenty of expertise at riding and maintaining motorbikes; and an elaborate tattoo on a very personal part of her anatomy. She never talked much about that period of her life. Doll Dumas said that if the only permanent damage done was a vulgar tattoo, then she should thank the Lord...and that's exactly what Shirleen ended up doing. She thanked the Lord!

After a couple of years of living on the wild side, Shirleen found herself stranded alone on the outskirts of a small town over in Mississippi. She was fed up with the lifestyle choices of those biker guys and refused to go any further. Even her best friend, Lucille, had roared off with that gang of hoodlums, hooting and jeering while they left poor Shirleen standing in the pouring rain by the side of the road.

It was a cold November morning so Shirleen began to search for someplace to get dry and warm. The first place she spotted through the rain was a small building up the road with several cars parked around it. As she walked closer she heard the sweet sounds of hymn-singing wafting out the windows.

Tears burned her eyes as she slipped inside the white clapboard church, and took a seat in the back. She hadn't realized it was a Sunday morning till then, and she couldn't remember the last time she'd heard a Bible verse. By the time the sermon was over, Shirleen had run down to the front of the church to be saved and be **BORN AGAIN!** What the poor girl had needed was a place where she could get warm and dry, and feel like somebody cared about her, but the way she likes to tell it, the Lord was waiting there for her with His arms wide open. Actually, the preacher was the one with his arms wide open and he was really handsome, according to Shirleen.

He and some of the older church ladies invited her to their Sunday potluck dinner. After filling her up on home-cooked fried chicken and casseroles, they convinced the wayward girl to return home to her mother and beg for her forgiveness.

She decided to make a collect call to Doll and ask her for help, being too ashamed to call her own mamma. Shirleen had not known until then about Herman Junior's sudden tragic death, having been out of touch for so long. She hated to tell Doll that Lucille had abandoned her in the middle of nowhere, but it was a great relief to Doll just to know that her daughter was still alive.

Doll immediately wired Shirleen money for a bus ticket home and made sure to mail off a donation to that little Baptist church. Shirleen arrived back in Peavine that fall, quieter and more humble than anyone had ever remembered. After a couple of weeks, even her mother forgave her and offered to take her back in. Shirleen politely refused the offer because she was determined to make it on her own and get a fresh start in life. Shirleen soon discovered that she loved "doing hair!" She honed her skills as a hair and beauty specialist by working at the only beauty parlor in town, Dee-Dee's Do's (owned by Dorine's sister). Unfortunately, Dee-Dee began to get jealous of Shirleen's remarkable talent for doing really BIG and HIGH hair.

"The higher the hair, the closer to Heaven," Shirleen would chant as another satisfied customer arose from a cloud of hairspray sporting an eye popping up-do. That didn't go over at all well with Dee-Dee.

Doll had been gleefully watching Shirleen's growing popularity and decided that the time was right to offer Shirleen a quiet little business loan so she could set up her own salon. The two of them discovered an absolutely precious little pink trailer at a Re-Po lot in Louisiana and had it hauled in to Doll's Home Sweet Homes on Wheels. That allowed Shirleen to live and work at the same place. It turned out to be very convenient for Doll to keep her waitress-black hair dyed to the roots and in perfect condition with Shirleen right next door. That gal could rat and spray your hair within an inch of your life, but she'd never cause any damage to the ends. Doll swore that when Shirleen did your hair, the only split end you'll ever have is the one you're a sittin' on!

All of the style-conscious women and young girls of Peavine became totally dependent on Shirleen's expertise, except those who didn't want to get on the wrong side of Dee-Dee. The little pink trailer was also the place to go if you needed makeup advice or the special lift and support of a Penny Rich Bra. Shirleen was the local distributor for the bras – another smart business move greatly encouraged by Doll.

One day destiny arrived in the form of a tour bus carrying a young up-and-coming country music singer with her band. They stopped in at Don's Diner for pie and coffee while Shirleen was there for a late lunch. Spotting that big tour bus pulling into the parking lot had caused her plenty of excitement.

Shirleen walked right over and introduced herself to the country music singer from Tennessee. My goodness, that little gal had a mighty big set of bosoms on her! She was as much in need of one of those Penny Rich bras Shirleen sold as she was a new hairdo.

From the moment Shirleen had entered the Diner the singer couldn't take her eyes off Shirleen's incredible bee hive. It was a sight to behold; gleaming blonde with plenty of volume, even on such a humid day. It was a perfect duplication of a hair style Shirleen had seen in "Amazon Women from Mars" at the drive-in over the weekend.

Meeting a country music star was Shirleen's big break. She offered to give the star a beauty session "on the house." By the end of two hours in the pink trailer, Shirleen had given her a whole new look, make-up and all. Delighted with the results, the singer offered to hire Shirleen as her personal stylist and asked her to go on tour with them right then and there.

Shirleen prayed about it for a few minutes before she determined that the Lord had meant for her to pursue a glamorous career of show-biz beauty all along. She ran over to tell Doll all about how "blessed" she was. After all, the singer's name was Dolly, so that had to be a good sign, right?

So that's how Shirleen got famous. The ladies of Peavine hated to see the pink trailer of beauty pull out of town, but most of them were happy for her, especially Doll Dumas. Dee-Dee, on the other hand, was a little conflicted over the whole matter.

CHAPTER SEVEN

Pastor Astor and KPEW Radio

Mary Lynn was impressed by the story of Shirleen but was skeptical about the amount of truth in it. The only comment she could think of was, "Well, my goodness. I never had thought of religion as having anything to do with show business, but I suppose Shirleen's situation was unusual."

Dorine burst out laughing. "Oh you do, hah!" She pointed with her thumb at the radio over on the corner of the counter. "Wait till you hear about Pastor Astor and KPEW."

Pastor Lyle Bodine Astor

When the sanctuary of the Fourth Baptist Church and Highway Prayer Club burned down in 1969, due to faulty wiring in the electronic bell tower, Pastor Astor, founder and minister of the church, insisted it was devil-inspired arson, pure and simple. He had developed an irrational fear that wooden buildings with windows were open targets for "Commie War-Protesters" to set on fire with their Molotov cocktails and stink bombs. Not that any anti-war protesters had been sighted anywhere near Peavine, but he had seen those stories on the news and was convinced he was a target, since he was a decorated veteran. A temporary location for services was established at the VFW Hut until funding for a new church building could be raised.

The congregation had begun to dwindle, because no matter how strong the spirit, it just wasn't very easy to raise money for a new building when it appeared they would end up worshiping in a cinder block bunker - the only kind of public structure that Pastor Astor felt secure in anymore.

Doll enjoyed listening to gospel music stations on the radio after Herman Junior passed; and got the notion that a ministry over the airwaves just might suit Pastor Lyle Bodine Astor to a "T." She suggested they make use of an old Dumas Oil Co. storage facility that had been abandoned for several years. It was a simple concrete building south of town, built on a small hill which would make it a prime location for a radio tower.

She explained to the stymied building committee that it wouldn't matter much how bad the place looked, if all you ever did was hear it. Doll had it cleaned up and furnished, with the help of some of the Oil Co. employees and the few remaining church elders. Her friend Marv helped get some information, and the church applied for an FCC license.

She bequeathed a generous donation to the church from the Doll Dumas Helping Hand Trust Fund, in memory of her dearly departed, Herman Junior. Pastor Astor was able to set himself up with a transmission tower and all the equipment he needed to transform that place into a real, sure-enough AM radio station! L.B. (Doll called him that because she'd start to laugh every time she said Pastor Astor) wanted his church's radio home to be called KPEW – "where your radio would become your very own private pew at the Fourth Baptist Church and Highway Prayer Club."

The call letters seemed even more fitting whenever the wind was blowing just right from the northeast, and the aroma of the paper mill in Pine Bluff would drift toward Peavine. *Peeeeyoooo* was more like it!

Before long, the programming that had started out as two-hour broadcasts during regular church service times - Sunday mornings and evenings, and on Wednesday nights and Bible Studies on Thursday afternoons - stretched into Wednesday through Thursday, 9 am to 7 pm.

Louise Dolesanger was hired as the music director for the radio station, as she had been organist and choir director for thirty-five years at the real church. She had been a musical entertainer playing the organ at Seymour's Tex-Mex for three years by then, and her knowledge and taste in music had expanded quite a bit. She and Doll got their heads together and ordered a large selection of new records... not all of it Gospel music, either.

Pastor Astor's eighteen year old son, Little Bo, played music between church service broadcasts. Every now and then Little Bo would sneak in some of his favorite secular tunes. The new station was the talk of Peavine and just about every household and business in the town had it on at some time during the day. Although the compliments were a delight to hear, it became obvious to the Pastor that Bo's musical programming was getting more listeners than the sermons and Bible lessons.

In an attempt to regain control of his ministry, Pastor Astor developed the habit of bursting into the control room when Little Bo would least expect it. He would open the mike on the air without warning, and start preaching just to see if he could save a few extra souls by surprise.

Then, lo and behold, the Pastor discovered the beauty and increased income of radio advertising! The way he would work the names of the local businesses into his radio sermons was pure genius. As the so-called donations began to pile up, he would pray fervently for certain dress shops, gas stations, and eating establishments. It wasn't long before the IRS got wind of that, and he had to change how he reported such generous gifts from his loyal followers.

Eventually Young Bo took over for the Pastor and developed an even more diverse format of secular music. Shirleen Naither was a real help with a collection of country music recordings, now that she had her Nashville connections. By 1975, KPEW was the best little radio station in the area. Bo earned enough off the station's revenue to donate money to build a nice little church sanctuary, with pretty stained glass windows right in downtown Peavine.

Old Pastor Astor had been forced to retire from the ministry after the IRS incident as part of his plea agreement. His other son, Joe Don, had felt the call and enrolled in the Abundant Life Bible College of Positive Preaching. Upon graduation he took over as pastor at the new church Bo built. It's called the New Church of the Vine and Joe Don is referred to as the Reverend Astor. "Thank God!" said Doll Dumas with a straight face."

CHAPTER EIGHT

Kristy and Misty, the Party Girls

The radio announcer spoke again. "Now we're gonna hear Doll's favorite party time tune, 'Rock Around the Clock', dedicated to the swingin-est Granny of all time. This request comes from Peavine's very own Party Girls, Kristy and Misty.

"MMMmm . . . I can hardly wait to taste their famous He-Man Rotel Cheese Dip tonight! They've brought a whole vat of it down for the big post-funeral celebration, so come hungry! Oh, Lordee!" Dorine heaved herself up from her chair. "I'd better go write myself a note so I'll remember to take that extra hot plate with me when I leave. I promised Kristy she could use it to keep the cheese dip good and runny."

"Does Kristy work here, too?" Mary Lynn asked.

"Heavens, no! She and Misty have their own catering business up in Benton. They're down here for the funeral and the party." Dorine stopped looking for her pencil, which was still stuck behind her ear, and looked toward the kitchen.

"If I don't go dig out that hot plate right now I'll end up running us late tonight. Be back in a sec, Mary Lynn." Dorine went into the kitchen and the door swung shut behind her. The sounds of her rummaging about in the cabinets emanated from the other side, followed by a loud crash and rattle of pots and pans. "I'm okay!" Dorine shouted.

Mary Lynn couldn't help laughing. She had been thoroughly entertained by Dorine. There was something very familiar and comfortable about sitting in the cozy diner and listening to the stories of the local inhabitants. Mary Lynn realized with a smile that Dorine reminded her a little of Aunt Carol, Lizzie's mother. Just like Dorine, Carol used to help at Harry's Side Car Café. She often took care of Mary Lynn, when she was a little girl, while her mother was at work.

The year before Mary Lynn's mother died, Carol remarried and she and Lizzie moved to Monroe. When they returned for her mother's funeral, Mary Lynn was invited to come live with them. She didn't think the new husband would think much of that. So she had stayed in Blytheville under Harry's watchful eye.

"A lot of good that did," she thought. "I wonder how my life would have turned out if I had taken them up on that instead of getting in over my head with Johnny."

The kitchen door swung back open and Dorine reappeared with her hat missing and her hair sticking out on one side. She set the heavy duty hot plate up on the counter in triumph. "Sorry about the racket. I usually stay out of there so I have the darndest time finding anything. That's my husband's domain not mine." She wiped her hands on her apron and came back over to the booth. "Now, what was I saying before?" She asked Mary Lynn as she lowered herself back down into her chair with a sigh.

"You were telling me about the catering business that Kristy has with her friend," Mary Lynn prompted.

Dorine cackled and slapped her knee. "If you think Shirleen Naither was the only one who's cleaned up her act, wait 'till you hear about Kristy and Misty!

Kristy and Misty

Kristy Lauder and Misty Bowers were the only tenants in Doll's trailer park that the citizens of Peavine would shake their heads over and complain about. Every Monday, there was another wild-girl story about the weekend antics of our local "Diabolical Duo", as Doll used to call them.

The problem with Kristy and Misty was, they were both bored . . . and pretty darn angry over that fact. Doll always said being bored and angry was one dangerous combination, so it's a good thing those girls were mostly harmless. They never hurt anybody physically. They got their kicks by making fun of the locals; especially a goody two-shoes or anybody they considered too big for their britches. Those girls had some mighty sharp tongues on 'em!

Their favorite putdown was to insult a man a by calling him a "TW". They reserved that term mostly for their ex-husbands; however they often referred to their boss as a TW - behind his back of course. Those two girls were just about as coarse as cornmeal, and liked to make fun of a person's anatomy whenever possible. The more belittling it sounded the better they liked it. (In case you haven't figured it out yet, TW stands for teenie weenie.)

Best friends all through high school up in Pine Bluff, the girls thought they were ready to enter adulthood together, when they married twin brothers that happened to be star linebackers on the varsity football team. There was a double wedding ceremony just one week after graduation. Since Bud and Bubba were heirs to their daddy's business, Kristy and Misty assumed they would have a life of glamorous leisure ahead of them.

However, it was not long after their honeymoons that the girls began to see how mistaken they had been. I guess you can chalk up a lot of their erroneous thinking to the foolishness of youth. After all, Kristy and Misty were only seventeen and the boys were eighteen.

Bud and Bubba were twins—not identical, but about the same size: huge. Kristy and Misty thought it was so cool that they had found two hunky twin brothers to marry, so they could all stay best friends and live next door to one another. The girls had been neighbors since third grade, so it was only natural to think that it would work.

All too soon it became obvious that aside from playing football, the brothers didn't have the ability to do much of anything else. They were expected to work for their daddy so they already had steady jobs but that was the other problem. One would have thought that when the girls heard the name of the company that Bud and Bubba's daddy owned they would have had a clue as to what kind of work their husbands would be doing. It was called Big Bob's Honey Hole Septic Service. That says it all in a nutshell.

Therefore, Kristy's and Misty's dream of becoming the wives of junior executives was totally unrealistic. Instead, they found themselves wedded to a couple of big lummoxes who dug out septic tanks for a living. Bud and Bubba hadn't seemed so thick-witted when they were all suited up for the big game, lumbering around the football field at the Pine Bluff High School Football Stadium. Now here they were, coming home every evening after a hard day of servicing Big Bob's Honey Holes. Just imagine the way those boys must have looked, and worst of all for their young brides - how they smelled!

Every evening, Kristy and Misty would doll themselves up and serve their husbands the latest recipes they had gleaned from the pages of their Betty Crocker cookbooks. The boys would gulp down dinner with hardly a word of conversation, belch copiously as a way of showing their appreciation, and leave the dirty dishes and their wives behind.

After supper the twins would get together at one house or the other and watch, listen, or talk about football for the rest of the evening over a couple of six packs of beer. Usually by nine o'clock,

Bud and Bubba each stumbled off to their connubial beds for about two minutes of wedded bliss, before passing out for the night. This situation was very unsatisfying to the girls.

It made matters worse that there was not enough money - after buying huge amounts of groceries and beer - for the girls to go out and buy the home decor items and the wardrobes of their dreams. In order to pad the boy's incomes, the girls got part time jobs during the day. Before long, they switched to full time shifts, preferably during the evenings, so they wouldn't have to be around Bud and Bubba any more than necessary. The boys didn't mind the girls not being around, as long as there was supper out on the table when they got home from work.

After about a year and a half of this, it dawned upon Kristy and Misty that all Bud and Bubba were inheriting from their daddy was an early onset balding pattern, and his particular body type: all gut and no butt. After a steady diet of Kristy's and Misty's junk-food suppers, and copious amounts of beer, the worst had occurred to the twins. Bud and Bubba those two big, simple yet loveable linebackers, had transformed into fat, balding, thickheaded septic tank diggers. To a young woman, that was just about as un-attractive as a man can be.

Kristy and Misty decided that they had squandered enough of their youth on the twins, and decided to file for divorces. They made plans to leave Honey Hole Septic Service and Pine Bluff far behind them and pursue a life of good times and excitement. They weren't sure where to find that life of excitement, but thought that New Orleans or someplace in Florida sounded exotic.

Poor old Bud and Bubba had been absolutely clueless about the girls' discontent. They stood there scratching themselves one evening, trying to figure out why letters from some lawyer was laying on their kitchen tables instead of their supper. Meanwhile, Kristy and Misty were speeding down the road to freedom and adventure in Kristy's new two-toned, tan El-Camino!

Speeding was not such a good idea, especially when traveling through Grady, Arkansas. The local sheriff eagerly awaited the approach of unfortunate lead-footed motorists who failed to notice the partially hidden 30-mph speed limit sign just outside of town. The fine for doing 75 in a 30-mile-per-hour zone certainly helped fill the Grady municipal coffers but it put a pretty serious dent in the Kristy's and Misty's "Road to Freedom Fund."

It was bad enough they had to shell out a small fortune for the speeding ticket but Kristy giving the finger to the sheriff as they pealed out only made him madder. His patrol car was much faster than they had counted on. So when he forced the El Camino off the highway it took a whole lot of sweet talking from Misty plus another hefty fine just to keep the girls from spending their first night of freedom in the Grady jail!

The girls showed up at Don's Diner early the next morning. Misty had taken the wheel of the El Camino, and driven 45 mph the rest of the way. They were pretty worn out and discouraged as they sat there counting the remains of their precious yet dwindling Freedom Fund.

Noticing the Home-Sweet-Homes Park across the way had a **TRAILER FOR RENT** sign, they thought they might as well go take a look at it. There was one old trailer from Madge's days still in the back of the park. It was vacant and partially furnished with cast-offs from Vaudine Fortney's Forever Formica - Used Furniture and Collectibles. Doll made a deal with the girls for a half month's rent. If they could find jobs the Freedom Fund could be rebuilt and Kristy and Misty could be back on the road to a better place in six months or sooner.

Doll had a soft spot for those girls, probably because they reminded her of her own wayward daughter, Lucille. She tried her best to help them out. Kristy got a job working at the diner for a while as the assistant cook but she couldn't get along with Don. Doll suggested that she switch over to Seymour's Tex Mex. That had more of an international feel to Kristy so she was happier there. Seymour's wife, Lolita, taught her how to make cheese dip and before long Kristy had developed at least five different varieties. Everybody's favorite was her "He-Man's Delight" made with Velveeta, Rotel and canned chili without the beans. Her secret ingredient was a heap of jalapeño peppers on top. Customers lapped it up and called for seconds.

Doll found Misty a job down at the Dumas Oil Co. answering the phone and helping with the office work. Eventually Misty could handle most of the payroll on her own. She would never admit it to anybody else, but she had a pretty good head for numbers.

It would seem as if the girls had done well to stop and settle in Peavine and they should have been happy and satisfied, but not so with the Party Girls. Their hunger for excitement and romance was far too powerful to allow that. There wasn't anybody or anything in Peavine suitable to fit their fantasies of life in the fast lane. Doll recommended they join one of the local women's bowling league teams. Unfortunately that only intensified the wild partying at Misty's and Kristy's trailer.

Their fellow team members, the Hell Kittens of Dumas Oil, were a pretty rowdy gang in their own right. They loved to come over to the trailer and celebrate their victories with beer and Kristy's great cheese dip and more beer. Sometimes, the Dumas Oil Co. Hellcats - the men's team - would join in too. Every weekend there was a noisy party and come Monday morning the yard around the trailer would be littered with trash and beer cans. Much as she hated to Doll would have to go knock on their door and demand they clean it all up.

By Tuesday or Wednesday things would be put right but on Friday night the party would begin all over again. All the neighbors were complaining about the noise, traffic and trashy behavior. Something had to change or she would lose her other tenants, so Doll decided to use a little psychology on Misty and Kristy, and hope for the best.

She happened to tune in to a big car race on TV one Saturday afternoon. The Daytona 500 brought the Party Girls to mind because she knew one thing the girls respected was skilled driving and fast cars. Kristy had been stopped for speeding at least three times by the Peavine sheriff in the first six months since they'd arrived.

Knowing the girls would be home preparing for the bowling team's weekend celebration, Doll went over to their trailer, presumably to issue her weekly warning about causing a commotion. This time she decided to tell them about the high-speed car race she was watching on the television. The girls were intrigued by Doll's description of all the race car wrecks so they came over to her place to watch it. (Their own tiny portable TV had been smashed by an errant bowling ball a month ago during one of their wild parties.)

Kristy and Misty sat in front of Doll's big color television enthralled by the spectacle of speeding cars fiery, crashes and sexy race car drivers. They ended up watching the rest of the afternoon. By the next week they were the biggest stock car racing fans in Peavine.

One of Doll's pals mentioned to the girls that she had gone to a stock-car race up in Benton, Arkansas at the local Speed Bowl. Although a lot of people seemed to enjoy it, she personally couldn't tolerate all the noise and exhaust fumes. You couldn't pay her to go back to another one. That's all it took to set the wheels in motion, so to speak.

Misty and Kristy cancelled all party plans for the next two weeks. They worked extra hours and saved all their money for a weekend excursion to the I-30 Speed Bowl up in Benton. It all worked like a charm. Within a month Kristy and Misty had decided to quit their Peavine jobs. Doll gave them a little loan to start up their own Nacho Concession stand at the Benton Speed Bowl.

Not since Shirleen Naither's conversion had Doll seen such a drastic change in attitude as in those two girls! They worked long hours and saved every penny. To her amazement they were able to pay back Doll's loan including interest within only two years.

By that time, they also had more realistic expectations and had gotten married to a couple of nice-looking part-time race car drivers - not twins or even brothers, just buddies. Benton suited all four of them very well a whole lot better than Peavine ever could have; and neither Kristy or Misty were heard to call anybody a "TW" ever again!

Teenie and Mavis Brice
Best of Show

CHAPTER NINE

AKC Toy Poodles and Dog Outfits

Mary Lynn laughed heartily over the "TW" reference. "That goes to show how much a little maturity and life experience can change a girl's attitudes about men."

"Lordee, does it ever!" Dorine agreed. "I wouldn't give Don the time of day until I turned twenty, and here I was working with him almost every day at his dad's little restaurant. It took me a while to get over my crush on Pastor Astor, but thank God I did!" Dorine shook her head and rolled her eyes to the Heavens.

"Oh no, really," Mary Lynn giggled. "I find it hard to believe you could have been attracted to a man like him."

"Hey, he may have been overly sanctimonious even back then, but he was mighty handsome when he was younger. Half the women in this town went to his church just to swoon over him during his 'Fires of Hell' sermons." Dorine gave a snort of derision. "I was a silly fool to fall for such an act, when all that time I had the love of my life right under my nose."

"When I was a young girl," Mary Lynn said, "I was sure my romantic life would turn out to be just like the movies. My mamma used to take me with her to the picture show from the time I was just a little thing. "If it starred Barbara Stanwick, we were there. She was our favorite, because she always managed to go from rags to riches and *still* end up with the man of her dreams."

Mary Lynn couldn't believe she was sharing her personal past with Dorine, yet it felt kind of comforting, especially after the rough morning she'd had. "Back then, the man of my dreams was a Dick

Powell or Van Johnson." She smiled at the thought of Leroy, standing behind the pharmacy counter at Struby's on the first day they'd met. "Instead, I ended up with my own version of Jimmy Stewart . . . and glad of it."

"That sounds like a better catch to me," Dorine said earnestly. "I guess the only film star I could compare to my husband, Don is, uh ... who's that feller that played Fred Mertz on 'I Love Lucy?'"

"William Frawly," Mary Lynn offered as she tried not to laugh.

"Yeah, that's him. Except Don's not cranky like that Fred, just looks like him, only taller and stouter. My Don's got the biggest heart in the world - real salt of the earth!" Dorine sighed as she gazed out the window.

In the silence that followed, Mary Lynn noticed the music on the radio had stopped.

The KPEW announcer began to chatter again. "And now, I'll bet you folks know who dedicated this next song in Doll's top 50 Favorites, 'How Much is That Doggy in the Window?' "

As the syrupy voice of Patti Page wafted across the room, Mary Lynn began to notice a peculiar, high-pitched wailing noise coming from behind a door over in the corner. "What's that crying-sound I hear?" Mary Lynn thought it sounded as if a small child or creature was in distress.

"That's just Dolly. She always tries to sing along with that old recording. It must remind her of her mamma." Dorine's face brightened with a wide grin. "You've got to see her favorite outfit. Mavis made it for her to wear when she comes to work with me. I know it's against health department regulations to have her in here, so I tell folks I'm legally blind, and Dolly helps me find my way around . . . which is partially true."

Mary Lynn had no idea what Dorine was talking about, but she just smiled and nodded her head as if she did. Meanwhile, the wailing sound got louder.

"I've got her a little bed in the broom closet there. She was sound asleep when you came in." Dorine twisted around in her chair and shouted in the direction of the closet door, which was slightly ajar. "Dolly, hush up, and come on out here so you can show this nice lady how pretty you look!"

The wailing stopped. The door opened wider, due to some industrious scratching. An ancient white toy poodle emerged, dressed in a pink skirt with a white apron that matched Dorine's uniform. An enormous pink bow was anchored with a rubber band to the frizzy pouf on the little dog's head.

The dog could have been wearing fuzzy pink slippers like Dorine's, because she mimicked her mistress's stiff legged shuffle as well as any four-legged creature could manage. She slowly approached the two women, and began to wiggle and wag her skinny tail, through a slot in the back of her pink skirt. Dorine reached down and tenderly picked up the fragile dog and sat Dolly up on her lap as if she were a child. Mary Lynn noticed that the dog's toenails were painted the same color of pink as her skirt.

"Oh my goodness, that is such a cute little dog!"

"Yes, she is adorable." Dorine naturally agreed with Mary Lynn's assessment. "You'd never guess she's sixteen years old, would you."

The elderly poodle gazed up at Dorine through eyes clouded with cataracts. "She doesn't look much more than a puppy," Mary Lynn lied politely.

"Where did you find a costume like that to match your uniform?" Except for the circus or Ed Sullivan Show, Mary Lynn had never seen a dog wearing clothes. "How do you get her to keep that thing on?"

"Dolly would feel naked without something to wear," Dorine

stated as if that were the most normal thing in the world. "The Brices make sure all the poodles in Peavine start off early learning to wear clothes. We never could find a way to keep shoes on them though. Their feet are too pointy and small."

"Who are the Brices?" Mary Lynn asked, knowing she was in for another story.

"Teenie and Mavis Brice are long time friends and tenants of Doll's trailer park. Those two are famous all over the country for their AKC toy poodles and dog outfits. They ran a thriving business here in Peavine back in the sixties and on up through the early seventies. Just have the one dog left now that they've retired. Take a gander at that picture of Teenie, Mavis, and Miss Pitty Pat Toodles over there on the wall by the entrance."

Mary Lynn got up and walked over to get a closer look at the small, framed photograph. It appeared to have been cut out of a newspaper and had yellowed with age, but she could still see clearly that the Brices were a different sort of couple from any she'd ever seen.

A short, delicate-looking man stood proudly holding a white toy poodle in a tutu. Both dog and man appeared to be fastidiously groomed, and neatly dressed. Standing beside them, also beaming with pride was an extremely overweight woman, twice the little man's height. She was wearing a loose-fitting, flower print dress and plain rubber flip-flops on her huge feet as she held up a tiny polka-dotted dress. Mary Lynn assumed it was one of the famous dog outfits.

"That picture was in the Peavine Evening Times, when Pitty won 'Best in Show' at the big Kennel Club Regional in 1963." Dorine said as she smoothed her dog's skirt and waited for Mary Lynn's reaction to the photo.

"My little Dolly is one of her pups." At the mention of her name

Dolly sprang into action, jumping up to lick a couple of doggy kisses on Dorine's chin.

"They sure look like a . . . uhm . . . an unusual couple," Mary Lynn observed as she studied the photo. All kinds of questions about the relationship of the Brices came into her mind, but she was too polite to ask them out loud. She couldn't help from wondering how and if the two of them ever had sex. "How did they meet each other? I mean they seem so . . . uh . . . to have such different backgrounds, don't they?'

"You're not the first nor last to ask that question, believe me!" Dorine shook her head and laughed. She seemed to have guessed what Mary Lynn was really thinking.

"They've got to be the oddest couple any of us around here ever did see, but they are perfectly happy and devoted to one another. Doll used to look at them and say, 'See, there's living proof that there's always a special someone for everybody. Teenie and Mavis are truly blessed to have been lucky enough to find each other.'"

"Of course, that sentiment was completely lost on Kristy and Misty. The first time Doll introduced them to the Brices, and said Teenie's name, those girls had to go running out of the room because they'd busted out laughing so hard their beer was blowing out of their noses. Hearing the name 'Teenie' was all it took to set them off."

Mary Lynn had to struggle to keep the sip of coffee in her mouth from blowing out her own nose. She recovered quickly by changing the subject.

"Well, it is interesting that such an unlikely pair would get together, so tell me about Teenie and Mavis."

Teenie and Mavis Brice

Nobody in Peavine actually knows how the Brices happened
to meet and marry. They had lived in Springfield, Missouri before
moving down to Jonesboro, Arkansas. Teenie and Mavis had married
late in life, but had been together for about twenty years before they
came to Peavine and settled in Doll's trailer park.

Up in Jonesboro, Mavis worked as a seamstress out of their home,
and Teenie had just retired from his job as a décor adviser at a local
furniture store. Mavis was able to design and sew just about anything.
She made all of her own clothes as well as most of Teenie's. This
spared him the embarrassment of being a fully grown man having to
shop for his dress suits in the boy's department. It also allowed Mavis
the freedom to wear her own style of super-sized comfort apparel.

They never had children, but they compensated by lavishing
plenty of love and attention on their toy poodles. As far as Teenie
and Mavis were concerned, those poodles were their children and
it became obvious they treated them more like little human beings
than dogs. (This delusion was probably the basis of the dog costume
fixation.)

After Teenie retired from his job at the furniture store, they sold
their home in Jonesboro. They bought a brand new Airstream so they
could travel to all the dog shows with their precious Pitty Pat.

Teenie and Mavis shared one passion, and that was AKC toy
poodles. They'd always had at least one of them as a pet all their years
together. By the time Teenie retired, they had become toy poodle
connoisseurs, and experts on their care and breeding.

Teenie had a natural talent as a dog show handler. Being small
was an advantage when you have a toy breed to work in front of the
judges. Teenie always attracted attention when he entered the show

ring. His rapport with his dog, plus a natural sense of showmanship, complimented Pitty Pat's pristine bloodlines. With plenty of free time on their hands since retirement, the threesome had all they needed to jump feet first into the exciting world of Kennel Club dog shows.

On the way between their fourth and fifth competitions, the Brices passed through Peavine. While stopping for lunch, they noticed how pleasant Doll Dumas' Trailer Park looked across the way under the shady pecan trees. It looked like the perfect place to set up a home base for their traveling life. Dorine gave Doll a ring as soon as she saw them bring their dog into the Diner.

Doll fell in love with Pitty Pat the first time she laid eyes on that delightful little creature. After Herman's death she had wanted to buy some kind of a dog to keep her company, but hadn't been able to decide which breed to get. She had always been partial to fancy-trimmed poodles, but thought a standard would be too big and rambunctious to live in a trailer. Until she met the Brices she had no idea they came in such a small size, and thought that teacup-sized Pitty Pat had to be the cutest dog she had ever seen in her life!

She invited Teenie and Mavis to come over to her trailer so she could show them her china poodle dog collection. She had been collecting them for years and had at least fifty of them in her special display case. Doll was a hit with the Brices right from the get go. That very day she rented them a prime spot for their Airstream, towards the back of the park. Teenie installed a nice little fenced-in play yard for Pitty Pat so she could get her fresh air and exercise, far away from the dangers of the highway.

Doll was eager to get a toy poodle of her own, so the Brices invited her to come along with them to their next dog show. Teenie offered to help her pick out one of the very best, top-of-the-line pups. Doll found her perfect pet poodle, and future husband for Pitty, at the

Kennel Club Regional competition in Little Rock. He was no more than a tiny black bundle of curls, and she named him Rufus P. They were all excited about the eventual breeding of the two dogs. Teenie thought mixing black Rufus P's genes with Pitty Pat Toodle's snow white genes would produce stronger, healthier litters with more variety. Doll liked to call it the first "mixed marriage" in Peavine.

Doll and the Brices became great friends. Whenever Doll arrived for a visit, Teenie would tell Pitty that her "Auntie Doll" had come to see her. Doll's pup grew up to begat a dynasty of prize winning AKC toy poodles. Teenie enlarged Pitty Pat's play yard behind the Airstream and built a pretty little love nest of a doghouse, in case the newlyweds needed some privacy. Doll kept Rufus with her of course, but she would take him over to play with Pitty every day. The intention was to get him used to the Brices and learn their ways of training.

The only problem was that Rufus never did learn to like wearing Mavis' dog outfits. He would tolerate Pitty in her clothes, but he'd pull his own off and chew on them first chance he would get. They finally settled on a letting him go about with only a red bow tie.

Doll marveled at how Mavis would make outfits for Pitty Pat, and the dog would wear them just like that was an entirely natural thing for her to do. Doll would howl with laughter every time she saw Pitty Pat prance around on her hind legs dressed up in her little pink tutu!

Mavis had sewn an entire wardrobe for Pitty Pat's trousseau, including a white tulle wedding dress and veil, and something sort of like a tuxedo to go with his bow tie for Rufus to wear at their wedding ceremony. The little rascal kept his top hat on for about five minutes before he tugged it off and ran around shaking it while Teenie chased and scolded him. The dog nuptials of Rufus and Pitty made for an event unlike anything anybody in Peavine had ever witnessed.

Teenie took plenty of pictures of the doggy bride and groom, and sent off the wedding photos to the other toy poodle breeders. Of course they wanted to order some outfits like that for their own dogs. After that, Mavis posed Pitty in all her new dresses for Teenie's camera. When they brought an album with the pictures of Pitty to the next Kennel Club show, Mavis was swamped with orders.

Within a year, everybody was getting busy. Mavis was busy sewing, Teenie was busy taking orders for dog outfits and interviewing prospective "adoptive caretakers" of the new pups, and Pitty Pat and Rufus were busy making babies!

By the time the first litter arrived - two black males and two white females – twenty-five residents of Peavine put their names on Teenie's list, each hoping to be lucky enough to be chosen by the Brices as proud owners of an AKC toy poodle. Teenie and Doll interviewed each one, and had Rhonelle do psychic background checks. An adoption agency could not have been choosier than Teenie when it came to a new home for one of his pups.

He finally narrowed it down to four deserving couples by the time the puppies were ten weeks old. Each one left with a custom made outfit by Mavis, and a stern warning from Teenie that he could drop by unannounced, at any time, to check up on their welfare.

As the puppies grew, they needed larger outfits, and then outfits for special occasions. Doll always hosted the annual birthday party/ reunions, so each dog had to have a new outfit for that. Then there was always: Halloween, Christmas and Easter outfits to make, too.

Mavis' Littlest Angel and Baby Jesus Poodle costumes were all the rage around holiday season. By the time Pitty had her third batch of puppies; Peavine had gone out-fit-wearing, toy poodle-crazy! Meanwhile poor Mavis was working her fingers to the bone, trying to keep up with all the orders for dog outfits. Doll recommended some of her friends, who were good at sewing, to help Mavis. She hired several of them to do the piecework and they finished the orders in plenty of time. The local housewives were delighted to help Mavis and earn the extra money. Thus a local cottage industry began to thrive in Peavine.

Word of Mavis Brice's Dog Outfits had spread nationwide because of the Kennel Club exposure, so it wasn't long before the Brices were contacted by a representative of a major poodle supply and accessory company from New York City. He paid $100 for each of her designs. This was a big thrill for Mavis. Being an extremely shy and humble woman, she had never expected such recognition of her artistic talents.

One day Doll had an inspiration: since Mavis' dog outfits were so famous, why not have a toy poodle style show right there in Peavine. By that time there were designer-dressed toy poodles all over the county, thanks to the Brices. This would be a fun way to get everybody together to show off their dogs without any of the stuffy rules and regulations of the Kennel Club competitions.

That was the beginning of Peavine's Annual Toy Poodle Pageant and Style Show, held every spring since 1969. Every year the event doubles the population of Peavine for a whole week! All of the area motels and eating establishments are swamped during Poodle Pageant time, and the locals love it.

Dorine's smile faded and she stopped talking. Noticing her mood change, Dolly peered up at her mistress and let out a whimper. "Now that Doll is gone," Dorine sighed, "the Pageant just won't be the same. It's been awful hard on Teenie and Mavis to lose her and they sure aren't getting any younger themselves."

A large tear rolled down from under Dorine's thick glasses and plopped onto Dolly's nose. The dog sneezed with a funny little snort, cocked her head to one side and began to squirm and whine so much that Dorine had to let her down. "Well, where do you think you're off to, young lady?" Dorine asked as the dog waddled briskly across the room. Mary Lynn was relieved to see Dorine was smiling again.

"I think she must want to go outside." Mary Lynn noted as Dolly began to frantically paw at the back door with her pink toenails.

"Oh I know what you want!" Dorine hefted herself up and shuffled over to the door, while honking into her Kleenex. "You want to get out there and see Whutzit, don't you?" She opened the door and Dolly ran outside. "Mary Lynn, you need to come over here and see this."

When Mary Lynn got to the door and looked out, she saw Dolly romping and yipping excitedly. The object of the toy poodle's adoration was the weirdest, ugliest dog Mary Lynn had ever come across. His face was smushed in and his lower teeth jutted out too far. He was black all over except where he was turning gray around his flat nose. His partly wavy fur had thinned to near baldness towards his skinny little rump and stump of a tail. He balanced on long trembling bowlegs with small pointy feet.

"What in the world is *that?*"

"Good question." Dorine snorted. "He may be ugly, but he's the sweetest-natured dog you'll ever meet. Come here, Whutzit!"

"His name is 'What's it'?"

Mary Lynn had to smile as the little old dog walked sideways towards them. He kept dipping and nodding his head as if to apologize for his ugliness.

"This here is Kristy's old doggy, the results of one of the Party Girls' more experimental pranks."

"Oh lord, what kind of prank?" Mary Lynn was thinking the worst.

"The girls were still living here when the Brices were really hitting it big in the dog breeding biz and you know how they were mostly up to no good in those days.

"Misty took in a female mutt they'd found running loose along the highway. Since she was pretty large and mean-looking they thought she would be a good guard dog. They got her fattened her up on Twinkies and bologna and with her being some combination of bulldog, lab, and no telling what else she did look pretty dangerous. Of course we all knew she wouldn't hurt a fly. Misty named her Two-Ton."

One Saturday night, the girls were bored because they didn't have dates. Poor old Two-Ton was feeling restless too because she was in heat and confined to the trailer. Kristy and Misty hatched a plan. They knew Doll was out to dinner with the Brices so they snuck over and dog-napped Rufus. They'd made up their minds that he needed to experience a little extra-curricular activity, if you know what I mean, and they just wanted to see what would happen.

They couldn't believe it but Two-Ton just lay right down on the ground and let little Rufus have his way with her. It sure didn't take long. They had Rufus back to his pen before Doll got home and no one was the wiser, until 2 months later.

The girls didn't even know Two-Ton was expecting but one morning there she was under the Party Girls' trailer with her one little puppy, Whutzit!

Misty and Kristy looked at the dog then back at each other. Both couldn't help but think of the size difference which reminded them of . . . well, Teenie and Mavis. Then Misty says, 'there may be a special someone for everyone and we just proved that where there's a will, there's a way.'"

Mary Lynn and Dorine burst into laughter .They watched out the back door of the Diner as Dolly and Whutzit began to race around in circles frolicking as if they were still puppies.

Doll and Granny Laurite

CHAPTER TEN

What a Hoot!

Back at the Moving Theater

Johnny had been having a fine time watching Dorine tell Mary Lynn stories about the inhabitants of Doll's trailer park. With his feet propped up on the seat in front of him, he alternately guffawed in laughter and stuffed juju beans in his mouth. He was looking forward to getting a good look at the Party Girls and the Brices later on. Since Laurite hadn't filled him in on all the details, he wasn't exactly sure why it was so important that Mary Lynn would end up in Peavine listening to Dorine on this particular day, yet so far it seemed to have had a beneficial effect on her.

The door in the back of the Theater burst open to the sound of Doll laughing hysterically. Johnny hopped to his feet and turned to see Laurite patiently pulling Doll along by the hand as she floated above her head like a Macy's Thanksgiving Day Parade Balloon. Johnny let out a low whistle as he watched Doll. She was not only floating, but also emitting a slight rosy glow of light.

"*That must have been one heck of a funeral to get her that high,*" he said in awe. He took a hold of Doll's other hand and helped Laurite to gently guide her back into her chair.

"*It was a pretty good one…as funerals go,*" Laurite said with a shrug. She took her seat on the other side of Doll and started eating popcorn as if nothing unusual had occurred.

"*Come on Laurite, it must have been a humdinger of an outpouring, for her to have already gotten on a glow like that.*" He turned to Doll who had settled down and was smiling contentedly. *"So, Doll . . . you liked your funeral okay?"*

That started off more giggles from Doll. *"Ooooh Lord! That big black wig was a hoot! I don't know where Shirleen got a hold of such a huge beehive!"* She bent over in laughter, as Johnny looked over her at Laurite for a clue. Finally Doll recovered enough to continue. *"I was full of reverence until they opened up my big, gaudy casket. Hon, there ain't enough hair stylin' or make up in the world to get that poor old worn-out body I left behind to look right!"*

Laurite smirked and nodded in agreement as she accepted a handful of Johnny's juju beans.

Doll wiped her eyes and sighed. *"I knew it was silly of me to agree to an open casket. I only did it to help pad the bill for Rupert Astor's funeral home and to give Shirleen Naither something fun to do when she got to town. I guess the joke's on me! I could have sworn I saw Shirleen glance up at me a couple of times with that mischievous smile of hers."*

Laurite patted Doll on the shoulder consolingly. *"No harm done to you now . . . right?"* Before Doll could acknowledge the first sign of sympathy she had experienced coming from Laurite, the little Creole pointed to the screen.

"We still got work to do. Gotta be sure that lady stays in town 'til de morning."

Doll looked up at the screen and watched for a minute. Dorine and Mary Lynn were chatting away together like old friends.

"It looks to me like Dorine is doing a pretty good job of putting her at ease." Doll started to ask why it was essential to have Mary Lynn spend the night in Peavine, but decided she would find out soon enough. She leaned back and pulled a cigarette from the pack that had just appeared in her hand. Johnny leaned in to give her a light.

"I've got to admit, having Dorine there was a stroke of genius, Doll,"

he said as he sat back and lit up a smoke for himself. Once again he rubbed his thumb across the engraved inscription before putting the silver lighter away in his breast pocket. *"She's the most entertaining human being I've seen in a long time."*

"Yeah, *Dorine is a master story teller,"* Doll smiled at the image of Dorine and Mary Lynn laughing about that funny little Whutzit as they sat back down for more hot coffee. *"Laurite has a psychic granddaughter, Rhonelle, and she is the one who suggested that I add that bit in my Last Wishes about her keeping the diner open."* She looked over at Laurite. *"Thanks for putting the idea in her head. At the time I just thought it would give Dorine a good excuse to get out of going to my funeral."*

"What's her problem with funerals?" Johnny asked.

"When Dorine was a little girl, she wandered into the dining room where they'd just laid out her newly deceased great-grandmother," Doll explained. *"In those days people would keep the dead at home for visitation until the funeral. She saw two big shiny coins holding down her granny's eyelids and helped herself to some ice cream money. That is the last time she would ever take something that didn't belong to her or go anywhere near a dead body. The sight of those eyes flying open gave her nightmares for years!"*

"I think that would have done it for me too!" Johnny snickered as he watched the screen.

"We all got to concentrate now," Laurite interjected as she focused intently on the screen. *"We gotta help Dorine and Don make Mary Lynn want to spend de night."*

CHAPTER ELEVEN

Dorine's Family Enters the Picture

The back door of the Diner burst open, startling Mary Lynn and Dorine. A large beefy man in a hat and overcoat stepped in just as three young children came tearing in past him. The foursome brought a blast of cold air and noisy chatter into the once quiet and cozy diner. Leaving the door ajar, he crossed the room to hang up his hat and overcoat on a peg beside the restrooms.

He appeared to be in his seventies (about the same age as Dorine) and was wearing a shiny navy blue suit, snug in all the wrong places. Loosening his wide short necktie with a jerk, he pulled it off over his head and flung it onto the peg next to the hat and overcoat. Unbuttoning his collar he rubbed his chafed neck with a sigh of relief. Then he struggled out of the tight suit coat, throwing it over the necktie with a look of disgust. It was obvious to Mary Lynn that it must take an act of God – or a funeral to get this man into a dress suit.

Whistling softly along with the tune playing on the radio, he ambled over to turn the volume up really loud. That act drowned out the argument the three children were having. The girl had snatched away a small electronic game from one of the boys.

"**Don, that's too loud!**" Dorine shouted to the man, whose back was turned to her, as he tied a large white apron around his middle. "**Don!** Dang it. **You've left the back door open!**" Completely oblivious to Dorine's shouts, Don opened the pie case, and pulled out a large pie with high fluffy meringue on top of it.

"**Don!!!**"

The children had thrown off their coats and were tugging at Don's pant leg to get his attention. "We want some **donuts**, Poppy!" the two boys shouted in unison.

"Lordee! Mercy!" Dorine got to her feet. "Don is so deaf; he couldn't hear himself fart in a jug!"

Mary Lynn wasn't sure she had heard Dorine right, with so much racket going on.

"Davie, Dwayne, Dora Lee, settle down now! One of you go and shut that door before Whutzit gets in here." Dorine rattled off the kid's names in a sharp tone that stopped them in their tracks.

Whutzit was gingerly poking his flat little nose in through the crack in the door, investigating any possibility of getting inside to play some more with Dolly. All the noise had revitalized the poodle and she was running around the children yapping at them.

"Git!" the little girl shouted at Whutzit. "You cain't come in here 'cause you stink too much!" Then she slammed the door in his face.

"Dora Lee, don't talk mean to that poor creature. He can't help it if he's old. Davie, Dwayne, and Dora Lee are my son, Danny's kids."

Dorine explained to Mary Lynn as she turned down the volume on the radio.

With the drop in the noise level, Don looked up startled. "Hey Dorine, I didn't see you before. Who's that you got with you?" Don smiled broadly at Mary Lynn and adjusted something in his ear that emitted a short, high-pitched, whiney noise. He looked over at Dorine apologetically. "I turned down my hearing aids while I was in the car with the kids. They was singing so loud, it near gave me a headache."

Dorine cast a sarcastic look at Mary Lynn and raised her eyebrows."I wish I could tune them out that easily sometimes. Don, this is Mary Lynn . . ."

At that moment, Davie and Dwayne started shouting and throwing pieces of donuts at each other. They dashed past Dorine and out the back door before Dorine could fuss at them. With the back door left open, Whutzit saw his chance and quickly scuttled inside. He and Dolly started woofing down the wadded up pieces of donut scattered across the floor.

"Oh well guess I'll let the dogs clean up that mess for me. Just hope it don't make them sick." Dorine got back up to go look out the window to see where the boys had gone. Mary Lynn watched the two dogs lick grease spots on the floor. She couldn't help wondering how many health department regulations were being broken.

"Gross me out the door!" Dora Lee said as she walked prissily in a wide circle around the dogs. "Granny Doh, I'm going over to the Cottage Office. You want me to answer the phone for you in case somebody calls?"

"Sure, honey, that'd be real nice." Dorine smiled at her. "Where's your Mamma and Daddy?"

"They're still at the church helping out Aunt Darla and Uncle Rupert. I was not gonna look at a dead person. Yuck! I almost did since it was Miz Doll but I didn't want to so Poppy brought us back." Dora Lee gave a little shiver, then straightened up and trounced out the door. Whutzit waggled up to follow her, only to have the door slammed in his face again.

"I don't blame her." Dorine shuddered and rubbed her arms, as she looked up at her husband "How was it, Don? Was it real sad and awful?"

"No, Honey, it was a really nice service, almost kind of cheerful. For once, Old Pastor Astor kept quiet and allowed his son to be in charge of his own church. Louise kept the music upbeat and you wouldn't believe how many people showed up! There must have been close to fifty or sixty folks standing up in the back, after they run out of extra folding chairs."

"*My stars!*" Dorine clasped Don's arm with both hands. "How . . . how did she *look?*"

"She looked great, Honey. Shirleen and Darla had got her all made up pretty. She had a kind of smile on her face and was wearing that big black beehive wig Shirleen had styled for her. Doll looked just like herself, Dorine. I think even you could have said so. Aw, now come on, Honey, don't get all tuned up again."

Dorine had started dabbing at her eyes and honking furiously into a fresh wad of Kleenex. Mary Lynn wanted to blend into the wallpaper but Don turned his attention from Dorine and came over to make a belated formal introduction. "Hey there, I'm Don, Dorine's Mister. Pleased to meet you Miz . . . uh . . . I didn't catch your name."

"Stanton, Mary Lynn. Mrs. Leroy Stanton but just Mary Lynn is fine. Pleased to meet you Don." She tried not to wince as Don gripped her hand in a strong handshake.

"Likewise. Now are you a friend or family of Doll?" Don asked.

"Neither one, I'm just a stranger from all the way up in Missouri."

Mary Lynn added quickly, "I wouldn't be here at all if I hadn't gotten lost on my way to Monroe." Then she looked past Don to the plate glass window.

"Oh, my gosh! It's already getting dark! Will you look at the time. I've got to get on my way, but I'm not sure how to get back on the road to Monroe."

The sun had already started to set and Mary Lynn couldn't see very well in the dark, especially on a strange road. She was starting to feel panicky again. How could she have sat there for so long when she knew it got dark really early this time of year?

She should have arrived in Monroe by now. Lizzie would be worried sick. Well actually Lizzie didn't ever get too worried about much of anything, but still . . .

"Why don't you just stay here in Peavine for the night and leave in the morning?" Dorine said, standing there waiting and watching Mary Lynn through her thick eye glasses.

A Vacancy at the Dew Drop Inn

"Well, I . . . uh . . . well, my cousin Lizzie is expecting me by tonight . . . and I . . . well," Mary Lynn stammered. She was taken off-guard by such a logical statement coming from the previously distraught Dorine.

"We have a phone right here you can use." Dorine continued with a sniffle. "You could call to let her know where you are."

"We still have a vacancy in the Dew Drop Inn Cottages," Don blurted out. "Number five is empty since Louise's daughter didn't show up. There's a special 'funeral rate' of twenty-five dollars a night but I'd let you have it for twenty."

Dorine moved forward and put her arm around Mary Lynn's

shoulders. "You know what would be really fun?"

"What?" Mary Lynn asked weakly.

"You ought to come along with Don and me to the big party tonight. Doll would have loved the idea of a complete stranger showing up at her memorial celebration. It's going to be loads of fun. Our friend Louise, Peavine's most beloved musician, will be performing on the electric organ with her grandson's new band, The Gay Caballeros." Dorine was all bright-eyed and bushy-tailed now. "My granddaughter Dora Lee is the leader in a big dance number Tammy's Tappers will be putting on after the dinner."

"And the food will be the best Peavine has to offer," Don added gleefully. "I'm bringing twenty of my best pies. I've been baking for the past two days. You'll get to meet everybody and I guarantee you'll leave Peavine the next morning all fat and happy!"

Both Don and Dorine laughed at that.

"He ought to know." Dorine poked her elbow at Don's big belly. "You're always 'fat and happy', aren't ya?"

"I guess it wouldn't do any harm to stay here." Mary Lynn thought that was the sensible thing to do. However she didn't want to intrude as an uninvited guest. "But I don't think I should be buttin' in on your party."

"There ain't no such thing as buttin' in at this party," Don insisted. "Everybody is invited including unexpected guests. Doll would have wanted it that way."

Don and Dorine were determined to get her to come along to the celebration with them, so, after a few more polite protestations, Mary Lynn gave in to their coaxing and decided she would stay the night and go to the party. After all, it would have been too rude for her to have said no.

Dorine cheerfully excused herself to go next door to the "Cottage

Office" (actually her and Don's home) to get the key to #5 and check on Dora Lee, Dwayne, and Davie. Mary Lynn went over to the cash register. Don had put the phone out on the counter before ducking back into the kitchen to allow her a bit of privacy.

Mary Lynn called her cousin collect, of course, and was surprised to learn that Lizzie had not expected her to get there until the next day. That was a relief to Mary Lynn, yet also puzzling. Hadn't Mary Lynn made sure Lizzie was aware of her arrival time? Mary Lynn always made sure someone knew when to expect her on the rare occasions when she was traveling solo. Just in case something terrible happened and she didn't show up on time, the state troopers could be called out to go look for her.

Mary Lynn returned to the booth by the window and sat down, gazing out the window at the lighted sign across the highway, "Doll's Day of Memorials". At that moment, Mary Lynn made the decision to leave all her worries by the side of the road and go ahead and enjoy the unusual situation in which she found herself.

As if to confirm the wisdom of her decision, Don came out of the kitchen with a big slice of lemon ice-box pie. "I thought you might like to try some of this," he said as he slid it onto the table. Of course Mary Lynn never could turn down a piece of pie and lemon ice-box was her favorite.

Don started to squeeze into the booth seat opposite her, thought better of it, and pulled up a chair from a nearby table instead. Mary Lynn noticed the small metal chair seemed to disappear when Don sat on it. "We'll ride to the party with Marv and Pauline," he said. "They have plenty of room in that big Cadillac of theirs."

"What about your grandchildren?" Mary Lynn was hoping to avoid squeezing into a car full of rowdy kids.

"They'll be going with their parents so they can go home early. My son Danny ought to be along pretty soon to pick them up. Darla and her husband Rupert will have to stay till everybody leaves the burial, I mean the internment." Don had a look of distaste when he mentioned this.

"Oh?" Mary Lynn wondered who Darla and Rupert were.

"Darla is our daughter. She ain't had kids yet and Rupert is her husband. He took over his dad's business, Astor's Eternal Rest Funeral Home. He's Peavine's only mortician." Don didn't seem too pleased to be sharing this information. "That skinny ole Rupert is pretty hard for Dorine to bear bein' as how she hates death and funerals so much. Of course that's probably what drove our Darla's fascination with it all . . . and Rupert."

Then Don brightened a bit. "At least she has other interests like her decorating business. It's called 'Denim and Lace Interior Design'. I got one of her cards here somewheres." Don struggled to fish a bent stack of small business cards from out of his trouser pocket, peeled one out and handed it to Mary Lynn. "Darla redecorated all our cottages a couple of years ago. Now she's started making her own line of potpourri. It's right stout smelling stuff though."

"How nice." Mary Lynn looked at the blue and white business card before politely before putting it into her purse. "She sounds like a very creative person to me. You must be proud of her."

"Oh yes I am. She's a very talented girl despite her obsession with the dead." Don shook his head. "People can pair up under some unusual circumstances. You just never know who your kids are gonna end up getting married to and sometimes it turns out to be a good match after all." "Look at our friends Marv and Pauline and all the dangerous adventures they've went through. Who'd have thought a couple of stylish folks like them would end up married to each other and living in Peavine?"

"That's who we're going to the party with, isn't it?" Mary Lynn recalled Don mentioning that they had a big Cadillac. "What kind of dangerous adventures are you talking about?"

Dorine had returned to the diner just as Don was mentioning Marv and Pauline.

"Hush Don," she cautioned. "Remember you have to be careful what you say about those two." Dorine looked over her shoulder as if someone might be listening in the empty diner. Convinced the three of them were alone she gleefully sat down opposite Mary Lynn in the booth. "I'm sure it's safe to tell Mary Lynn about it though.

Intermission at the Moving Theater

"*I believe Don is as personable as Dorine is,*" Johnny said appreciatively as he relaxed back into his blue velvet seat and propped his feet up on the back of the one in front of him. "*I believe the pair of them has pretty much hooked Mary Lynn into staying over for your big Memorial Bash.*"

"*They are a force to be reckoned with, that's for sure.*" Doll smiled warmly at the image of her two dear friends. "*I'm gonna miss my daily dose of Dorine and Don. Their good food and conversation was one of the treasures of my day. Even after I got too sick to go over to the Diner, they'd bring me over something special to tempt my taste buds. God love 'em.*"

"*I've never seen Mary Lynn so at ease, when she's off on her own like this, at least not in all the years I've been watching over her,"* Johnny noted with satisfaction.

"Have you been watching her ever since you, uhmm . . . passed?" Doll wasn't sure she had worded that correctly, but she wanted to know. She was curious about what Crossing Over must have been like for Johnny, when he had left the World of the Living in such an abrupt and unfortunate manner.

Johnny turned and gently looked Doll in the eyes as if he knew what she was thinking. *"I have witnessed almost every moment of Mary Lynn's life since I left my body in the wreckage of that car. It was my choice, to stay near her the only way possible, under the circumstances."*

"Bless your heart," Doll sympathized. *"Was it . . . all this real hard to take?"*

"At first there was a terrible moment of remorse," he said as he returned his gaze to the screen. *"At the same time, I knew things would eventually turn out as they were meant to be. Since then, I've discovered quite a sense of peace here in my own personal Moving Theater."*

"This is all yours?" Doll was surprised to hear that, but recalled Johnny had remained there while she and Laurite attended her funeral.

"It kind of formed around me early on and it's only fitting since Mary Lynn loved for me to take her out to the movies. Laurite only showed up right before you arrived." He flashed his bright grin at Doll. *"It sure has been a pleasure having the company of you two ladies here."*

Laurite made an odd grunting sound and got up from her seat. *"I know plenty about dis Marv and Pauline."* She brushed off her skirt and adjusted the red kerchief on her head. *"I already checked dem out for Rhonelle."*

"That's right. You and Rhonelle did do a background check on them for me." Doll nodded to Johnny. *"Knowing a psychic comes in right handy*

when you run a trailer park. I sure do appreciate all the help you gave Rhonelle, especially with finding Lucille and Tammy."

Laurite gave the slightest hint of a self-satisfied smirk before turning away to vanish into the darkness. "She sure comes and goes a lot." Doll sighed as she settled back to watch the screen again.

"Yep," Johnny agreed. "I'm about to get used to her ways after the past couple of days. But for now, I want to hear about Marv and Pauline." Johnny turned toward a small lit window behind them that Doll hadn't noticed before. "Could we go back and watch this one partly as a Real Time Specialty please?"

Doll looked back at the screen and saw the picture blur and reform. The scene at the Diner faded and was replaced by an image of a younger Marv at the race track, sitting alone on a bench with his head in his hands.

CHAPTER TWELVE

The Saga of Marv and Pauline

Hialeah Race Track, Miami, Florida 1969

Marv was in big trouble! Because of a long spell of bad luck and too many IOUs he was over his head in debt to his bookmakers. Realizing it was only a matter of time before the local collection thugs caught up with him, Marv was feeling pretty desperate.

Earlier that day a mysterious stranger had come to the restaurant where he worked as a waiter, leaving a $50 tip with a note attached telling him to bet on Slippery Sue in the 7th race. Marv thought this indisputably was to be his long awaited lucky day! He left work early to catch a cab ride to the track. He got there just in the nick of time to throw his entire savings (seventy-five dollars, counting the fifty) at the teller and put it all on Slippery Sue to win.

The filly was going off at 60 to 1 odds. Perfect! This would be the beginning of the end of all Marv's problems. He knew that horse would have to win. The mysterious note had said Slippery Sue was a sure thing, and those professional high rollers were privy to information that regular stiffs like Marv could only hope to overhear in the Jockey Club.

"THEY'RE OFF!"

For Marv those were the two most exciting words in the English language. What a race it was! Sue slipped up behind the leading horse right away. Halfway 'round the track, she scooted up ahead of the second horse by a length. Marv was ecstatic! As far as he could tell, Sue was doing everything right.

When she pulled out to four lengths ahead of the pack Marv was jumping for joy and screaming his head off. Slippery Sue was the most beautiful filly he had ever seen and she was about to put him on the road to "Easy Street" until the unthinkable happened. Slippery Sue . . . slipped! She must have stepped on a soft spot on the track, because down she went. Her jockey leapt clear of danger. Sue was shook up a little but got back to her feet and continued the race without a rider. She would live to run another day.

On the other hand Marv feared he would soon be a goner. Standing there in shocked disbelief he didn't see any way he was going to come up with the amount he owed by ten o'clock that night. Without the money, it would be curtains for poor Marv.

The poor fellow didn't have any way to get out of town or even a ride back to his apartment. He had sold his car months ago and he didn't even have a dime for a bus ride. He might as well just stay there in the "Equine Cathedral" and wait for the hit men to come and get him. Marv sunk down onto a bench beside the paddock and put his head in his hands. His eyes filled with tears and squeezed shut as he prayed harder than he ever had in his life:

"Just get me out of here in one piece, and I swear I'll never gamble or set foot anywhere near a racetrack ever again. I mean it God, I promise. Just please don't let Snookie's boys hurt me too bad. (That's my bookie, Lord). Just give me one more chance, that's all I'm asking." Of all the prayers Marv had sent up to Heaven while at the racetrack this was definitely the most earnest of them all. Unbeknown to Marv, seated at the other end of that bench was exactly the "Angel of Mercy" he had been praying for.

Pauline Peavey

Pauline sat at the opposite end of the bench watching Marv. Actually she had been watching Marv with renewed interest for the past three weeks. She needed Marv as much as he needed her. He just didn't know it yet. Pauline was the girlfriend of Little Larry, a former jockey and the brother of Big Louie, owner of the steak house where Marv was employed. Little Larry also was just about the meanest man in all of south Florida. Larry had seemed quite charming and completely harmless when Pauline first met him a year ago, when she was a seating hostess at the Crab Shack, in Panama City.

He came in for lunch every day for a week. Each time he would flirt shamelessly with Pauline and hide generous tips in her hand when she showed him to his favorite table with a view of the beach. By the time he was ready to return to Miami he had sweet-talked Pauline into going back with him. He promised he would get her a real nice job working at his brother's swanky restaurant in Miami.

Pauline was "free, white, and single," as she liked to say. Unfortunately she was also trusting, blonde, and clueless. Pauline and Little Larry hit the road together in style. The fact that his vehicle of choice was a brand new white Cadillac convertible with red leather seats made the offer even more appealing. Pauline needed a place to stay in Miami so he gave her one of his own apartments down by the beach, free of charge.

A week later when he presented her a bracelet with a real diamonds she felt like Marilyn Monroe! Pauline thought this was all too good to be true and brother was she was right! The time came when Little Larry insisted that Pauline return his affections. She supposed that she was obligated since he'd treated her like a princess. She decided he wasn't that bad-looking even though he was barely five feet tall. Unfortunately that's when Pauline's troubles began. (Short men can occasionally turn out to be ill- tempered little Napoleons. Fortunately, Teenie Brice is proof there are exceptions to that rule.)

Little Larry had great deal of insecurities because of his small stature. He would get insanely jealous if Pauline even looked at another man so she took great pains to give Little Larry plenty of attention. She even quit her job as the seating hostess at Big Louie's Steak House to please him but nothing was going to reassure Little Larry.

Men were prone to gawk at Pauline due to her blonde hair and great figure. Little Larry enjoyed taking her out to show off what a bodacious girlfriend he had acquired but when he saw how much all the other guys were enjoying her, his mood would turn sour. As soon as they got back to her place he'd fly into a rage and end up hurting Pauline. The first time he hit her, she was astonished that a little guy could be so strong and quick. Eager to apologize he always said how sorry he was afterwards. Sorry indeed!

The next day Larry would send Pauline flowers and a "make-up" gift, most often an expensive piece of jewelry. Each time he promised it would never happen again and each time it became harder for her to trust anything he promised. Things went on like this because Pauline couldn't see any way out. Not only was Larry little and mean he had a lot of influence with the local Mafia. He made it a point to remind her of that all too often.

Over a six-month period Pauline suffered two black eyes, three broken ribs, a sprained wrist and numerous bruises to her shins. She also had accumulated earrings, a necklace and a brooch - all in diamonds to match her bracelet, a closet full of expensive clothing and a fur stole. She was also given plenty of money to decorate the apartment so Little Larry could use it as an impressive location for his shady business dealings.

It was after the last beating that Pauline began to form her plan. First of all, she would need to find herself a good man to help. She chose Marv. Pauline had gotten to know Marv while she was still working as the seating hostess at Big Louie's Steak House. He seemed to be quite the gentleman, especially when she compared him to Little Larry. He was also fairly handsome and well-preserved, for a man of forty. Pauline was surprised to find out he had twice been married and divorced.

She wondered what personality flaw would have caused Marv to have two wives walk out on him. He did seem to always be broke and asking to borrow money but Pauline chalked that up to double alimony payments to his ex-wives. One day she happened to overhear Marv in a desperate conversation with Snookie (the bookie) and the missing piece of the puzzle fell in place. She realized Marv had an out-of-control gambling habit. Whenever he got any extra money, he'd be off to the bookie or the race track, and end up losing more than he won. He was continually searching for that most elusive, underrated and overlooked horse . . . the long shot! Oh yes, Marv was going to fit in perfectly with Pauline's plan to get away from Little Larry.

After Pauline quit working at the Steak House to ease Little Larry's jealousy she began to discreetly keep her eyes and ears open whenever she played hostess to some of Larry's shady business meetings. She soon figured out a lot of things about where and how Little Larry got all his money. She discovered the source of a large part of his income was from fixing the results at the local race track.

She began to study up on all of the horses running at the track. After a few seemingly innocent questions, she was able to find out the names of trainers and jockeys that were in tight with Little Larry and the hoodlums he had working for him.

For the past two months, Pauline had been going to various pawnshops to hock the diamonds Little Larry had given her. She was careful to buy some rhinestone imitations to wear in place of them in case Larry noticed. She had to do these transactions under the cover of going to the beauty shop or grocery store so it took her awhile to get herself enough money together for the second phase of her plan.

Pauline had been able to keep tabs on Marv by going by the Steak House for take-home meals for her and Little Larry. She was there waiting on some steak sandwiches to-go one afternoon when she saw that Marv was clearing a table vacated by a group of professional handicappers on their way to the track.

When he left the dining room to go into the kitchen with a load of dirty dishes, she walked by and slipped a fifty dollar bill in a cocktail napkin under a plate. Then she sashayed around the corner and hid by the ladies' lounge. Pauline watched Marv's face as he read the note she had written on the napkin. He looked up and when he couldn't see Louie (Pauline had checked to be sure Big Louie was down the street ordering more booze) Marv kissed that napkin, shoved it into his pocket and tore out the door of the Steak House.

Bingo! Pauline was now ready for Phase Three of her plan to escape from Little Larry. After Pauline and Little Larry had eaten their steak sandwich lunch back at the apartment, Pauline fixed them some coffee. What Little Larry didn't know was that Pauline had sprinkled the contents of several of her sleeping capsules into the sugar bowl. Little Larry liked to put about five spoonfuls of sugar in his coffee. Pauline always had hers black. As soon as Little Larry lay down for what was going to turn out to be a very long nap, Pauline flew into action.

She packed as many valuables as she could find and only her best clothes. Very carefully she removed Little Larry's gun that he always kept in his vest pocket as he slept on the sofa. She donned a black wig, scarf, raincoat, and glasses. She had been hiding the disguise for weeks in the back of her closet. She put the gun in her purse, loaded up Larry's car from the back of the apartment and drove like a bat out of hell to the racetrack. She arrived at Hialeah Park Race Track right after the third race and started looking for Marv.

Going back to poor Marv sitting on that bench at the racetrack with his head in his hands, he didn't even notice when Pauline scooted over next to him. She had to wait a minute to steady her breath and calm down before she spoke. For the past forty-five minutes, she had been running willy-nilly all over the track searching for him. It was critical to her plan to find him before the end of the seventh race and she almost didn't make it in time. When she finally spotted him sitting there on that bench she knew her plan might succeed after all.

Beside Little Larry's gun stowed in Pauline's purse was a stash of a little over six thousand dollars. Most of it was in large bills sewn into the lining of her ordinary-looking black handbag that matched her ordinary-looking black coat. Marv had never seen Pauline wear anything that wasn't brightly colored or animal print so with the black wig and sunglasses, her disguise was complete.

"Hey Marv, you look like you could use a friend." Pauline's disguise was so clever that when she first spoke to Marv he was so startled by her appearance he almost bolted right then. "Wait, Marv! It's me, Pauline," she whispered as she lifted the large pair of sunglasses so he could see her face a brief second or two. "You know, Little Larry's girl."

That frightened Marv even more because he was well aware of Little Larry's brutal reputation.

"What do you want from me?" he stammered. "Just give me a little more time. Don't send Little Larry's boys after me, please."

"Marv, will you shut up!" Pauline cut him off. "I'm here to help you and I really need for you to help me! Just listen for a minute . . . Okay?"

So Marv sat and listened while Pauline outlined the rest of her escape scenario. He realized his best and last chance for redemption had miraculously arrived. There sat his very own angel, clad in black leather and he'd do whatever he could to make this work and he would never even look back.

SO, here's what they did . . .

Walking as slowly and nonchalantly as they could, they left the track and walked out to the parking lot. They drove Little Larry's car to a bus station and unloaded it. They left the car in a no-parking zone and went into the station and called a cab.

They took the cab to the airport and boarded a flight to New Orleans where they stayed for one night. While they were there Marv wrote two letters and mailed them off. One was to big Louie, apologizing for running out on him but explaining that he'd needed to return to New Orleans because of a death in the family.

The other letter was to Snookie saying he was no longer beholden to him because of this money he had just inherited from his uncle. In the envelope was a cashier's check for the money he owed (thanks to Pauline).

Pauline bought a used Chevy and she and Marv drove north. They stopped in Vicksburg at a little jewelry store and bought a couple of inexpensive wedding bands so they could pass for a married couple. When they got to Tallulah, Louisiana, Pauline decided it was safe to ditch the wig, but she kept the sunglasses on. Marv wouldn't stop again until they ran out of gas at Peavine. The engine was overheated so they left the car at a service station and walked over to Don's Diner for a late breakfast.

Back at the Moving Theater

Doll was on the edge of her seat when the picture on the screen blurred and faded. "Woweee, I knew they had a pretty narrow escape of some kin, but I never knew poor Pauline had been abused like that!" Doll shook her head. "That poor girl . . ."

It was so strange. Rhonelle had told me the night before to be expecting some strangers to arrive soon, and that I was supposed to help them out.

"Very interesting, indeed," Johnny agreed. "Let's see how Mary Lynn is taking all this. She's always had a horror/fascination with the Mafia."

He turned back to the projector and snapped his fingers. The screen sparkled and the small circle of light grew until they were once again looking in on Dorine avidly telling a spellbound Mary Lynn about the day Marv and Pauline arrived.

"Doll and I watched them coming up the street, and we knew they weren't from anywhere around here," Dorine said. "Doll was sitting at the counter there having her mid-morning coffee and cigarette when they came in. Her curiosity just seemed to get the better of her so she moseyed right over to where Marv and Pauline were sitting and introduced herself."

"That's just like Doll," Don chimed in. "She could get past anybody's shyness, given half a chance. It was pretty obvious them two was nervous about something so she was right careful in how she approached them."

Dorine took over at this point. "Maybe it had to do with the fact that Marv and Pauline were just worn out from running but after an hour of commiserating with Doll they must have decided this was just about the safest place for them to be. Doll had made a deal with them to fix up and rent one of the vacant trailers she happened to have available."

Mary Lynn seemed a bit surprised by this. "How could she be so sure they were trustworthy after just meeting them?"

Don winked at Dorine and they both said, "Rhonelle."

Mary Lynn was on the verge of asking who that was, but decided she'd probably hear about her later.

Dorine hunkered up her shoulders and leaned in so as to beat Don back to telling the story. "At first, they only planned to stay a few months but after a few weeks Marv and Pauline took a mysterious weekend trip up to Little Rock. When they returned to Peavine they announced happily that they were going to stay and open up the Nu-Tu-U Flea Market with Flair."

"Marv and Pauline were aglow with happiness acting like a couple of newlyweds. Later I found out that's exactly what they were! They had taken care of a lot of business up in Little Rock that weekend. Pauline was able to gradually unload the fine furs, clothing, and a few knick-knacks she had taken with her from Miami. She did this by mixing them in with various items she picked up at rummage sales and some things Doll had left over from the old Dumas estate. Marv indulged his gambling urges by playing the stock market instead of the horses. He got a few good tips from some investor buddies up in Pine Bluff and has ended up doing pretty well by it."

"Hey, what's wrong there, Mary Lynn," Don noted in alarm. "You look downright pale!"

Mary Lynn had begun to tremble a little and her eyes were big as saucers. "But . . . how did Marv and Pauline know they would be safe here? I mean, the Mafia for God's sake. They never give up looking for people who run out on them or do them wrong!" She had seen that movie, 'The Godfather' and been unable to sleep for a week."

"Oh . . . that. Well . . ." Dorine looked around the deserted diner, and lowered her voice to a whisper. "Have you ever heard of the witness protection program the FBI has?" Her eyebrows arched knowingly as she nodded her head at Mary Lynn.

"You mean . . . Marv and Pauline . . ." she whispered wide-eyed.

"Not their real names." Dorine stated with an air of intrigue. "We all know them as just our own Marv and Pauline Hampton but their true identities were changed. Let me backtrack a little."

Dorine leaned back in her chair with a smile. "The night they spent in New Orleans wasn't at a fancy hotel. They went straight to FBI headquarters as soon as they landed at the airport. There were five undercover agents there waiting for Marv and Pauline, who escorted them to the local office."

"Wow," was all Mary Lynn could think to say.

"Back in Florida," Dorine continued. "Pauline had been approached by one of Little Larry's so-called business partners during one of his parties she had been hostess for at her apartment. This guy got her alone in the kitchen while she was freshening up some drinks.

It didn't take long for him to convince Pauline that the only way for her to escape from Little Larry was to turn State's witness against him and all the guys in his gang of hoods!

"This 'guy' was an undercover agent who wasn't ready to blow his cover yet so he needed to recruit Pauline. She helped work out the famous 'Pauline Plan' during visits to Julio, her hairdresser.

Turned out Julio was working for the feds too. That gave her the time, place, and support to pull all that off. She and Marv are smart but not smart enough to have gotten away with all this on their own.

Mary Lynn was just stunned. "What about Little Larry? Did he go to jail?"

"He's dead. No, Pauline didn't kill him with the sleeping pills; she's way too kindhearted for that. The testimony Pauline provided made sure that Little Larry was sentenced to forty years in a federal prison. He picked one fight too many with some convicts that weren't afraid to fight back. Imagine Larry's surprise! As for Snookie and all the rest of the gang they squealed like a bunch of little girls to the Feds and I guess you could say they're harmless now."

"That's what I call some pretty wild and dangerous adventures," Don added.

"*Oh Lord,*" Doll was watching Mary Lynn closely. "*I hope they haven't overdone it with this story and scared her off.*"

Johnny squinted at Mary Lynn then started to laugh. "*I think the fascination has overcome the horror this time. That's my girl,*" he said as her turned the silver lighter in his hand.

CHAPTER THIRTEEN

Denim and Lace Interior Design in Cottage Number Five

Mary Lynn sat in stunned silence after hearing the story of Marv and Pauline. She had never known anyone personally with such an exciting past. Now her reluctance about going to the party with Don and Dorine was replaced by an intense curiosity about Marv and Pauline.

"I can't wait to meet them," she said honestly. "What time are they getting here?"

"Well, Lordee!" Dorine squinted at her pink and gold wristwatch. "It's already five-thirty. They're picking us up at six-fifteen so we'd better get moving if we're going to be ready in time."

"I'll go get your bags for ya, Mary Lynn," Don offered.

"Oh, thank you. I have them on the back seat. Here're my keys." Mary Lynn dug around in her hand bag and handed a wad of car and house keys to Don. "Will there be time for me to freshen up before we go?" She was also hoping to change clothes. "Dorine, how dressy is this party?"

"You don't need to get all gussied up," Dorine said as she and Mary Lynn headed out the back door. "Just wear something festive and be sure it's comfortable, nothing black or dreary either. Doll's instructions were that this is supposed to be a celebration not a pity party."

As they walked across the small lawn Dolly and Whutzit caught up with them. The dogs scampered so closely around her feet that Mary Lynn had to be careful not to trip over them. A neat, white picket fence enclosed the yard and adjoined the five little stone cottages. This comprised the Dew Drop Inn.

"These are just darling!" Mary Lynn exclaimed when she saw the cozy-looking stone cottages. They had pink awnings and shutters, pink window boxes with pink plastic roses, and pink doors with white numbers painted on them. Each one had a small drive and gravel patch for parking beside it. Three of the cottages still had cars parked alongside them. All but one, the number five cottage, had lights glowing behind lace-curtained windows.

"I can't wait for you to see what a nice job our Darla has done with the décor," Dorine said with pride. "She pulled out all the stops when it came to fixing this place up for the tourists. She figured it would be a good way to advertise her skills as a decorator."

"Don gave me one of her cards. 'Denim and Lace' sounds very…" Mary Lynn tried to find the right thing to say. "Country and cozy is what I think of."

Dorine liked the sound of that. "That's real clever, Mary Lynn. I ought to tell Darla to add that to her radio ads."

Don was just pulling Mary Lynn's car up to the parking patch beside cottage number five as the women arrived. He got out and grabbed Mary Lynn's two bags from the backseat and met them at the door. "Hope you didn't mind me moving your car back here for you, Mary Lynn. You got the cottage key, Honey?" he asked Dorine, who nodded and held out a key tied to a large pink plastic key tag with #5 scrawled on it.

As Dorine unlocked and opened the pink door to Cottage #5 a potent odor of cloves and cinnamon mixed with a strong artificial pine smell assaulted Mary Lynn's sensitive nose.

"Phew!" Dorine exclaimed as she tried to wave the smell away from her. "This dang stuff Darla makes near 'bout takes my head off.

She keeps on sneaking it in here in hopes of selling it to my guests...
Lordee!"

Holding her nose with one hand, Dorine picked up a china bowl
filled with red and green wood shavings from the small dressing table
near the door. Scooting a wastebasket over with her foot she dumped
the bowl's contents into it. Don swooped over after switching on the
lights and set the wastebasket outside the cottage.

"See you gals in thirty minutes," he said as he went quickly out the
door. Both dogs cautiously approached for a sniff at the wastebasket.
Whutzit yelped and ran off while Dolly had a sneezing and snorting
fit. Mary Lynn was glad that she wasn't the only one offended by the
malodorous potpourri.

"We'll leave the door open and crack the window a little. That
ought to clear this stink out pretty quick. Darla must have damaged
her sense of smell being around all those terrible chemicals they use
at the mortuary." Dorine frowned and shuddered as she bent down to
turn up the little gas space heater near the door to a small bathroom.
The bathroom was complete with pink towels and a matching pink-
and-white flowered shower curtain.

"Now," she said as she stood back up with a grunt, and wiped her
hands on her apron. "Dolly and I'd better get along and change into
our party togs. Come on Dolly." The poodle waddled over to Dorine
to be picked up. "Let's us go on, and let Miz Mary Lynn get settled."
Dorine waggled Dolly's pink-toe-nailed front paw at Mary Lynn and
grinned. "We'll come back to fetch you in about twenty minutes."

"I'll be ready." Mary Lynn said. She stood at the open door
watching Dorine shamble across the lawn holding Dolly under one
arm and carrying the offensive wastebasket of potpourri in her other
hand.

After propelling in more fresh air to the cottage by using the front door as a large fan of sorts, Mary Lynn decided she could tolerate the aromatic remains of Darla's "Smells of the Season" that still lingered in the room and closed the door. She put on the latch and switched on a nearby lamp.

Darla had done a fairly nice job of decorating the cottage. The walls were painted a pale pink with white trim. The wood floor was painted white, and a small hooked rug with pink roses was beside the bed. The double bed had a thick floral-print comforter on it and about a dozen small decorative pillows with a variety of combinations of prints, chintz, crochet, and lace in pinks and whites.

Across from the bed was a large recliner with a handmade pink-and-white quilt thrown over it. A floor lamp with a pink shade stood beside it. Mary Lynn didn't see a TV in the room but a table near the lamp had a variety of magazines and paperback books neatly laid out on it.

"Darla should definitely stick to decorating," Mary Lynn decided, "and give up on the potpourri business." Turning to her suitcase on the luggage stand at the foot of the bed she opened it up to find something to wear. Packed on top was the flashy sequined sweater Leroy had given to her for Christmas just three days ago. Mary Lynn had brought it for their New Years Eve date. It would be just the thing to wear to the party tonight, she thought happily.

She could also wear her red knit pants and new shoes she had bought on sale right before Christmas. She pulled them out of the side pockets of her suitcase, and laid them on the bed beside her red slacks, and the beloved sequined sweater. The shoes were red satin flats with sequins and beads on them. They glimmered and glowed in the soft pink light. Mary Lynn sighed with satisfaction at the sight. Along with pie there were two other things she never could pass up: shoe sales and sequins.

Sparkly things were like a magnet to her and Leroy was well aware of that fact. He did a great job picking out that sweater for her. Unlike her friend's husbands he always managed to find something special for her. Leroy's thoughtfulness never ceased to amaze her.

Most people would never guess from his serious demeanor and avid enthusiasm for outdoor sports that he would be the type to always know just what his wife wanted as a gift. Even when they were newlyweds and pinching every penny Leroy could always come up with something pretty that she really appreciated.

"I can count myself as really lucky since most husbands don't even have a clue as to what women really want." Mary Lynn mused as she held up the sweater to herself, and looked at her reflection in the mirror over the dressing table. "I must have had an angel on my shoulder the day I walked into Struby's Drugstore in Baton Rouge and got that job at the lunch counter."

Leroy had been the assistant pharmacist. Even though he was only a few years older than Mary Lynn she had been very intimidated by him. That seemed funny to her now. She later found out that he had been so smitten with her that he could barely get up the nerve to start a conversation with her. He ordered a whole lot of lunch specials and ice cream sodas before finding the courage to ask her out. After dating only two months they were going steady.

If it hadn't been for Leroy, Mary Lynn didn't know if she could have ever been able to recover from Johnny's tragic death and the dark years that followed. It was because of his love and quiet encouragement she had gone on to make something of her life.

Leroy suggested that she take night classes so she could finally earn her high school diploma. After that she continued her education with a business course at LSU while he finished his pharmacy degree. She learned enough to manage the accounts and payroll at Struby's Drug.

A year after they got married they moved away from Baton Rouge and Leroy took over his father's drugstore in Cape Girardeau. Mary Lynn helped him out with the bookkeeping even after the kids were born.

She was fully aware of how fortunate she was to have ended up with a husband like Leroy. He was a far better man than she thought she deserved. Suddenly, tears welled up in her eyes. More than anything right then, she just wanted to hear his voice.

"What am I doing standing here blubbering like a love-struck teenager? I need to get myself ready to go to that party. What would Leroy think if I were to call him, all silly and sentimental, right in the middle of his 'duck retreat' with the guys? He'd think I'd lost my mind!"

Still, she definitely planned to call him as soon as she got to Lizzie's tomorrow.

Chapter Fourteen

The Arrival of the Powder Blue Coupe de Ville

"Knock, knock!" sang Dorine from outside the cottage door. "Are you decent?"

Mary Lynn patted at her hair one last time and sang back, "Just a minute!" She gave herself a third once-over in front of the narrow full-length mirror before reaching over to unlock and open the cottage door.

"My lands, you look as sparkly as a Christmas tree," Dorine exclaimed when she saw Mary Lynn standing under the porch light with her sequined sweater flashing like a disco ball.

"And look at your pretty shoes! Where did you get those? They probably pinch your feet."

Mary Lynn was still taking in Dorine's party outfit, a pink sweatshirt with a white poodle appliqué and a pair of pink fleece sweat pants. The fuzzy pink house shoes had been replaced by gold bedroom slippers and white socks. A pink bow with gold curly ribbon cascaded down the back of Dorine's frizzy gray hair. Large earrings in the shape of white poodles dangled from her ears.

Dolly was tucked under Dorine's arm with her head poking out of a bulky pink bunting. She also had a pink bow with gold curly ribbons secured by a rubber band on her topknot.

"At least they don't have high heels. I myself haven't worn heels in twenty years. Are they comfortable?" Dorine was still looking at Mary Lynn's new shoes.

"Oh yes, as a matter of fact, they are as comfy as a pair of . . . um . . ." Mary Lynn started to say bedroom slippers. ". . . a pair of tennis shoes!"

Dorine was relieved to hear that. "Marv and Pauline are here and Don is already in the car. They are all waiting on us over in front of the Diner."

As Mary Lynn followed Dorine across the lawn to the Diner, she saw a large powder-blue Cadillac Coupe de Ville purring in the gravel parking lot. Her heart began to beat faster at the prospect of meeting the infamous Marv and Pauline, as well as the other residents of Peavine.

Once again, Mary Lynn was amazed at her new found sense of adventure. She was actually about to ride in a car with two people who had a dangerous past and she was looking forward to it. Not sure what to expect, Mary Lynn was most curious as to what they'd look like. Just as they got to the car, a tall, dark-haired man in a light blue leisure suit hopped out of the driver's seat and came around to open the car door for them.

Marv introduced himself to Mary Lynn. As he shook her hand he looked just a tad too deeply into her eyes. His black hair was slicked straight back and a gold chain glinted against his tanned chest. His wide-collared polyester shirt was open and unbuttoned far enough to reveal a few gray chest hairs. "Hmmm, Marv must be hitting the Grecian Formula bottle on a regular basis," Mary Lynn thought as she averted her stare and got into the back seat.

Don was on one side so Mary Lynn scooted over to the middle to leave room for Dorine and Dolly. Pauline turned and looked around at them from the front seat and said how glad she was to have Mary Lynn join them for the party. Because of the dim light all Mary Lynn could see of Pauline was that she was very blonde, very made-up, and had on flashy earrings.

It was difficult to guess the ages of either Marv or Pauline. She would take a closer look once they got to the party. Dorine handed Dolly to Mary Lynn and slowly lowered herself onto the car seat. Marv stood patiently holding the car door until she was settled. Then he closed the door with the solid "thunk" that only a heavy plush car door makes. In a cloud of Pauline's Estee Lauder cologne fumes and in the comfort of Marv's Coupe de Ville, they glided off down the highway to the VFW Hut for the posthumous party in honor of Loretta "Doll" Dumas.

"What a weird night," thought Mary Lynn. "I can't believe I'm doing this." Little did she know that this was only the beginning of weirdness for Mary Lynn Stanton.

CHAPTER FOURTEEN

Welcome to the Doll Dumas Memorial Bash

O*kay, I got ever ting set up for us now.*" Laurite had reappeared beside Doll and Johnny.

"*What do you mean set up now?*" Doll turned to look at Laurite.

"*Looks like we're going to your big party,*" Johnny said with a smile as he extended his hand to her.

"*You're going with us this time?*" Doll was getting excited about her Memorial Bash.

"*Yep, I'm going to go this time. How are we doing this, Laurite?*"

"*Follow me.*" She led them down the aisle past the front row of seats, up the steps to the stage and right into the movie screen.

Doll grabbed Johnny's arm and held it tightly as they stepped into the sky high above the light blue car speeding along the road below. She squeezed her eyes shut and buried her face in his shoulder.

"*Ooooweee! Sorry Hon, I'm not real keen on heights.*"

"*That's OK. You should have seen me when Laurite took me on one of her junkets for the first time . . . and I used to be an Air Force pilot!*" Johnny patted Doll consolingly.

Laurite simply folded her arms and floated regally alongside them, her black skirt billowing like a parachute. Johnny did a double take when he caught a glimpse of something and burst out laughing.

"*Not to be disrespectful Laurite but are those red bloomers you are wearing?*"

Far from being embarrassed, Laurite pulled her skirt aside to display the bright red satin underwear, modestly gathered with lace just below her knees. *"Was a gift from my fourth husband – he the best one! Tanks for noticin',"* she said with a grin so wide that her gold tooth shone in the darkness.

At that point Doll forgot to be scared and had to take a peek. As her eyes opened she caught sight of the building below .Multicolored Christmas lights outlined the roof of the VFW hut, giving the drab cinderblock building a festive appearance. Since the parking lot was already full of cars, Marv pulled up to the front of the building to let everybody out.

He hopped out of the car and was holding the back passenger door open before Mary Lynn could get her purse and coat gathered up. Dorine lurched and struggled until she managed to get out of the car with the help of the ever solicitous Marv. By the time Mary Lynn was able to climb out from the middle of the back seat everybody else was waiting for her.

This was the first time Mary Lynn had been able to get a good look at Pauline. She certainly did not look like somebody you'd find in a place like Peavine, Arkansas. Glamorous was the first word that came to mind when she looked at Pauline. Definitely in her prime Pauline's figure was stunning. Mary Lynn attempted to suck in her own tummy and smooth her sweater a little lower over the hips. She wistfully remembered that once she had possessed a pretty nice set of curves too.

She guessed Pauline had to be pushing forty but didn't look or dress her age. Her party outfit included tight-fitting slacks, stiletto pumps, topped off with a clinging mohair sweater. Diamonds flashed and sparkled on her neck, wrists and ears. Mary Lynn was trying to count how many bracelets Pauline was wearing when Pauline came up to her and grabbed her hands, spreading Mary Lynn's arms wide to get a better view of her sequined sweater. "Look at how darling Mary Lynn looks in this divine outfit!" Pauline gushed in her high sweet voice. "You are an absolute vision honey. Where on earth did you find this gorgeous top?"

Mary Lynn felt like the Belle of the Ball, being made over by such a fashionable person as Pauline, who seemed sincere in her admiration of the beloved Christmas sweater. "Leroy, my husband, gave it to me," she said proudly. "He noticed I was drooling over it in the Dillard's catalogue and surprised me with it on Christmas Eve. I was able to wear it to church and Christmas dinner. Good thing he knows what size I wear." Mary Lynn giggled and blushed with pride.

"You are so lucky," exclaimed Pauline. "Every time Marv tries to buy me clothes, they turn out to be at least two sizes too big. Finally he just gave up and started buying me jewelry, didn't you, Sugar Daddy!" Pauline sidled up to Marv, and he put his arm around her shoulder.

Pauline abruptly changed gears. "Ya'll, I'm going to run on in and be sure Ozelle and Sally got everything set up on the buffet. Kristy said they'd probably need some help. See you later alligator," she said as she kissed Marv on the cheek. He gave her a little love tap on her shapely derriere as he let her go.

"Look a there, Don" Marv said with pride and admiration as he watched Pauline sashay up the steps and into the VFW. "You could bounce a quarter off her rear end."

Don seemed to get the gist of Marv's comment and nodded appreciatively.

All of this had the effect of making Mary Lynn feel frumpy and lumpy again. She fell back behind Don and waited with Dorine while Marv drove off to find a parking place. Mary Lynn held Dolly for

Dorine while she heaved herself up the stairs to the front entrance.

"You go ahead on Don and save us a table before you go check on your desserts. Mary Lynn and I'll be along directly. "I hate these stairs," Dorine huffed as she made it up the five steps, one at a time. "We can put Dolly down once we get inside and find some place she won't get stepped on. I'll bet a few of her friends will be here tonight."

Mary Lynn handed Dolly back, grateful to be making her entrance with Dorine rather than being totally eclipsed by the radiance of Pauline.

Doll noticed Johnny had eyes for no one but Mary Lynn as the three spirits stood together at the door of the VFW.

"We split up for now," Laurite announced before she disappeared into the crowd. She was on a mission to contact her psychic granddaughter, Rhonelle.

"Will anybody be able to see us walking around amongst 'em like this?" Doll felt noticeably different here at the party than she had during the odd experience of floating above the crowd at her funeral earlier that afternoon. *"I'm feeling pretty, uh . . . solid at the moment."*

Johnny took Doll's arm and walked her over the threshold. *"Rhonelle and a few of the dogs are the only ones that are likely to pick up on your presence at this point."*

Sure enough, the party guests were flowing right past them. They were all oblivious that the ghost of the honoree was standing right there in their midst. Suddenly Doll was overcome by a strong urge to find her own granddaughter, Tammy.

"I guess I know who I'm supposed to go 'haunt' now," she said. *"You mind if I leave you here, Johnny?"* Doll could feel herself being pulled towards the opposite side of the room.

"I'll be fine. You go on and enjoy yourself. I'll be over there with Mary Lynn." He grinned and tipped his hat. *"I'll catch up with you and Laurite before midnight."*

"I found us a table right over there by the desserts." Don had found Dorine and Mary Lynn as soon as they got in the door and began to steer them through the crowd. "This 'un is far enough from the stage so the music won't mess with my hearing aids. There 'tis right over yonder by that long table in the back."

Mary Lynn's jaw dropped as she took in the sights and sounds of the VFW Hut. At least a hundred people were talking and laughing at tables arranged around a dance floor. On the stage at the back of the room was a large woman wearing a rainbow-hued skirt and a huge Mexican sombrero. She was busily checking out the various amplifiers and extension cords.

"Hey, Louise," Dorine shouted to the woman as they neared the stage. "We can't wait to hear the Gay Caballeros band!"

"Hola Don and Dorine," the woman called out as she trotted over to the edge of the stage. "You'll love the new arrangement of 'Mexican Hat Dance' Gary and I have worked up. It's going to be a real show-stopper! Speaking of stops, I'd better go check out the new electronic jazz organ he's brought for me to play on." Before Dorine could introduce Mary Lynn, Louise skittered away and was intently studying the various controls on her new instrument.

"Lordee . . . Louise is already into her 'show-time' mode. She sure is thrilled that her grandson has followed in her musical footsteps. Bless his heart, he's the only one in her family that seems to care about his grandmother and she truly dotes on him. Louise never batted an eye when he brought his . . . uh," Dorine leaned over to Mary Lynn's ear, and shouted in a quieter tone. ". . . brought his boyfriend, Jay, to visit a couple of years ago."

"That was sweet of her." Mary Lynn had become much more tolerant of that kind of thing lately. Besides, she was too busy gawking at all the lavish decorations as Don led them to the table to think much about the sexual preferences of the Gay Caballeros.

Twinkling white lights were strung tent-like above the dance floor with a disco mirror ball suspended from the ceiling. More white lights were looped across the stage along with teal and mauve crepe paper garlands. At each corner of the stage stood a white flocked Christmas tree, decorated with little blue lights, gold baubles, and mauve silk bows. Topping each tree, were some odd-looking, frizzy-haired angel dolls. Mary Lynn stopped and squinted up at them before she realized they were little poodles in white dresses with wings.

"Cute, aren't they?" Dorine noticed Mary Lynn looking at them. "Those Poodle Angels have been a real hot seller. Teenie came up with the idea and Mavis hand-makes each one."

They were so appealing, Mary Lynn wondered if she could manage to buy one for herself as a souvenir.

"Here we go. How's this, ladies?" Don indicated they had arrived at their table. "You and Mary Lynn sit over to this side so's you can see the stage. I'm gonna sit right here and watch the dessert table."

He was already peeking past Mary Lynn to see what pies had been laid out.

"This will be a great opportunity for me to conduct a little research. I'm tryin' out somethin' new tonight – chocolate pecan pie – it's one of my better recipes, if I do say so myself."

"Don's a pie specialist," Dorine told Mary Lynn. "Honey, go on and do your inventory so you can keep count but," Dorine grabbed Don's sleeve to get his attention, "after you do that go find Marv and ya'll get us something to drink from the bar. Is a Whiskey Sour okay with you, Mary Lynn?"

"Sure, I'll have one if you are." Mary Lynn was not expecting cocktails but wouldn't mind having a little nip to help her relax.

"GET US TWO WHISKEY SOURS HONEY, OKAY?" Don nodded to indicate he heard as he twiddled an adjustment on one of his hearing aids before heading off towards his array of pies.

"These tables are so elegant." Mary Lynn was still preoccupied by the lavish decorations. Their round table was covered by a teal-colored cloth, white votive candles, and a centerpiece of mauve tulips and gold-painted ivy. A bunch of gold, teal, and mauve helium-filled balloons floated four feet above the table, tied onto the vase holding the flowers.

"Who put all of this together?" Mary Lynn knew from the experience of decorating for her daughter's wedding reception that to pull off a party such as this took a lot of work and money.

"Darla did almost all of the planning herself," Dorine said with pride. "The actual setting up and flower arrangements were done by the boys at the local florist shop, Violet Expressions. That's them with some of their little friends over there at that table by the stage."

Mary Lynn looked over to where Dorine was pointing and saw the group of musicians in Gary's band sitting at a table with two other nice-looking young men.

"That one with the blonde hair and glasses is David who owns the shop," Dorine sighed. "He was pretty upset when he found out Darla had chosen this color scheme. There weren't any roses to match so he had to settle on tulips, and they barely got here in time."

"He seems to be enjoying himself now." Mary Lynn noticed David was laughing hard and pointing to the stage where the organ was set up with a vase of David's mauve tulips on it. "I wonder what's so funny."

Dolly began to wiggle and whine. She had just sighted one of her poodle pals at the table beside them and wanted out of her bunting. As Mary Lynn's attention was focused on helping Dorine fluff up Dolly's pink party tutu it was a moment or two before she realized that someone was standing beside her left elbow staring down at her in great agitation.

CHAPTER FIFTEEN

Rhonelle Dubois - Former Exotic Dancer Turned Psychic

O H!" Mary Lynn gasped and gave an involuntary jerk as she looked up into the face of a tall woman glaring down at her with large heavily lined dark eyes. Like "burnt holes in a blanket" is how Leroy would have described them. A bushy halo of salt and pepper curly hair surrounded her intense face and fell below her narrow shoulders. A brightly colored shawl was clutched at her large bosom by a gnarled hand covered in silver and turquoise rings. Beneath the shawl, she had on a purple spandex ballet-style top and a long purple skirt.

The woman stood there alternately staring at Mary Lynn then closing her eyes and humming under her breath. This was such odd behavior that Mary Lynn couldn't think of a single thing to say. By the time she had mustered up some bright and cheery greeting the woman abruptly turned and walked quickly away.

"Looks like you made quite an impression on Rhonelle," said a voice near her left ear.

"What? Oh!" Mary Lynn was startled by Marv as he suddenly appeared beside her with the cocktails.

"Good Lord!" Mary Lynn gasped. "What is wrong with that woman? She scared the Begeezus out of me!"

"Rhonelle has that effect on most people until you get used to her," Dorine whispered with a nervous laugh before taking a generous pull on the whiskey sour Marv had set before her. "But don't let her

Rhonelle aghast

scare you. She's harmless, right Marv?"

"Is she mentally ill or something?" Mary Lynn asked Marv and Dorine, suddenly concerned.

"Well, I guess Rhonelle isn't much crazier than any other person who's a psychic," Marv noted with a chuckle.

"A psychic? She isn't a real one is she?" Mary Lynn wasn't quite sure she believed in that sort of thing.

"She's for real all right. I can vouch for that." Marv said, as he took his eyes from the retreating back of Rhonelle and turned his steady gaze on Mary Lynn. "She's as authentic as they come. Funny thing is, she never realized what a talented telepathic and clairvoyant she was until after she settled down here in Peavine."

Topics such as ESP made Mary Lynn feel tense and shivery yet she was compelled to find out more about this bizarre woman. "Where did she come from, I mean before she came to Peavine?" Mary Lynn craned around to sneak a peek at Rhonelle only to quickly shrink back behind Marv. She had no sooner caught a glimpse of Rhonelle standing at the bar across the room when she realized those dark eyes were staring right back at her.

"New Orleans, the Big Easy," Marv answered as he leaned back in his chair and took a sip of his gin and tonic. "For years she made a pretty good living as a strip . . . I mean uh . . . an exotic dancer in a club down on Bourbon Street."

"You don't mean it!" Mary Lynn was shocked. First she hears about a former gangster's moll and now a stripper! She began to wonder just what kind of a town Peavine had become.

Marv laughed over Mary Lynn's prudish reaction. "It wasn't such a bad thing to be doing that kind of work, not near as sleazy as it'd be nowadays. Back in the 50's and 60's striptease was much more of an art form. Rhonelle was quite a looker when she was younger. She's showed me some of her old posters. I understand she was also a very talented dancer, claims that's what allowed her to do more teasing and less stripping."

Both Dorine and Marv started to laugh at the horrified expression on Mary Lynn's face.

"Aw come on Mary Lynn, get over it!" Dorine snorted between sips of her whiskey sour. "Rhonelle was only doing what she had to do to survive the world she was brought up in. Who knows, if I'd had her looks I might have done the same thing in her situation."

"Done what?" Don had just arrived back at their table after overseeing the layout of the desserts. He had a big paper cup filled with beer in one hand and was hurriedly adjusting his hearing aid with the other.

"I'd have been an exotic dancer!" Dorine said as she wiggled her shoulders. Dolly looked up and whimpered. Everybody else at the table, including Mary Lynn, suddenly burst into laughter at the thought.

"Hey! I had what it takes to get attention when I was a young thing," Dorine announced coquettishly.

When Marv could finally stop giggling, he wiped the tears from his eyes and continued. "Oh me, Dorine, that's an interesting picture you've put in my head. Where was I? Okay, let's see . . . Rhonelle never did know who her daddy was. She grew up kind of wild living in the French Quarter. She and her mamma, who was a striptease dancer, lived with her Creole grandmother. 'Old Granny Laurite' is what everybody called her. She was a famous palm reader and worked at that little tea room down in the French Quarter."

"I think I know where that is!" Mary Lynn interrupted. She had seen it every time she went to New Orleans and was always tempted to go check it out but never had the courage to go inside. "It has a sign with a tea cup and a hand on it that says Palms Read."

"That's the one." Marv continued. "Granny Laurite had herself a loyal following in her day. Most were wealthy ladies from the Garden District, what you'd call the 'old money' families. In addition to the female clients some of New Orleans' most influential politicians and businessmen would come to see her for advice and . . . uh . . . other kinds of favors.

"There'd always been rumors about Rhonelle's granny." At this point Marv lowered his voice so Mary Lynn had to lean in closer to hear. "It was common knowledge in the Quarter that Granny Laurite was actually some kind of a Voodoo Queen!"

"Now I know you're pulling my leg." Mary Lynn was certain there was nothing to all that voodoo foolishness. "I don't believe in that sort of thing anyway." She stated primly.

"Don't be so sure about that Mary Lynn. Wait till you hear the rest of this." Dorine said as she downed another big gulp of her whiskey sour. "Go on Marv, tell her."

"Rhonelle inherited her mother's dark beauty and dancing talent. It was her grandmother who passed along to her the gift of 'the sight' as they called it. Often those traits skip a generation. Rhonelle was a good deal brighter than her mamma ever was and learned most of her skills by simply keeping her eyes and ears open. She picked up all she ever knew about dancing from watching back stage at the strip club where her mother was a dancer. Laurite taught Rhonelle how to do tarot card readings when she was only a child.

"By the age of eleven Rhonelle would go to the strip club and practice her readings on the other dancing girls. They thought it was an amusing game for a little girl until they began to get spooked over the things she told them. She did a Tarot reading for her mamma one afternoon just for laughs, they said. What Rhonelle saw when she laid out the cards upset her so badly she swooped up them up before her mother could see. She ran away and set fire to the whole tarot deck out in the alley. Sadly that still couldn't stop what was going to happen.

"That very night, her mamma was murdered in a fight with another dancer over some good-for-nothing scoundrel they were both sweet on. The other girl pulled out a knife and stabbed her right in the heart. When the terrible news reached Granny Laurite her face went all strange. She was furious at Rhonelle for not coming to her just as soon as she had read the cards on her mother. She forced the girl tell her who it was that killed her mamma and to find out the name of the man they were fighting over.

"Laurite instructed her to return to the club and steal something that belonged to the woman and bring it back to her. Nobody paid much attention to a child like Rhonelle. The police were at the club and everything was still in an uproar so it was simple for a little girl as dark and quick as Rhonelle to sneak into the dressing room and pick up one of the murderer's tasseled pasties."

"What's a pasty?" Mary Lynn asked as she leaned forward listening intently to the bizarre tale of Rhonelle's childhood.

"Oh Mary Lynn, you can't be that innocent!" Dorine was getting a bit loose lipped by now. "You know what pasties are. They're those tasseled thingies that strippers paste onto their . . ."

"Oh yes, those things. I know what you mean, Dorine." Mary Lynn blushed slightly.

"Anyway," Marv went on. "Rhonelle ran all the way back to her Granny Laurite with that pasty hidden in her pocket. She also had a scrap of paper with the name of the man that was the cause of the fight. She dutifully handed them over to her Granny Laurite. The only words of comfort the old Creole offered to her distraught grandchild, as she ordered her to go to bed, was not to worry because she would see that justice was done.

"Within two days the murderous dancing girl was found dead in her jail cell. They say she died of a bleeding ulcer. Three days after that the man they were fighting over was grievously injured in a freak accident at work on the docks by the river. So, what do you think about Voodoo now, Mary Lynn?" Marv asked her as he attempted to hide his smile.

"I think you all are just trying to scare me." Mary Lynn tried to sound casual as she took a ladylike sip of her cocktail. "What happened to that poor little Rhonelle after her mother was killed?"

Marv rubbed his chin and took a few sips of his drink. "Dorine, isn't that about the time she was thinking she was gonna grow up and be a nun?"

"*A nun?*" Mary Lynn exclaimed as she almost choked on her drink.

"I believe it was about then, Marv." Dorine had to laugh. "The first time I heard about that part of her past I was sure it was a joke!"

"Yeah, well," said Marv shaking his head. "It does sound pretty much like Rhonelle had herself a conflict of interest. Having her mamma killed like that was so traumatic and the poor child was loaded with guilt. She felt like her mother's death was all on account of her not warning her or telling her granny."

"I can sure see how she would feel that way after what her grandmother told her." Mary Lynn now felt defensive of Rhonelle, the poor little orphaned girl. "If she was such a great fortune teller, why didn't she see her own daughter's death and warn her?

"That's a good point. Maybe that's why Granny Laurite couldn't offer up any comfort to the motherless child. She was feeling too guilty. After her mother's violent demise, Rhonelle wouldn't have anything to do with fortune telling. She avoided being around her granny and fell into a screaming fit whenever she laid eyes on a pack of tarot cards!

"Rhonelle came to believe that the only way she could find redemption for herself was by total immersion in the Roman Catholic Church - a great place to work on your guilt issues. The nuns at the convent school had charitably decided to make Rhonelle into their pet project. The sisters were determined to save her from a sinful life by holding her to the blessed bosom of the church.

"Mother Superior labeled Granny Laurite a wicked heathen. However she didn't mind holding her holy nose while accepting the large donation of Laurite's tainted money to fund her little granddaughter's tuition. For a while there it appeared Rhonelle was well on her way to becoming a devoted daughter of the church, until her hormones got her into trouble."

"Oh my . . . isn't that always the case," thought Mary Lynn as Marv went on with the story.

"By the time Rhonelle had turned twelve she was beginning to look very well endowed for her age. The nuns were noticing that the altar boys were paying way too much attention to their little Rhonelle, who didn't look like a little girl anymore," Marv said with a wide grin. "Those sisters didn't approve of that at all," said Dorine pursing her lips and arching her eyebrows. "Even though the poor girl hadn't done a thing to be ashamed of except starting to grow up like nature intended. They came down hard on her over everything. They started a making her feel even guiltier than before and she didn't have any idea why."

"That's when she started going back over to Bourbon Street every afternoon after school." Marv said. "That's where her heart truly was."

Mary Lynn looked over at Rhonelle by the stage. Little Bo had some jazzy music playing on the sound system. Rhonelle was having an animated conversation with two of the Gay Caballeros and her hips were moving slightly to the beat. As if on cue she turned around to smile and wave at Marv.

"She was one poor mixed-up kid." Marv grinned and waved back at Rhonelle. "She'd finally reached the conclusion that her only true friends were the girls working at the strip club. It was like coming home. Whenever she came by the dancers were delighted to welcome their little mascot back to where she belonged."

"They were mighty proud of how good she was filling out too." Dorine chuckled. "Nobody there tried to make her ashamed of her body, that's for sure!"

"Yeah," Marv agreed. "In a contest between nuns and strippers the nuns are gonna lose out every time."

"I'll drink to that!" chimed in Don, who'd been so quiet all this time that Mary Lynn had thought he couldn't hear the conversation.

"What did her grandmother think about all that?" Mary Lynn asked.

"She didn't appear to care what Rhonelle did." Marv said as he stirred around the ice in his drink. "Granny Laurite spent all of her time and energy on her clients. She'd become obsessed with her work after her daughter's death. When old Granny died a few years later, it didn't appear to be much of a loss to Rhonelle. By then she was a wild and beautiful sixteen year old vixen! She dropped out of the Convent School at age thirteen and had been spending most of her time at the club.

"She found some money left by her granny hidden in a tin box under a floorboard. It didn't amount to very much, which was surprising. Rhonelle spent most of it on new dance costumes and a place to live. She got herself set up in an apartment above the strip club, with a balcony overlooking Bourbon Street. To this day, she says she can't go to sleep without hearing some kind of music playing."

"And she was only sixteen?!" Mary Lynn had to admire the girl's courage. She realized Rhonelle was about the same age she had been when she suddenly was left on her own. Nevertheless, New Orleans sounded like a far more menacing environment than Blytheville. "Wasn't that a dangerous place for such a young girl to be living alone?"

"Not with that big ole Cajun, Richard, the club's bouncer looking out for her." (Marv pronounced it Ree-chard.) "Nobody could get past him. Rhonelle turned out to be a very good judge of character. Her psychic abilities were still working even though she refused to acknowledge it. She just naturally knew who to trust and who not. The club's owner also kept his eye on her. He wasn't about to let anything happen to the newest and hottest 'sin-sation' on Bourbon Street."

"You mean she started to striptease dance when she was only sixteen?" Mary Lynn didn't believe that was legal, but those days in New Orleans she doubted anybody cared what age a girl was, so long as she looked good.

"Oh yes," Marv said with a laugh. "As long as she wasn't drinking alcohol or doing anything too lascivious they could bend the rules. Besides, she looked more like she was in her twenties. That was the beginning of a long and successful career for Rhonelle. I believe she was performing right up through her mid to late thirties. None of us really know for sure how old she is now because she keeps her age a secret. However, she didn't have to be a psychic to figure out when the time had finally come for her dancing days to end. Dorine, what was it she used to say?" Marv rubbed his ear trying to recall.

Dorine leaned forward on her elbows. "She said that she knew it was time to quit when her 'assets began to fall'. Time and gravity always takes a toll on the body over the years." Dorine nodded meaningfully at Mary Lynn. Marv and Don slapped the table in laughter.

"I'll drink to that, too," Don said and took a big swig of his beer.

Mary Lynn sat up straighter so she would look a bit less like she was sagging. "But you still haven't told me how Rhonelle ended up here in Peavine," she said, changing the subject.

"I was coming to that part. Rhonelle had several lovers over the years but never did tie the knot. Most of her old friends had retired and didn't hang around the club anymore. A has-been stripper can be a mighty pathetic creature. Rhonelle knew she had to move on but had no idea where to go or what to do.

"She vowed to look for some kind of a 'sign' that would give her a hint as to what her new life would be . . . no scary or psychic kind of sign, just some kind of an indication about which path she should take. So for the next few weeks she kept her eyes and mind open. She lounged most of the day on her balcony, watching the tourists and drunks walk by below. She wandered around the quarter, night after night, going to one club after another, but no sign presented itself.

"Finally, she gave up on her search and decided that the next morning she would take a job at the costume shop down the street. Her savings had dwindled so she had to get back to work doing something. On that fateful night, instead of going out, Rhonelle did something she rarely ever did. She went to bed early. Just after she shut her eyes . . . and she swears to me this is the truth . . . no sooner had she closed her eyes when everything went silent. The ever-present sound of bump and grind music just stopped.

"That was mighty peculiar to Rhonelle. She still was living in the flat over the club where music could be heard till the wee hours. Her eyes flew open, and she sat bolt upright. Standing at the foot of her bed, was the 'sign' she had been waiting for. Her old Granny Laurite was standing there, and she looked as real as you or me!"

Mary Lynn's mouth went dry. Nobody at their table was laughing this time. They all just nodded slowly and took sips of their drinks. Dolly woke up from her little snooze, poked her nose up over the edge of the table, and whined at Dorine.

After a dramatic pause, Marv continued. "If I'd seen such a sight, it would have scared me out of my britches. Rhonelle says it was the most natural thing in the world to see her dead granny standing there smiling down at her. She was actually glad to see the old woman.

"Granny Laurite had come back from the 'Other Side' to give Rhonelle the sign she'd been waiting for. Told her not to worry about a thing because she was sent there to guide Rhonelle the way she should have done years ago while she was still living in this world."

Mary Lynn scanned the faces of Don and Dorine for any smirk or rolling eyes that would indicate that they were all in on this tall tale, but they were as solemn as church. This was definitely no joke they were playing on Mary Lynn. Rhonelle's tale was a story they all had heard before and for some strange reason accepted as the truth.

"So then," Marv went on, "Granny Laurite told Rhonelle that she was to pack up and leave New Orleans the very next morning. She was to drive towards Baton Rouge and head north as far as she could get. When she couldn't go no further she would be where she was supposed to be."

"And that ended up being Peavine, right?" Mary Lynn said, still expecting a punch line.

"It almost was. Her old T-Bird stalled out on her about three miles down that a way." Marv said pointing back over his shoulder. "Rhonelle coasted to a halt in what appeared to be the middle of nowhere. Out of the blue, Granny Laurite appeared in the headlights, standing by the road, waving at Rhonelle to follow her."

"You got to remember that nobody but Rhonelle can actually see Granny Laurite, but I can always feel it when she's around!" a suddenly sobered Dorine explained to Mary Lynn. "It's really spooky."

"I'm sure it is." Mary Lynn agreed politely, still waiting for everybody to burst out laughing.

"And to make it even spookier," said Marv with hint of a smile. "Rhonelle arrived here on a dark and stormy night."

Sure she did, thought Mary Lynn.

"Granny Laurite led Rhonelle through the rain and wind right up to the door of Doll's trailer. If you think that woman looked frightful to you just now; imagine the sight that greeted Doll when she opened her door that night! There she stood, tall and big-eyed with that bushy head of hair standing on end. Doll says Rhonelle was babbling like she was in some kind of trance or something. She was about to slam the door on her and call the sheriff . . . thought she'd escaped from a loony bin or something . . . when she heard Rhonelle mention the name 'Hermie'. That was Doll's pet name for her husband.

"Rhonelle kept on babbling and started to tell Doll things nobody else could have known. She mentioned real personal stuff about Doll and Herman. She even mentioned Madge! It was then that Doll grabbed Rhonelle, yanked her into the trailer and locked the door. After several cups of hot coffee, generously laced with whiskey, Doll and Rhonelle were able to settle into a somewhat saner conversation. Doll soon realized that Rhonelle was pretty weird all right, but not crazy.

"Rhonelle proceeded to tell Doll her whole life's story, even the part about her Granny Laurite's ghost. She told Doll that her Granny was with her now to help her communicate with the Other Side."

"And Doll fell for all that? You mean she believed everything this complete stranger told her?" Mary Lynn couldn't understand how Doll could have been so gullible.

"Of course she believed her," Marv said, a little taken aback that Mary Lynn was still skeptical. "Doll says Rhonelle sat there talking about things between her and Herman Junior that nobody else alive could have known. She even had a few messages passed along, by way of Granny Laurite, from her dear departed Herman."

"Don't you think she just wanted to believe Rhonelle because she missed her husband?" Mary Lynn asked, still unconvinced.

"I'm sure that's what got Doll to listen to her at first." Marv conceded. "Pretty soon she began to see the benefits of having a real genuine psychic added to her little community of trailer folk. The fun of shaking up Pastor Astor and his pack of self-righteous fuddy-duddies was another advantage.

"Rhonelle also turned out to be extremely valuable when it came to getting background checks on prospective tenants. Pauline and I were the first ones that she tried out her abilities on." Marv grinned and shook his head. "I can imagine how scared and lowdown we must have looked when we showed up that morning. Turns out Rhonelle had told Doll the night before we arrived to be expecting us."

"I'm sorry, but this is all just a little too farfetched for me." Mary Lynn had never had gotten into all that 'New Age' kind of thing, and wasn't about to start now. She turned to Dorine and Dolly, hoping to find a way to change the subject.

Dorine had been sitting very still. Her eyes were huge behind those thick glasses of hers, as she looked at Mary Lynn and said, "What Rhonelle told Doll was that she knew about the young woman who had run away and been lost . . . and she would find her and get her to come back to Peavine, and that is what caused Doll to take her in on that dark and stormy night."

Mary Lynn was not much of a drinking woman, but she shakily picked up her whiskey sour and drank it all down before setting the glass back on the table.

"Hey ya'll, what's going on?" Pauline had just arrived at their silent table. "This party is supposed to be FUN, remember! We'd better go on and get in line. Ozelle and Sally just put out the catfish and bar-b-q."

"*Good grief, Laurite! Can't you get your granddaughter to dial it back a notch?*" Johnny was standing with his hands gently laid upon Mary Lynn's shoulders in an attempt to transmit soothing vibrations, when the old Creole popped up beside him. "*Rhonelle even looked scary to me when she came up to the table with that act. What's wrong with her? She's supposed to be helping us.*"

Laurite stood there with her arms folded across her chest and a bare foot tapping impatiently. "*Humph!*" She grunted as she nodded her head towards Marv and Dorine. "*Dey doan know nuthin' 'bout me.*" Then she changed her mood in a blink and turned to Johnny with a grin. "*Rhonelle could see you standin' there behind Mary Lynn and jus' got surprised is all.*" She looked across the room at her granddaughter who smiled and waved back at her and Johnny. "*She thinks you a mighty fine lookin' spirit! No worry, she'll be OK now.*"

"*Rhonelle could see me - but how could that be? All these years, Mary Lynn has not once been able to see me.*" He wasn't sure why, but to have been seen and acknowledged by a living human made him feel hopeful for the first time since his Crossing Over.

CHAPTER SIXTEEN

At the Buffet Line

S ally's just put out a batch of catfish and hushpuppies - hot out of the fryer!" Pauline said, whacking Don on his broad shoulder.

"Well, it's about time!" he replied, as he swiveled around to grin at Pauline. "I'm 'bout near to starvin'." Don looked up and inhaled deeply. "That must be Ozelle's prize-winning bar-b-q brisket that I'm a smellin."

Marv stubbed out his cigarette and swigged down the last of his drink as he slid out of his chair. "Let the feast begin!"

The creepy, somber mood brought on by the telling of Rhonelle's story, quickly dissipated with the prospect of the spectacular array of culinary delights awaiting them at the buffet line.

"Come on ya'll, we'd better get in line before all those little old ladies do." Dorine grunted as she braced herself on the table and stood up with the assistance of both Don and Marv. Dolly had jumped down was dancing around excitedly on her hind legs like some tiny, pink-tutu-clad ballerina. "Whew! I'm not used to such a stout drink," Dorine said. She steadied herself by leaning on Marv with a little help from Pauline at her back. "Don, will you carry Dolly for me?"

"Sure Honey. Come on baby." Dolly obediently jumped up into Don's open arms as he leaned down towards her. He stood up, tucking the tiny dog under one large arm, and offered his other to Mary Lynn. "Let's go on ahead and save a place in the line. It'll take Dorine awhile to get there."

"Ya'll go on." Dorine was still clutching Marv's arm and waved everybody else on. "Marv and I'll be there directly."

Pauline turned to Dorine. "You want me to just go load up a plate for you, sweetie?"

"Nah, I need to get up and stretch my legs a bit." Dorine continued to shuffle along putting one foot ahead of the other, getting nowhere fast.

"The buffet line is over this way," said Don, as he and Mary Lynn followed Pauline out across the dance floor. As they passed near the stage, Mary Lynn glanced over at the table where the Gay Caballeros were gathered. Rhonelle was sitting there surrounded by the admiring young men. She was flirting and laughing, and it seemed they were all having a fine time. Rhonelle looked up as Mary Lynn walked by, beamed a lovely smile and winked, before turning back to the man sitting next to her.

Mary Lynn started to comment to Don on this complete turnaround in Rhonelle's behavior. However, his attention was riveted upon the large posse of frail, elderly ladies slowly making their way toward the start of the buffet. They moved as one unit at a snail's pace, yet too close to the buffet for Don to head them off without appearing to be rude. Pauline came to a dead stop in front of Don and Mary Lynn with her hands out like a crossing guard.

"Well, that does it! The 'Blue Hair Brigade' must have been watching like hawks for a signal from Kristy that the food was ready." Pauline turned back to Don. "Tell you what I'll do. I'm going to go on up there and see if I can help get the serving line sped up a little. You two get in line behind them and I'll go see what I can do."

"Okay." Don said with a sigh, and a long low rumble coming from his mid section. "We'll just have to cool our heels while all those old biddies pick over each and every item offered to 'em." He looked back to check on Dorine and Marv's slow progress across the room. "This is just what Dorine was hoping to avoid, but this way she can take her time gettin' here."

"What did Pauline call them . . . what Brigade?" Mary Lynn looked ahead at the food service line. At the start were two ladies, each using walkers. They still seemed to be moving faster than Dorine, until they stopped to talk to a large black gentleman sitting in a wheelchair beside the first set of hot food servers.

"Yeah," Don chuckled. "We call 'em the 'Blue Hair Brigade,' affectionately of course," he said, looking back at Mary Lynn, concerned that she'd think he was making fun of the elderly. "Dorine come up with the name for that gang, because they always do everything together. They seem to be pretty well organized to boot. They got that bus driver from the Mansion Rest and Retirement Center at their beck and call. Look at 'em. They sure are happy to see Ozelle back in health good enough to grill again! That's him, sitting there at the front of the line."

Mary Lynn carefully studied the gentleman in the wheelchair and his interaction with the Blue Hairs. He was smiling broadly and nodding to the elderly ladies. One of them leaned forward to tell him something that must have been humorous, because he reared back and let out a generous guffaw that carried across the room.

His hair was mostly gray and his glasses were even thicker than Dorine's. His left arm and hand were held tightly up to his side and shook with a slight tremor. The large white apron he wore was generously smeared and spattered with sauce and charcoal soot.

"The stroke he had six months ago liked to a kilt him." Don said as he shook his head and smiled. "But nuthin' was gonna keep Ozelle from supervising his bar-b-q grill for Doll's party."

Mary Lynn noticed a handsome black woman, also wearing an apron, come up and stand next to Ozelle. It appeared she was trying to gently steer some of the Blue-Haired-Brigadiers forward along the line "Is that his daughter up there beside him?" she asked.

"Lord no!" Don laughed. "That's his wife, Sally. His daughter's down there next to Kristy and Misty."

Mary Lynn looked on down the line and saw two old hard-looking babes. One was dishing up cheese dip and nachos, the other was laying out a fantastic-looking array of what appeared to be pigs-in-a-blanket and barbequed cocktail sausages. They were laughing enthusiastically over something that the pretty young black woman, standing between them had said. Hmmm, thought Mary Lynn, it must have been some joke about the "teenie weenies" they were serving. She knew those two could be none other than the infamous Party Girls, Kristy and Misty.

"The Washington's sons, Ozzie and Emory are over by the catfish and hushpuppies," Don said, as he looked longingly towards the piles of delicious food.

"Ozelle and Sally's children look like nice young people," Mary Lynn noted.

"They're not as young as they look. They take after their mother on that," said Don. "Little Doc Ozzie, that one there serving the slaw and beans, he's their oldest. He's been a full-fledged medical doctor since; let's see . . . since 1965, at least."

"Really?" Mary Lynn was impressed. She thought he didn't look like he could be much older than his thirties.

"He graduated high school by the time he was fourteen and whizzed through college and Med School in record time. So I guess you could say he started his practice pretty young, at age twenty one. He takes after his daddy in the brains department."

How unusual, Mary Lynn thought. "Does he have many patients? I mean as a young, black man in a small southern town like this. I just wondered."

MADGE'S MOBILE HOME PARK | 151

"He's the head of Peavine Family Medical Clinic, first of its kind for our community!" Don beamed proudly. "He's been running it for the past ten years . . . brought in four specialists. They got all the latest, fanciest medical equipment too. Before Doc Ozzie, Peavine didn't have many doctors. We had to go up to Pine Bluff or over to Monticello, if a person was really sick."

"Ozzie's younger brother Emory is the administrator of the Mansion Rest Home and Retirement Center. He's got degrees in law as well as business. Their baby sister Lettie is the new principal of the Peavine Elementary School. I don't think those students mind too much gettin' sent to the principal's office."

Mary Lynn was impressed by the fact that all three of Ozelle's children were so successful and well-educated. Any family would have had to struggle to achieve that. The fact it was a low-income black family from deep in south Arkansas made the accomplishment even more impressive. Mary Lynn knew Doll Dumas must have lent a hand in this, and she was eager to find out how.

At that moment, the food line came to a standstill. Several Blue Hair Brigadiers were picking over the various canapé selections Misty had just put before them, asking about the ingredients of each and every one.

"So, Don," Mary Lynn asked casually, "what was the connection between Ozelle's family and Doll Dumas?"

CHAPTER SEVENTEEN

Emory Ozelle Washington and Sally Lou Evans

B oth Ozelle and Sally grew up at the Dumas Family Plantation. Ozelle's parents were the Mansion caretakers, and Sally's were the cook and butler. The Dumas family was thought to be putting on airs, keeping so many servants around, but the property was large enough that they needed plenty of help to take care of it.

"The Washington and the Evans families each had their own small cottage to live in, right there on the Mansion grounds. When Ozelle's and Sally's parents got too old to do their jobs, their children took over their chores, as was expected in those days.

"Herman Junior went away to college and then onto several different law schools, leaving his father (Herman Senior) to rely heavily on young Ozelle to keep things running smoothly out at the Mansion. Ozelle also worked part time at the Dumas Oil Company office. Whenever Mr. Dumas went on business trips to New Orleans, Ozelle accompanied him as his valet. The truth was Ozelle actually functioned more as a secretary to the old man.

"Although Ozelle had only been able to go to school up to the fifth grade, he was sharp as a tack. His mind soaked up knowledge like a sponge. It wasn't long before he began to pick up on the finer details of running the Dumas Oil Company and the Cotton Farm land. He taught himself to use a typewriter, so he could type up confidential letters to important business associates for Mr. Dumas.

"One can imagine the reaction of the local white folks if they were to have seen a big, strapping young black man in field hand clothes and glasses, behind a typewriter, clackety-clacking away ninety to nothing. It would have caused a stir sure enough, so as a cover, Ozelle only worked in the oil company office at night. Everybody assumed 'Big Mo,' as Mr. Dumas called him, was only doing janitorial work."

"He was called Big Mo?" Mary Lynn's cheeks reddened as she looked back towards Ozelle sitting in his wheelchair with dignity, despite his infirmities. "That sounds so . . . demeaning."

Don grimaced and shook his head. "That's the way Mr. and Mrs. Dumas thought of colored people, and anybody else who worked for 'em. They believed they were high class and everybody else was below them. Herman Junior and Doll weren't anything like that."

"Perhaps Mr. Dumas was intimidated by Ozelle's size as well as his intelligence," mused Mary Lynn, still gazing at him, deep in thought.

"Uh, yeah, I would think so." Don agreed. "Ozelle was the biggest black man I'd ever seen, but he took care to act as meek as possible so as to not scare any of the white women. His thick glasses and quiet manner kept him out of trouble."

"That was smart of him." Mary Lynn stepped back into line behind another Blue Hair who had cut in front of them, claiming her sister had been saving her a place.

Don sighed loudly and rolled his eyes. He was helpless against the Brigadiers.

"It's a shame he couldn't have continued his education. Did you say he left school after fifth grade?" Mary Lynn brought Don's attention back to Ozelle.

"In a way, he did keep up with his schooling, on his own." Don said. "He read as many of Herman Junior's discarded textbooks as he could get his hands on while he worked odd jobs around the Dumas Mansion. The Washington's cottage had bookshelves covering every bit of wall space from the floor to the ceiling. They were filled with books on every subject; from science and law to cooking and gardening tips. Young Ozelle loved to read. I sometimes wonder if that's what could've caused of his poor eyesight? It was those weak eyes of his, and some quiet intervention by Mr. Dumas on Ozelle's behalf that got him rated 4 F when the war came along.

"That wasn't out of any kindness toward Ozelle, mind you. Mr. Dumas knew there was no way to talk Herman Junior into staying home to help him with the business, so the old man was really just looking out for his own interests. Ozelle knew more about taking care of the Dumas' Mansion and Oil Company business than Herman Junior could ever hope to. So the old man had become completely dependent on this young black man to keep everything working smoothly. But, he would never have admitted that to anybody.

"On the occasions of the large Dumas family bar-b-q, or the yearly Dumas Oil Company parties out at the Mansion, Ozelle would be in charge of all the grilling. He just loved grilling! Had his own secret blend of bar-b-q sauce that he'd created by combining recipes from those gourmet cookbooks he was always reading. He's won countless bar-b-q cooking contests using that sauce. That's the wonderful aroma you're a-smellin' right now, rising off his famous beef brisket." Don paused, closed his eyes and sniffed in a deep breath. "I swear, I'm 'bout to start slobberin', I'm so hungry!"

Mary Lynn looked at the line of Blue Hairs ahead of them, and saw it was at a standstill. Most of the ladies were clustered around the trays that Kristy and Misty just had put out, pointing and asking questions. One elderly lady took out a folded piece of aluminum foil from her huge handbag and placed several of the pigs-in-the-blanket in it to "save for later."

Pauline rolled her eyes and shrugged her shoulders as she looked back at Don and Mary Lynn.

"I declare," Don said in quiet exasperation. "You'd think they were starving 'em over there at the Mansion House the way those old biddies hoard food!" His stomach let out another noisy growl. "Beg pardon, Mary Lynn, I never should have skipped my lunch."

"So, how did Ozelle and Sally get together?" Mary Lynn asked Don, hoping to distract him from his hunger. "She must be quite a bit younger than he is, isn't she?"

"She is a good deal younger but that hasn't seemed to matter. Sally's always been mature for her age." A smile returned to Don's face as he watched Sally graciously hand out catfish, hush puppies and greetings to the gang of little old ladies hovering around the deep-fried entrees.

"She was about twelve years old when she began to fine tune her cooking skills by helping out her mamma with all the meals at the Dumas Mansion. Sally was the youngest child and the only daughter of Gussie, the resident household cook. There was a peach cobbler that old Gussie used to bake that you'd swear had been made by angels. I've never been able to duplicate it, but Sally's recipe comes mighty close.

"As Gussie's arthritis worsened, especially in her hands, she'd sit in the corner of the Mansion kitchen in an old red rocking chair, barking out orders to Sally about what to fix and how to do it right. Pretty soon, Sally could do most all of the food preparations without being told how. That's when she began to experiment a little and come up with her own recipes. She had to give up on school after seventh grade to help her mamma full time. That was okay by her, cooking had become her main interest . . . until a few years later when she began to develop a crush on Ozelle.

"Sally was only fifteen at that time, and Ozelle was a grown man.

He usually had his nose buried in a book when he wasn't busy working for Herman Senior, so he hadn't thought much about girls. Sally came into her good looks by age seventeen. That gave Ozelle cause to finally take notice of her. After all, for the past two years she'd been using every excuse she could think up to bring some of her tastiest jams and pickles over to Ozelle's ma and pa. Ozelle didn't court Sally proper until she got to be eighteen. Gussie told Sally it wouldn't be fittin' until then. Once the official courting began, they were married within a year.

"Ozelle and Sally had some big plans back then. They were gonna build their own house, with a little bar-b-q shack out back of it. They'd set up a few picnic tables and call it 'The Brisket Basket'. That way there'd be a nice little café for the colored community to come to. Ozelle had already bought himself a nice piece of land down south of town along the highway.

"After quietly saving his money all those years, he was really looking forward to starting a new life with his young bride . . . away from the Dumas Mansion. He'd been at old man Dumas' beck and call long enough. He knew that Herman Junior was going to be coming home from the war. Ozelle was hoping that by stepping aside the son would take his rightful place and learn how to run the oil company.

"Doll (she went by Lucille Lepanto back then), was doing maid service out at the Mansion by then too. She and her mother had helped serve at parties and clean house for Herman Senior and Adeline for years. By then she was a single mother needing to earn a living, so Ozelle trained her on all the details of running the Mansion household. It was a big old place and needed a lot of maintenance.

"Doll and Ozelle had everything worked out, or so they thought; until Herman Junior came home from the war with that gold digging hussy . . . Madge."

"Oh, that's right, Madge arrived." Mary Lynn nodded her head soberly as she pictured the uproar that followed. "What happened to the newlyweds, I mean Ozelle and Sally?"

"They weren't married yet. You see, they had wanted to wait and get their own home first. Then everything went haywire around them. Ozelle never could find the right time to tell Adeline and Herman Senior that he and Sally were gonna quit. The whole family was in such swivet, Ozelle felt sorry for them.

"He and Sally snuck away to their preacher one evening and secretly got married. Ozelle felt that would be the honorable thing to do. He sure didn't want the wrath of Gussie to come down on him, should anything improper happen to occur (if you know what I mean)," Don added quietly.

"That was gentlemanly of him." She tilted her head as she considered Ozelle, still chatting cheerfully with the Blue Hairs surrounding him. "But didn't the situation improve? I mean . . . everything was OK after Madge disappeared, wasn't it?"

"Now that you mention it, things did eventually turn out far better for Ozelle and Sally." Don rubbed at the stubble thickening on his double chin. "I just never did look at it as all being because of Madge coming to Peavine." This was a startling admission to be coming from Don.

"What do you mean?" Mary Lynn asked eagerly. This was the first positive thing she had heard concerning the notorious Madge.

"Well," said Don, as if realizing it for the first time, "it's just that if Herman Junior had not returned from the war with Madge in tow, Ozelle and Sally would have gone ahead with their plans. They would have quit their jobs and moved away from the Dumas Mansion to set up their small bar-b-q place. I guess they probably would have done alright, and maybe their kids would have had a chance to get college degrees in spite of it all. Come to think of it, if it hadn't been for Madge coming along to stir things up, Ozelle never would have ended up owning the very Mansion he'd worked in most his life."

Mary Lynn was completely confused and wondered if she'd heard that correctly. "Did you say that Ozelle . . . that man there . . . owns the Dumas Mansion?"

"Well, he did for a time," Don nodded enthusiastically. "Let me go back and tell you how it all happened. After Madge upped and disappeared, the situation actually got worse out there at the Dumas Mansion. There was so much gossip and suspicion over why and how Madge had left that Adelaide was too embarrassed to go out anywhere. She took to hiding up in her bedroom all day.

"Doll was so distraught by it all that she quit working at the Mansion and took a job at the Too-Tite Tavern. For some strange reason she blamed herself for causing Madge to leave. Herman Junior was absolutely useless. He'd got to drinking heavily while Madge was around. After she disappeared he just stayed drunk most all the time. This had Herman Senior and Adeline beside themselves with the worry and their health begin to decline."

"That sounds terrible to me," Mary Lynn said, interrupting Don. "I still don't see how Madge did anything but make things a whole lot worse for all of them."

"It sure seemed like it back then," Don admitted. "But if things had been hunky dory instead of going to hell in a hand basket, Ozelle and Sally would have been long gone from there. By this time, Sally had discovered she was expecting their first child. They had to get themselves a place of their own because they'd been living with Ozelle's parents and that wouldn't do any more. When Ozelle came to Mr. Dumas to tell him he was quitting, the old man was so desperate to keep him and Sally that he offered up the whole east wing of the Mansion for them to use as living quarters and big raises too.

"That old rascal knew that if he was to let Ozelle leave all he had left was Herman Junior. Junior was in such a sorry state that he wouldn't be any help with the Oil Company. Old man Dumas had to finally admit to how dependent he was on his Big Mo, and that wasn't easy. Ozelle and Sally stayed on at the Mansion. The east wing of the Mansion, their living quarters, had to be enlarged as their family began to grow.

"Adeline and Herman Senior passed away within a year of one another. Ozelle and Sally saw to it that all the proper arrangements were made. Herman Junior begged Ozelle to stay on and help him with the oil and cotton businesses his daddy had left him. Herman Junior had wanted to make Ozelle the President of the Dumas Oil Company. He could take care of the cotton fields because he knew a bit more about farming.

"Ozelle wisely figured it would only stir up trouble with the Oil Company employees, were it to be known they had to work for a colored man, so they kept things as they were. Herman Junior held the title of ownership of the Dumas Oil Company, but in secret they filled out all the legal papers that put Ozelle in control of all major decisions. As the fog of drunkenness began to clear from Herman Junior's brain, he rediscovered his beloved Doll Lepanto.

"Ozelle actually was enjoying his work at the Oil Company now that he was in charge and not just following Old Man Dumas' orders. He and Sally were comfortable living in the Mansion with their three children. When Doll and Herman Junior got married, the most natural thing in the world was for Ozelle and Sally to stay on when Doll asked them to. Herman Junior was so grateful to Ozelle for staying on that he built a nice swimming pool out on the back lawn so their kids could learn to swim that summer.

"The four of them became very close friends over the years after Doll and Herman were married. Doll had never been around colored people that much and got a brand new understanding of what life was like for them by listening to Ozelle and Sally. She discovered how kindhearted and intelligent Ozelle was and how much he regretted never getting to go to college. Doll never had thought much about education or how hard it was to find a decent school for your kids if you were colored. It was then that she and Herman Junior quietly set up college trust funds for all three of Sally and Ozelle's kids.

"After Herman Junior's sudden and tragic death Doll never would've made it through the dark days that followed if it hadn't been for Ozelle and Sally. When Doll made the decision to liquidate her inheritance, she had Ozelle handle the transactions for her. She insisted on paying him twenty percent of the total."

"Gosh," Mary Lynn was attempting the math in her head of what twenty percent of the entire assets of an oil company and cotton farmland must have amounted to. "That had to be a nice chunk of money!"

"Right on, Mary Lynn," Don said, raising his eyebrows. "Look there behind you. I think this line is beginning to move a little now."

"Oh, it sure is." Mary Lynn had to take about a dozen steps to fill the gap between herself and the two Blue Hair Brigadiers ahead of them. "So is that how they were able to buy the Mansion?" she asked Don, eager to hear the rest of this story before they got up to Ozelle.

"You could say that. See, when Doll told Sally and Ozelle about her plans to move to Madge's old trailer park, she said she didn't need to live in that big mansion or to make any more money. So she sold it to Ozelle for one dollar! Wouldn't take no for an answer. She already had the papers drawn up. So that's how Ozelle and Sally Washington became the owners of the Dumas Family Mansion."

"My word!" exhaled Mary Lynn in wonderment. "Do they still live there?"

"Nope. Not anymore. The place has gone through quite a few remodeling adjustments since then. First it was a small private school for kids of any color who wanted to come, and lots of 'em did. The west wing upstairs was made into rooms to house the teachers they recruited in from the colleges Ozelle went to scout out. After integration, the new local public schools were built and the Mansion House private school closed. They maintained the boarding house for teachers. Ozelle went around the country visiting colleges, looking for the best young teachers he could find. Having free room and board at a mansion made his offers pretty hard to turn down.

"Eventually some of the older retired teachers wanted to know if they could come and live out there too. That's about when Ozelle and his second son looked around town and realized there was a sore need for some kind of a retirement facility here in Peavine. The old Mansion was renovated into the Mansion House Rest and Retirement Center."

"Is that where all the Blue Hairs are from?" Mary Lynn asked Don as quietly as she could into the nearest of his hearing aids.

"Yep," he said with a snicker. A look of optimism spread across Don's face as he noticed the pace of the line picking up again. "It looks like Pauline has recruited some of 'Tammy's Tappers' to help the ladies!"

Mary Lynn saw a contingent of about a dozen young girls of all shapes and sizes strutting across the room wearing sequined and feathered dance costumes and tap shoes. They converged upon the Blue Hairs as they progressed to the end of the buffet line. Each girl took a tray from the elderly ladies and carried it over to their table for them, their pink tap shoes clacking in a noisy procession.

"Cute, ain't they!" Don beamed proudly as he saw his granddaughter, Dora Lee, at the lead of the pack of flashy little toe-tappers. "They'll be puttin on a great show in a bit. Now, where was I?" Don said, trying to get back to his narrative. "Sally and Ozelle moved out and built their own home on that piece of property Ozelle had bought way back when he and Sally were first married. They ended up buying more of the land surrounding it so there'd be enough room for a big house. The property values in that neighborhood shot up when they built their own large palatial home.

"Ozelle finally got to open that little bar-b-q place he'd always dreamed of. You'll see it on your way south of town. It's called the 'Brisket Basket' just like they'd planned. Some of their grand kids run it for 'em now." Don looked around and discovered that the line had been moving while he talked. They were almost up to Ozelle's wheelchair at the head of the buffet line. "Thank goodness. I was a feared I was gonna blow away afore I got here!"

"Oh, come on Don, it'd take a mighty big wind to get you to budge," Dorine said as she edged into line beside Mary Lynn and Don.

"You're right about that, Honey!" Don laughed and made room for Marv to get in the line too. "Where've ya'll been? You took yer time gettin here." Don transferred a suddenly awakened Dolly back into Dorine's arms.

"We had to show Teenie and Mavis where our table was," answered Dorine.

"Mavis is waiting there for us so she can save our seats," Marv said.

"Hey there Ozelle, you look like you're feeling fit!" Dorine said as she leaned over to lay a kiss on his shiny black cheek. Mary Lynn noticed Dolly sneak in a few licks of the bar-b-q sauce smeared on Ozelle's apron.

"Well, hello there, Miz Dorine and Miz Dolly," Ozelle boomed in his deep voice. "Sure is good to be back at the grill. Good to see ya! How ya'll doing this evening?" He turned his gaze to Mary Lynn and smiled his wide, friendly grin. "Who's this you got here with ya?"

Dorine pulled a suddenly shy Mary Lynn over to introduce her to Ozelle. "This here is Mary Lynn."

"Stanton," Mary Lynn finished nervously for Dorine, as she clasped Ozelle's good hand in both of hers. "It . . . it sure is an honor to meet you."

"Nice to meet you too, Miz Stanton," Ozelle squinted up at Mary Lynn through his thick glasses. "Are you from around here? You seem kind of familiar?"

Before Mary Lynn could answer, Dorine butted in. "She was traveling through and got lost on her way to Monroe."

"I'm from Missouri. Cape Girardeau," Mary Lynn added.

"Don and I told her she'd be a fool to miss out on this party, so she's staying at the Dew Drop so she could come with us," said Dorine, smiling broadly.

"Well, that's just grand, just grand," Ozelle said with a wink to Mary Lynn. "Miz Doll, God rest her, would've loved that."

Mary Lynn was so captivated by this man she almost forgot to pick up a tray . . . if Marv hadn't handed her one. "How about that, Mary Lynn," he whispered into her ear as they moved forward. "You just met the richest man in the county."

Don leaned away from the vat of hot food with his plate piled high with steaming bar-b-q brisket, and hollered back at Marv. "You said the Brices are here? Where's Teenie?" he asked, looking around for him.

"I'm right here." piped a nasally, high-pitched voice from behind Marv.

CHAPTER EIGHTEEN

Here Are the Brices . . .
But where is Christabelle?

"S peak of the Devil and he'll appear," chanted Teenie Brice as he stepped out from behind Marv. There he stood, all four feet and eleven inches of him, counting the stacked heels on his yellow patent leather loafers and the pouf of gray hair on his toupee. "Well, hello there!" Teenie said cordially, as he saw Mary Lynn standing next to Dorine. "You must be Mary Lynn, our mysterious stranger, I'm Teenie."

Mary Lynn turned at the sound of his voice and looked down at the delicate little man. Unfortunately, she had just arrived at the part on the buffet line being manned by the notorious Kristy and Misty with their vast platters of 'Teenie Weenies.' An expanding bubble of hysterical laughter was forming in Mary Lynn's mid-section, threatening to burst forth if she dared open her mouth. She began to panic at the thought of embarrassing, not only herself, but also Mr. Teenie Brice, who was standing there smiling and blinking curiously at her.

"*Teeeeeeeenie*, you rascal, we've been dying to see you!" Kristy was jumping up and waving gleefully from behind the buffet.

Misty trotted around from the serving area, squealing with delight as she made a bee-line for Teenie. "Come here you little booger and give me some sugar!"

To Mary Lynn's astonishment, Misty grabbed Teenie up into a tight hug and swung him around till his feet left the floor. She set him back down with his hairpiece askew and a very pleased expression on his face.

"Control yourself, Misty, there's enough of me to go around for everybody." he said nonchalantly as he patted his hair back on straight.

After a two-second pause of silence, the people nearby erupted in laughter.

"Saved by the Party Girls," Mary Lynn sighed under her breath as she dabbed the tears of laughter from her eyes with her cocktail napkin.

Teenie put his fists on his hips and looked up at each Party Girl with an expression of mock seriousness on his face. "Girls, how's that little Whutzit doing? Have you been giving him the tonic I sent for him, like I told you to?"

"He's doing just great, Teenie," said Misty beaming down at him. "And he just loves that tonic, don't he, Kristy?"

"Yeah, he slurps it right up, so long as we mix it into his daily beer," added Kristy from behind the weenie tray.

At this disclosure, Teenie pursed his lips and narrowed his eyes as he looked from Misty and Kristy sternly, then reconsidered before he spoke. "I guess that's OK - probably helps his arthritis some."

"Glad you approve, Teenie," said Dorine. "'Cause, you and I both know these girls will do as they please."

"Just be sure you don't ever give the poor thing whiskey again," Teenie said as he shook his forefinger in warning at the Party Girls, "or you'll have to answer to *me*!"

"Yes sir!" they both said in unison as they saluted before dissolving into another bout of raucous laughter. Teenie joined in with a high-pitched giggle this time.

As soon as they got their plates full to overflowing, Dorine properly introduced Mary Lynn to Teenie. By now Dorine was able to shuffle along at a decent pace. Don was carrying both their plates so Dorine could carry Dolly (whose tiny nose was quivering at the aromas of bar-b-q and catfish). Pauline fixed herself a small plate of catfish and coleslaw as she finished her stint of serving duty. The party of six, plus one poodle, made their way back across the room to their table close to the array of pies.

Mavis Brice sat there patiently waiting for them, totally absorbed in the process of slowly eating a slice of Don's chocolate pecan pie. Teenie quietly explained to Mary Lynn that Mavis was a very shy about eating in public. "She had her supper before the party, but she never can pass up some of Don's pie for dessert."

In the chair next to Mavis was a tiny, charcoal-gray poodle with her paws up on the table. The poodle was fully clad in a lavender tulle skirt and a head bow adorned with gold sequins. Mary Lynn noticed the nails on her paws were painted lavender and wondered once again at the tedious nature of attempting to paint a dog's toenails.

Mavis was wearing a huge caftan with a pink and lavender paisley print swirling across it. Her only jewelry was her wedding ring. Mary Lynn thought Mavis looked several sizes larger than she was in the old photo from the diner.

"Mavis!" The large woman looked up with a start as Pauline squealed out her name. "You look wonderful in that dress! This is a whole new style for you isn't it?"

Mavis ducked her head as a little smile creased her round cheeks.

"We decided to make something a little different for the party, didn't we, Hon." Teenie proclaimed with pride as he came up to Mavis and started twitching and smoothing the fabric across his wife's broad shoulders. "Don't you just love the way these colors bring out her eyes?"

Everyone nodded and complimented Mavis, but Mary Lynn had

yet to glimpse Mavis' eye color.

"Hon, this here's Mary Lynn, the lady I told you about who is staying over at Don and Dorine's cottage.

"Mary Lynn, meet Mavis, the Love of my Life," Teenie announced as he set his plate next to Mavis and sat down.

Mavis ducked her head towards Mary Lynn and said in her high whisper of a voice, "Pleased to meet you."

"It's a pleasure to meet you, Mrs. Brice," Mary Lynn said as she took her seat on the other side of Teenie. "I am so impressed with your poodle outfits and those poodle angels on the trees by the stage are adorable! If there are any left, I sure would like to buy one to take to my cousin in Monroe."

Mavis' smile widened and she put her hand to her mouth and said something to Mary Lynn across the top of Teenie's head that Mary Lynn couldn't understand.

"Beg Pardon?"

"She still has some left at the trailer," Teenie translated for Mary Lynn. "We can bring them over to the Diner tomorrow morning for you to look at."

"Oh, thank you. That'd be real nice." Mary Lynn was beginning to get the impression that Teenie often did Mavis' talking for her.

They each took their places around the table: Mavis next to Teenie, Mary Lynn on Teenie's right, then Marv and Pauline next to Don and Dorine. The two poodles, delighted to be together, were scrambling up and down and around the chair on the other side of Mavis. There was still one unoccupied chair between the poodles and Dorine, who was craning her head and squinting as she looked around the room. She turned back to the Brices.

"Teenie, where's Christabelle? Wasn't she going to ride over with you and Mavis?"

"W . . . e . . . l . . . l . . ." Teenie drawled with an air of drama. "I've got something to tell you all about Christabelle."

Everyone at the table scooted up and leaned forward to hear what Teenie had to say. That is, everyone but Don, who had turned down his hearing aids again upon leaving the buffet line. He was concentrating on shoveling down large bites of bar-b-q brisket. "Mmm, Mmm . . . Man, this stuff is tasty! Worth the wait!" Don said with his mouth full.

"Don!" Dorine jabbed him with her elbow to get his attention and put her finger to her lips in a shushing motion. "Teenie is trying to tell us something important."

"Oh, sorry about that!" Don gulped and twiddled with one of his hearing aids, without a pause in his eating.

"Go on Teenie, what's up?" Marv asked with concern.

"Well . . ." Teenie gave an even longer dramatic pause, and looked meaningfully at each one of them before continuing. "She's done took to her bed."

Dorine let out a gasp and clutched her hand to her breast. "She's sick is she? Funerals make me downright ill, don't they Don? That's why I don't like to go to 'em."

"Uh hmmm," Don continued to work his way through the pile of ribs on his tray.

"Well, she's not sick exactly, just kind of in shock." Teenie leaned back in his chair, obviously relishing the effects of his pronouncement. "You know, they had the reading of Doll's will this morning."

"Oh Lordee, I wondered about how that went!" Dorine clasped a hand to her breast and rocked back and forth in her chair.

"Excuse me," Mary Lynn's curiosity got the best of her. "Is Christabelle a relative of Doll's?"

"She was Doll's private nurse. She took such wonderful care of her. Especially toward the end when things were so bad," Dorine explained mournfully.

Teenie regained Mary Lynn's attention by tapping lightly on her arm. "Christabelle Tingleberry is just about the most cheerful and caring person on the face of this earth, very cheerful, isn't she?" Everybody around the table smiled and nodded in agreement before Teenie continued telling Mary Lynn about Christabelle.

"She came to work at the Mansion Rest Home about ten years ago. She used to be head geriatric nurse at the hospital up in Pine Bluff, but her ways of handling her patients didn't go down quite so well with the hospital administrators. They had too many rules for Christabelle."

"They didn't like the way she dressed neither." Mavis added quietly.

"That's right, Hon. She was always wantin' to wear her signature red and green outfits. Never did like those white uniforms."

"Christabelle was born on Christmas Eve," Mavis added for Mary Lynn's benefit.

"Yes." Teenie nodded, "she was . . ."

"Born right afore midnight, like the baby Jesus," Mavis added with a bit more confidence in her voice.

"That's right," Teenie continued, "and because of her very special birthday, Christabelle decided it was her Christian duty to hold the Christmas Spirit in her heart and spread its cheer every day of the year."

"She loves my poodle Christmas tree angels," Mavis added, warming a little more to Mary Lynn.

"She sure does and they are so cute, who wouldn't adore them!" Teenie patted Mavis' large flabby arm affectionately, as everyone at the table nodded and smiled in agreement.

"Anyway, I digress . . ." Teenie came back to his original subject. "In Christabelle Tingleberry's world, every day was Christmas. Most of her patients couldn't have known the difference anyway, so whenever Christabelle would pop in on those poor old people singing out a 'Merry Christmas' every morning, it just made everybody so happy.

"She'd bring each patient a little gift to open, and unwrap it for 'em if they weren't able to. Christabelle loved giving gifts! She'd wrap each one up beautifully the night before."

"She always went to the after-Christmas sales up in Pine Bluff, to stock up on paper and ribbons," Mavis added sagely.

"Yes, Hon, she did. That's the only day of the year that she liked to have off, isn't it?"

"She didn't take off this year though," Dorine said with a slight tremor to her voice.

"No, not with Doll's passing away, she just went out to the Mansion Rest Home to see what she could do to help," Teenie sighed theatrically.

"Tell about the fish tank," Mavis said to Teenie.

Mary Lynn thought for sure she had misunderstood Mavis, until she saw everybody, including Dorine smile and look cheerful again.

"Oh, that's right. Mary Lynn probably don't know that story, do you?" Teenie asked.

"Did she say 'fish tank story'?" Mary Lynn wanted to be sure.

"This is so funny." Teenie let out a high giggle. "See, about two years ago, Christabelle decided she wanted to do something extra nice for the Mansion Home. She'd read somewhere that watching fish in a tank . . ."

"Aquarium," Mavis corrected.

"Yes, with those pretty tropical fish in it," Teenie went on never losing a beat, "is very soothing and therapeutic for patients with some

kinds of . . . uh mental disorders. Most of Christabelle's patients had
some form of . . ."

"Dementia," (Mavis again)

"Yes. Anyway, Christabelle ordered a great big tank with one of
those air pumps in it to keep the water good and bubbly and several
lovely fish to live in it. They had it set up in the lobby so everybody
could enjoy it."

"It was nice for her to do that." Mary Lynn was impressed by this
act of generosity.

"It was, it was but about a month later, when Mavis and I went
out there to take our new little puppy Pitty-Too to visit with the old
folks, that's our favorite volunteer project," Teenie told Mary Lynn,
"we noticed the fish tank was gone. We asked Christabelle what'd
happened to it and . . ."

Teenie started to giggle so much he had to pause to collect himself.
Mary Lynn noticed Mavis giggling with silent laughter, her hand
pressed to her mouth.

"When we asked what had happened to the fish tank," Teenie
said. "Christabelle told us they had to take it out of there because they
kept finding too many of the patient's dentures in it every morning!"

"They thought the bubbles were Polident," Mavis explained before
the whole table laughed heartily along with Mary Lynn.

"That just cracks me up every time I hear that story, Teenie!"
Dorine said wiping her nose.

"Now, tell Mary Lynn about Christabelle's dark secret," Mavis
prompted.

"W e l l . . ." Teenie began in his dramatic story telling voice
again.

"Remember, I was telling you how Christabelle just loved to bring
presents to all her patients every day?"

Mary Lynn nodded. "How was she able to manage that?" she asked.

"We were beginning to wonder about that very thing. At first she would just get real simple, inexpensive items, like new combs, fresh baked cookies, socks, and key chains, stuff that was useful. A lot of the time she would sneak 'em back out at supper time and re-gift it the next day to someone else. Most of the poor things didn't know the difference anyway. But then, we started noticing her gifts were getting much more expensive and didn't make sense at all."

"Tell what she gave 'em," Mavis prodded.

"Yes. They were weird things to give old folks in a nursing home. Things like . . ."

"Eight-track tapes and video tapes," Mavis inserted.

"Now I ask you, what in the world would some old person do with a tape that teaches you to do something called 'Country Line Dancing.' How could they even watch it?"

Dorine told Mary Lynn, "Hardly anybody round here even has one of those things you use to play those movies on. What are they called?"

"VCR," Mavis said.

"That's right. Doll got herself one of those," Dorine said shaking her head. "For some reason it was always blinking the number 12:00 over and over."

"I made a little cozy to cover that up for her, so it wouldn't disturb her at night." Mavis said.

"Yes, you did," Teenie nodded earnestly at Mavis. "And she was ever so thankful for it."

"Anyway, it was all making us a bit suspicious - Christabelle spending so much money on such odd merchandise, and then turning around to give it all away so's she could buy more things.

"If it hadn't of been for Cutie Boy, there's no telling how long before we would've discovered Christabelle's secret."

"Cutie Boy is Christabelle's little fox terrier," Mavis informed Mary Lynn before she could ask.

"Yes," Teenie continued as he raised his eyebrows and pursed his lips. "That breed is not nearly as refined as a toy poodle, but he does have a lot of personality. Mavis has made him the cutest little Santa Claus suit to wear whenever there gets a chill to the air."

"He doesn't have much hair and gets to shivering a lot," Mavis added, blushing at Teenie's compliment. "I was just tryin' to make him a bit more comfortable."

"Well, he sure loves to wear that thing," Teenie said, smiling up at his wife. "And it does keep him from bein' so shivery all the time. But anyway, that's what uncovered Christabelle's dark secret, Cutie Boy's shiverin.

"Bein' an AKC certified dog breeder for all these years I've accumulated quite a store of canine health care experience and pharmaceutical samples, so whenever anybody has a problem with one of their dogs they usually call me first."

"Teenie knows more than most vets do!" Mavis added quietly, filled with fierce pride in her little husband.

"Oh, Hon, that's not true," Teenie fussed unconvincingly. "Except maybe when it comes to small dogs, and AKC toy poodles most certainly," he added unabashedly, as he fluttered his eyelids at Mary Lynn before returning to the subject of Christabelle.

"So, one night about a month and a half ago . . . no, three months ago, Christabelle called me late of a Sunday night, and she was all upset. At first I thought Doll had taken a turn for the worse. Christabelle was spending all her time with Doll by then. Because Doll's cancer had got so bad, Christabelle took a leave of absence from the Mansion so she could provide Doll full time nursing care and keep her from having to stay out of town in some hospital.

"But, it wasn't about Doll this time. Christabelle was over at her own trailer. It was Cutie Pie that was ailing and could I please come over to see what was causing the poor little thing to be having such terrible shiverin' fits. I dashed on over there with my vet kit to see what I could do. When I got there Christabelle was a wreck. Her hair was on end, her makeup was smeared, and it looked like she'd been crying.

"This was extremely unusual behavior for Christabelle. No wonder Cutie Boy was shaking so bad. He could tell something had really upset his mistress. Being low to the ground like I am, I notice a lot of details that a taller person would overlook. I immediately saw that there were credit card bills and large envelopes scattered all across the floor of Christabelle's living room. I'd never had the occasion to come into her trailer before that night, but I thought it a might odd that a lady as well-dressed and orderly as Christabelle was would have tall stacks of boxes all over the place, so's all there was room for was a little path through them.

"At first I just thought she had gotten behind in her gift-giving, what with having to spend so much time caring for Doll, but then I noticed these were not typical gifts, even for Christabelle to be giving out. I saw cases of books on learning new math and counted at least twenty expensive-looking collectable dolls still in their boxes.

"I just stood there and put my hands on my hips and said, 'You have got to tell me what's really going on here. Your little doggy is so worried over you that he's having himself a nervous breakdown and you don't look too far from the verge yourself.' Well, she just broke down and cried right then! I gave Cutie Pie one of my canine tranquilizer tablets immediately 'cause he was in such a terrible state. He was tremblin' and whinin' upon seeing Christabelle's extreme distress. The pill knocked him out pretty quick. Then I had Christabelle sit down and start telling me from the beginning how things had got to this state of affairs."

"Oh Teenie," she wailed. "It all started out with me entering that Publishing House Sweepstakes! It just seemed so exciting thinking I might actually win. I thought if I ordered more of their books and gift items, I might have a better chance of having those nice people come to my trailer with balloons and flowers, and that great big ole check!"

"It's just another form of gambling!" Marv said suddenly, in such a serious tone it startled Mary Lynn. "Christabelle didn't realize it, but she was just as much a gambling addict as I was, only it took a different form is all. That's why Teenie called me over to talk her down."

"But, what was she doing that was so bad?" Mary Lynn was confused because she had bought plenty of things from those publishing companies that had sweepstakes. Just this past Christmas she'd ordered a couple of sets of books to give her grandchildren.

"What she was doing," Marv said vehemently, "was buying chances to win a jackpot!"

"Calm down now, Marv." Pauline gave his arm a squeeze and rolled her eyes at Mary Lynn. "Marv is a vigilant anti-gambling crusader. The only trouble with Christabelle was she got too carried away with . . ."

"She was addicted to it." Marv corrected Pauline.

"Well, yes, Sugar. She was addicted to buying things she didn't need just to keep playing the sweepstakes game and she certainly couldn't afford to be doing that."

"The night she called me," Teenie piped in, "she realized she had maxed out her credit cards by mail-ordering all that merchandise and she didn't know how in the world she was ever gonna pay off all her bills. She was so embarrassed and ashamed and had been hiding this from all her friends for two long years."

Marv spoke up again. "Teenie and I sat up with her most the night trying to help the poor woman figure out a way to clear up her debt problems." Marv leaned back and flashed his smile again. "I got on the phone the next day and talked those sweepstakes crooks into letting Christabelle return about half the stuff she'd bought that was still in the original unopened condition. That got her a refund credit of pretty near $1,800. Pauline put the rest of it in her flea shop, NU-TU-U to see if she could sell it."

"It's not moving very fast," Pauline said quietly to Mary Lynn. "Too many other people have ordered the same stuff themselves."

"We had not intended to let Doll get wind of all this but Tammy accidentally ended up telling her about it," Teenie said, shaking his head. Then he brightened suddenly. "So this morning, Marv and I got calls from Doll's lawyer about special instructions Doll had recently added to her 'Last Wishes.' It turned out Doll had written in a nice bequest for her cheerful and kindhearted private nurse, Christabelle Tingleberry!"

"That was a very generous 'bequest,' wasn't it, Teenie," Marv said grinning at everybody. "It was more than enough to pay off all her credit card bills."

"The most fun part about it all," Teenie shrilled, clapping his hands, "was that Doll told us to go get balloons and roses from over at Violet Expressions and have David draw a picture of a big blank check on some poster board . . ."

"We filled in the amount, and that's how Christabelle found out how much Doll had left her," Marv said, grinning. "You should have seen the look on her face when we came to her door with all that paraphernalia!"

"How much was it, Marv?" Dorine asked, after a honk into her wadded up teal paper napkin. "Did Doll leave her a lot of money?"

His grin grew wider as he leaned forward so he could speak somewhat confidentially. "Let me just put it this way, Christabelle has finally won herself a sweepstakes."

*"**Let us pray.**"* a deep, sonorous voice boomed forth from the speakers up on the stage, followed by a loud microphone feedback squeal.

"Lordee!" Dorine said, squinting in the direction of the noise. "Who let Pastor Astor get loose up on that stage?"

CHAPTER NINETEEN

An Interlude of Devout Holiness

A hem . . ." Tap . . . tap **thunk!** "Hawwuuuk . . . ahem, ahem . . ." A series of prodigious throat clearings and microphone tapping boomed forth from the stage. "I said, **let us pray**." This pronouncement coming from the venerable Pastor Astor brought a halt to all conversation and eating in the VFW's Great Hall. An uncomfortable silence settled upon them all, punctuated only by the occasional cough, whining child or poodle.

Mary Lynn bowed her head and stared at her hands in her lap. She glanced at her half-eaten plate of dinner that was quickly growing cold. She snuck a look up towards the stage. From what she had heard about the Pastor, he had to be close to ninety years old. He was a tall impressive man, even though he was somewhat stooped with age, and his black suit hung loosely on him.

His magnificent mane of gleaming white hair was combed up into a perfect pompadour. His arms were now raised in an exhortation to the heavens above and he was just getting warmed up.

"Bless all of this abundance placed before us, Lord!" the Pastor intoned sincerely. "We want to thank you **especially** for the life and **many** generous works of our **dear** departed sister, Loretta Doll Dumas.

At his mention of Doll, scattered shouts of: "Amen, Uh huh," and "**Yes**, Lord," rose from various people in the audience.

"**And** remind us **all**, Lord that **death** can come to find us at any **time** and any **place** and we must be prepared to come before **God** as a **saved** disciple of His word!"

"Oh Lordee," Dorine muttered. "Here we go." Then she heaved a big sigh, as Pastor Astor built to yet another crescendo.

"So in order to be ready for that inevitable day that **will** come . . . **that final day of judgement**. . ."

At this point, the Pastor became so excited that it caused his dentures to slip with a great clacking sound, magnified by the microphone clutched in his hand. As he paused to shove his uppers back up with his thumb, three young girls sitting at the table next to Mary Lynn began to giggle, keeping their heads bowed and eyes clenched shut.

Don was still holding a roll in his hand poised over his plate. He had been just about to sop up the last of the sauce on his plate when interrupted by Pastor Astor's invocation, turned sermon. Everyone else sat and watched their food grow cold and congeal on their plates.

Meanwhile, the Pastor began to advise everyone to "get **saved** before it was **too late**" and then he went on to describe several versions of "the fires of **Hell**."

Softly at first, as if it was a part of Pastor Astor's sermon, the sound of organ music began to swell behind his droning voice. The tune of "Rock of Ages" built ever so gently, and some of the audience began to hum along.

"Nobody knows better how to bring Pastor Astor back down to earth than Louise Dolesanger," Mavis observed quietly.

"Thank the Lord for Louise!" muttered Dorine.

"Amen," whispered everybody else at the table.

By now, the music was loud enough to drown out the Pastor, and Louise segued into a rousing version of "Amen, Amen." The audience began to clap in time with the music and sing along with gusto. A top-heavy, brassy blonde woman, wearing a low-cut sequined western shirt and tight jeans stepped up on the stage with a microphone. She went up to Pastor Astor, who seemed delighted with the sudden audience participation, waved at the crowd and shouted out, "Let's hear it ya'll for the one and holy, Pastor Astor!"

There was thunderous applause, especially from Don, who sopped up his gravy with his roll and stuffed it in his mouth to free both hands. The Pastor smiled beatifically, waving his blessings at the crowd, as an attractive young woman in a short sparkling dress came up to lead him safely off the stage.

Marv whistled loudly through his teeth. "Let's hear it for Lucille and Tammy!" he said as he clapped and laughed.

"Yes, siree!" said Don. "Hey, anybody ready for some pie?"

Laurite returned to stand beside Johnny at his post behind Mary Lynn. The old Creole stuck out her bottom lip and shook her head as she glared in the direction of Pastor Astor being led docilely back to his table.

"It's people like that preacher man who give the After-Life a bad name, right Laurite," observed Johnny with a twinkle in his eye.

"He gonna be in for a BIG surprise when his time come," Laurite gave a curt nod and spat over her shoulder.

"Hey! Watch where you're spitting!" Doll had just appeared behind Laurite. She wasn't really bothered though. In fact she was absolutely delighted with her surroundings. *"At least Don's got the right idea. I can't think of anything more heavenly than his coconut cream pie!"*

CHAPTER TWENTY

Tammy's Tappers and the Return of the Prodigal Daughter (Lucille Lepanto)

I'd like to have a piece, but I've already had my dessert." Mavis looked longingly towards the table laden with Don's delectable pies.

"I'd better wait on mine, Don," said Pauline as she hopped up from the table. "I promised Tammy I'd help with the girls."

Blowing a kiss over her shoulder, she trotted across the dance floor toward the stage. Mary Lynn was beginning to understand how Pauline stayed so slim. The woman hardly sat still for more than a few minutes; barely giving her a chance to eat.

"Dorine," Teenie piped in. "Isn't your little Dora Lee going to be performing tonight?"

"She's the lead dancer in her group, and has a solo in the grand finale!" Dorine beamed with pride.

"*Don!*" she hollered to get his attention. "*Bring me a piece of the coconut cream. Do you want one, Mary Lynn? It's his best. Bring two and hurry! You don't want to miss Miss Dora Lee!*"

Don nodded and gave a two finger sign, as he expertly ducked through the crowd gathering around the dessert table.

"Okay everybody, can I have your attention, pau-leeze!" The brassy blonde woman in the sequined shirt was back up on the stage. "It's almost time for that special treat we've all been waiting for."

A buzz of excitement filled the room, especially among the three little girls at the table nearby.

"Who is that?" Mary Lynn asked Dorine, indicating the woman making the announcements on stage.

"That's Doll's daughter, Lucille. The pretty young gal coming out from behind the curtain is Tammy, her granddaughter, the delight of Doll's life," Dorine added softly. "I'll tell you more about them after the dance revue."

Don returned to the table, juggling three plates with huge slices of coconut cream pie. He passed out extra forks, and sat down chuckling.

"The word is Little Bo has some stunt up his sleeve. I cain't wait to see what that is!" Don pointed toward the stage just as Little Bo cued up some records, hurried off the stage, and darted into the Men's room. "I get the biggest kick outta that guy. He's the best radio host they've got on KPEW," Don explained to Mary Lynn.

"He better not steal any thunder from the Tappers," Dorine retorted as she stabbed her fork into her pie. "They'll be dancing their little hearts out for Granny Doll and Miss Tammy."

"Oh my, will you just look at that girl!" Teenie sighed, as Tammy walked across the stage to stand in the spotlight beside Lucille "She's an absolute vision in that new dress."

Mary Lynn had to agree with him. Tammy was a lovely young woman. She stood with perfect posture and poise as her mother handed her the microphone. She was wearing a figure-hugging aqua blue sequined mini dress that flashed and sparkled. The light shone off her gleaming blonde hair like a halo.

A collective sigh of admiration rose from the audience as the house lights dimmed and Tammy stood alone on stage. The murmurs were immediately followed by applause and whistles.

"Hi, ya'll. . . . Hi!" Tammy said sweetly, in an almost childlike nasal twang as she waved to the audience. "Thank you soooo much for comin' out tonight!"

"We love you Tammy!" all the young men seated at the Gay Caballero table shouted in unison. Tammy blushed prettily and giggled as she blew them a kiss.

"Thank you, I love ya'll, too!" There was applause and laughter at this. "Okay . . . okay . . . Now, ya'll know my Granny Doll wanted us to have a real good time tonight . . ."

(More applause)

"Thank you, thank you so much! Anyway, I wanted to have the girls do a special dance revue especially in honor of my Granny who taught me sooooooo much about life and all that good stuff."

"God bless you Tammy!" shouted someone from across the room.

"Well thank you and bless you too," she gushed with a self-conscious giggle.

"She is such a sweet girl," said Teenie sincerely.

"I . . . uh . . . mm . . . oh yeah, Miz Rhonelle, my buddy Amber and I worked up a very special program for you tonight, dedicated to my Granny Doll." There was a smattering of polite applause, followed by a pause that was about to become uncomfortable as Tammy stared blankly at the audience, still flashing her radiant smile. "Oh yeah," she said suddenly. "It's called 'Ode to Shirley Temple, to the Tunes of Elvis.' I hope ya'll like it!"

She skipped over to the side of the stage and handed the microphone back to her mother, who took over as MC. "Here they are folks, Peavine's brightest new stars . . . Tammy's Tappers!"

A line of twenty little girls in pink and white sparkling dance costumes clacked noisily out from behind the curtain across the back of the stage. The crowd cheered enthusiastically.

Little Bo burst out of the men's room at this moment and Don howled with laughter as he watched him dash up onto the stage. Bo had transformed into an Elvis impersonator complete with black wig, sunglasses, a white cape, and bell-bottomed jumpsuit. The audience yelled and hooted as Bo strutted around the stage before taking his place behind the turntables. Don let loose with a loud, two-fingered whistle that made Mary Lynn jump.

"Look at that rascal," Don shouted gleefully. "He's really outdone his self tonight!"

"Hush up Don." Dorine elbowed her husband sharply. "The girls are about to start the show."

With a nod from Tammy, all the Tappers struck a pose in unison - right arms up, left toes pointed forward. After a few seconds of crackling noises coming from the speakers below the stage, 'Jail House Rock' blared forth. Don and Dorine watched with rapt attention as their little Dora Lee calmly led the dance line forward into their first routine. Don never touched his hearing aids or dessert throughout the entire performance.

Tap dancing to a medley of Elvis hits was not an easy accomplishment but the little girls pulled it off without a single blunder. Mary Lynn marveled at the expertise of the Tappers, especially Dora Lee.

"Oh look at her GO!" Don put his fingers in his mouth and whistled loudly as applause rose again. Dora Lee was doing a series of turns while balanced on one foot, followed by four cartwheels before landing in the splits, right on the beat of the final note of "Blue Suede Shoes."

After the grand finale, Dora Lee hopped up and quickly curtsied to the audience, followed by the rest of the dancers stepping forward in line to curtsy daintily. The entire crowd was on their feet in an exuberant standing ovation. Even Dorine jumped up from her chair without a single grunt. Teenie was standing on the seat of his chair, until Mavis made him get down.

The Great Hall of the VFW Hut filled with shouts and cheers as Dora Lee came forward alone for a solo bow (after checking with Miss Tammy first, of course). Dora Lee bowed again, grinning proudly. She and all the other Tappers turned toward Miss Tammy, waving and pleading for her to come join them in the spotlight. Tammy joined her students, alternately applauding and hand-fanning at the tears streaming down her cheeks.

Lucille got on the microphone again and called out over the applause, "Rhonelle, Amber! Ya'll belong up here too."

A wiry, overly tanned young woman with frizzy orange hair and a vivid green satin dress sprang onto the stage and energetically hugged Tammy and each one of the girls. Rhonelle sauntered nonchalantly across the dance floor and stepped onto the stage beside Tammy and Amber. The three women joined hands and bowed to the wildly applauding crowd. David, the floral designer, took this opportunity to run up on the stage and present huge bouquets of flowers to the three of them.

After the last of the Tammy's Tappers disappeared behind the curtain and the applause had finally died down, Lucille got on the mike again. "OKAY, everybody, this is your last chance to grab some dessert. Then you'd better belly up to that bar, or drink you some coffee, **'cause we've got a whole lot of partying left to do!**"

(Cheers, hoots and whistles at this!)

"In just fifteen minutes I want ya'll to be ready to start cutting the rug! That's the way my Mamma would've wanted it."

There were more cheers as people began to scoot their chairs back. Little Bo cued up some slower Elvis tunes. He had decided to leave on his costume for the duration of the evening.

"Don, I think I'll have a piece of that coconut cream pie after all if you think there's any of it left," Mavis said in her loudest voice yet.

"If there ain't any on the dessert table, I'll go cut into that extra pie I hid out in the kitchen." Don moved nimbly through the crowd. Mary Lynn could see traces of the old quarterback in the way he zigged and bobbed his way across the room. It was pretty impressive for such a large man.

Mary Lynn saw this as her chance to get the lowdown on Doll's daughter and granddaughter. "So, Dorine, tell me about Lucille. I thought you told me she'd run away from home when she was a teenager."

"That's right," Dorine said, glancing towards the stage where Lucille was laughing and talking to Little Bo behind the DJ stand. "She was only seventeen when she and Shirleen Naither ran off with that motorcycle gang. Doll and Herman Junior had only been married a few years then. I hate to say it, but it was kind of a relief to all of us to get Lucille out of town.

"Lordee, by the time that girl was twelve, she was nothing but trouble! Of course, it broke poor Doll's heart when Lucille ran off like that; she's her only child. Herman Junior had been generous enough to claim Lucille as his legally adoptive daughter, but she wouldn't have a thing to do with him; that is unless she needed some more of his money. She may have resented Herman Junior but she sure loved his money! Most of the time, Doll wasn't even aware of how much Herman Junior had been handing over to the girl. Things came to a head around Lucille's sixteenth birthday when Herman and Doll bought her a red Mustang convertible. She tore all over the county speeding, with the car full of her wild bunch of friends. Doll and Herman seemed powerless when it came to Lucille.

"She got drunk one weekend and wrecked the car. Thank the Lord nobody got hurt, but her red convertible was ruined for good. That was about two, maybe three weeks before she ran off."

Mary Lynn's mouth was hanging open in astonishment. Dorine shook her head and squinted over at Lucille up on the stage.

"I know it is hard to believe all that about Lucille, seeing how she is now. She's changed a lot but she'll never deny that she was a mess in her youth. Lucille claims that her past is a part of who she is and she wouldn't be the person she is now without being able to accept who she used to be too."

"Really?" Mary Lynn pondered this. "I've never thought of a shameful past quite like that."

Dorine raised her eyebrows. "Well, I'm not sure exactly what Lucille meant, it sounds to me like that New Age jargon. Anyway, where was I? Oh yeah, the red convertible. Both Herman and Doll agreed, they'd refuse to buy her a new car until she'd proved she could behave herself. So what did that dang sassy girl do? She up and run off with some hooligans to get back at them!"

"Two years went by with only a few phone calls from Lucille, made secretly to Herman Junior - usually at his office. She'd sound all sorry and desperate and ask him to wire her some money so she could get home, but she'd never show up. After a while, the phone calls stopped.

"Herman Junior passed away, yet Lucille never showed up to claim her part of the inheritance. Nobody could find her. It wasn't until Shirleen Naither came back to Peavine with her tail between her legs that Doll got any news about her long lost daughter. She was so relieved to hear something; she didn't care what, so long as she knew Lucille was still alive.

"Don and I had given up on ever seeing the return of Lucille, but not Doll. She was getting pretty low on hope of finding her, until that stormy night when Rhonelle showed up."

"What did Rhonelle have to do with it? Did she see Lucille in New Orleans?" Mary Lynn was reminded of the low life on Bourbon Street.

"Naw, Lucille wasn't ever a stripper, if that's what you're thinking - although it wouldn't have surprised me if she had tried something like that." Dorine suddenly lowered her voice and her eyes got bigger, as she leaned closer towards Mary Lynn. "You remember what Rhonelle said to Doll that first night she met her? It's what caused Doll to yank that spooky woman right into her trailer. She said she knew about the young woman who had run away!"

"Oh!" Mary Lynn's eyes were as big as Dorine's now. "You mean she was talking about Lucille?"

"Turns out, she was," Dorine said raising her eyebrows and nodding seriously. "Rhonelle claimed the spirit of her Granny Laurite had instructed her to say those exact words to the woman who would open the door. That was how Rhonelle could be sure she'd arrived at her true destination."

"It sounds like the ghost, uh . . . her grandmother was giving her good advice, heh, heh." Mary Lynn gave a nervous laugh and tried not to look toward where she had last seen Rhonelle.

"It did Doll a world of good to have somebody tell her with certainty that Lucille was alive and eventually would be found. I don't know why but none of us ever doubted what Rhonelle told us. That may sound odd to you but there's just something about her. About three months later, Marv and Pauline showed up at the Diner. Rhonelle had predicted they would be the right people to help locate Lucille. Granny Laurite had told her that the time had finally come when Lucille was ready to be found."

"Psychic clues aren't all that easy to interpret," Marv said suddenly at Mary Lynn's elbow. She had not realized he had been listening to Dorine. "That's where I came in handy. I don't know if Dorine has mentioned it, but I've got some pretty close contacts with folks at the FBI." Marv leaned in close to Mary Lynn to whisper this last bit of information.

Mary Lynn glanced at Dorine before shaking her head and looking properly impressed.

"I had a couple of my buddies at the Bureau check out a few things real quiet-like. We didn't want to get Lucille into any hot water, just wanted to find out where she was. Of course I never did tell those guys how we'd gotten our 'tips' on the girl's whereabouts from a psychic. To their credit and Rhonelle's, it only took a couple weeks of looking before we got a positive ID and location on Lucille. For the past few years she'd been working at a little roadhouse bar and grill outside of Austin, Texas."

Marv squinted up at the stage and watched Lucille playfully bump hips with Little Bo. Marv swirled the ice in his glass and swigged down the last of his gin and tonic.

Mary Lynn waited anxiously for him to continue.

"We didn't want to tell Doll anything about Lucille until Pauline and I had a chance to go down there. We wanted to see for ourselves what kind of a frame of mind she was in, you know, after hearing from Dorine what she'd been like before. It'd been so many years since anybody had heard from her, we weren't sure what we might find. There was no use gettin' Doll all built up over nothing."

"Did you take Rhonelle with you?" asked Mary Lynn.

Marv shook his head and gave a snort of laughter. "We didn't want to take the chance of scaring Lucille off. Pauline and I made up some excuse for a trip on the weekend before Christmas and drove down to Austin. I was pleasantly surprised when I finally met the infamous Lucille Lepanto. She looked older than I'd expected, like a woman who's been 'rode hard, and put up wet' as the feller says. She wasn't a monster though, just a hard-working woman. Come to find out, she had a little girl of her own to support, with the daddy long gone. We was really taken aback when we saw little Tammy for the first time! She must have been about five then, just as sweet and pretty as you saw tonight."

"Rhonelle didn't know about a little girl," Dorine added. "Says her Granny couldn't tell her everything, had to leave a few things for us to discover on our own."

"When Pauline and I appraised the situation, we decided we had better do some heavy-duty talking to Lucille and convince her and little Tammy to come back to Peavine with us. Lucille broke down into tears, and admitted she'd wanted to come home to her mamma, especially after she had Tammy. She was deeply ashamed of herself because of the way she had treated Doll and Herman Junior what with running off to live on the wild side all those years. She just couldn't bring herself to ask them for help. If it hadn't been for the kindhearted owner of the roadhouse taking pity on her, Lucille doesn't know what would've happened to her and her baby girl. She gave Lucille a job serving beer and a place to stay."

"That was the beginning of the new Lucille. All she wanted out of life was to be clean and sober so she could be a good mother to Tammy. She hoped that some day she could make up for all the bad things she'd done to Doll and Herman. She didn't even know until we told her that Herman Junior had died years ago. Pauline told Lucille it looked to her like she was a doing a great job as a mamma and the best way to make things right with Doll was for her and Tammy to come back to Peavine with us."

"Oh, Lordee!" Dorine honked into her napkins and wiped away

fresh tears. "What a scene that was! Don and I were over at Doll's trailer that Christmas Eve of 1970 when Lucille walks in after being gone all those years. Doll jumped up and threw her arms around Lucille and both of them started crying to beat the ban. H o o o n k . . . sniff . . . sniff. Oh, what a precious memory!

"Then Pauline and I brought in little Tammy. She goes to tugging at Lucille's coat and crying too, wanting to know what was wrong with her mamma." Mary Lynn saw Marv blink away a few tears of his own, as he stopped to clear his throat.

Teenie and Mavis had been listening quietly, until now.

"Doll just couldn't believe it!" Teenie exclaimed dramatically. "Mavis and I agreed it was truly a Christmas miracle. Not only had her long-lost daughter been returned to her safe and sound, she also discovered she had the most darling little granddaughter ever!"

"I believe it was the best Christmas of Doll's life." Dorine sobbed loudly. Don looked up from his last few bites of pie in alarm and tweaked his left ear.

Teenie took this opportunity to retake control of the conversation. "Now, come on, Dorine. You've got to pull yourself together, for Tammy's sake, at least," Tut-ted Teenie as he reached up to put his arm around her shoulder.

"Here, Honey, I got a hankie you can use," Mavis said quietly as she passed a large lace-trimmed handkerchief over to Dorine who honked gratefully into it. (She had used up all the nearby paper napkins.)

Teenie turned back to Mary Lynn. "We all feel like Tammy is our own child. I never saw a more beautiful little girl. She was always so full of love for everybody we just naturally loved her back. Her favorite thing to do was dance! She and her Granny Doll would watch old Shirley Temple movies together on the TV. Tammy hopped right up and tried to dance along with each one of the tap numbers.

"Doll got her the cutest little pair of pink tap shoes for her sixth birthday, and Mavis made her a darling little frilly costume. Whenever Shirleen Naither came to visit, she'd crimp Tammy's hair up in them bouncy little curls just like Shirley Temple used to have! We got treated to a whole bunch of performances of 'The Good Ship Lollipop,' didn't we?"

Everybody at the table smiled and nodded as Teenie prattled on as if he were a proud grandfather. "Tammy could mimic all the dance routines she saw in those old movies just by watching them a few times. Rhonelle recognized Tammy was gifted at dance real early on and started giving her some lessons. Now, before you get all shocked over that Mary Lynn, you have to remember that Rhonelle was a very talented dancer. She only did that other stuff just to make a living." Teenie shuddered at the thought before continuing. "Doll looked after Tammy every afternoon and evening while Lucille was at work."

"She didn't have to go to work," Mavis leaned forward to tell Mary Lynn. "Doll would have supported them, but Lucille insisted on paying her own way."

"She sure did." Teenie agreed, nodding vigorously. "Lucille was going to prove to all of us how much she'd changed and wouldn't take any money from Doll. She even paid her rent for the trailer next door to Doll's that we all fixed up for her and Tammy. Lucille got herself a job at the Too-Tite Tavern, same place her mamma had worked when Lucille was a little girl. When the owner decided to retire Lucille applied for a bank loan all by herself and bought the place from him."

"Meanwhile, Tammy was expanding her dance expertise by going into baton twirling and cheerleading. She stayed in high school an extra year just to help out the band. She was the drum majorette, and a cheerleader."

"How was she able to do both things at the same time?" Mary Lynn asked. "Did she only do cheerleading at the basketball games?"

"Not our Tammy!" Teenie swelled out his little chest with pride. "Maybe she wasn't all that accomplished at 'book learning' but her talent and energy for twirling and cheer were unsurpassed."

"She had plenty of help at the football games, especially." Mavis said, smiling.

Teenie sighed dreamily. "Oh, Mary Lynn, if only you could have seen her out on the football field during those halftime shows. She wore those little sequined outfits Mavis made special for her (I don't know what kept her from freezing to death) and her pristine white majorette boots with the tassels on 'em."

"The lights would dim as she lit up them fire batons. What a thrill it was to see that girl in action! As long as I've been watching her perform, she has never dropped a baton. Tammy was the only real reason anybody ever went to those boring old football games."

"Speak for yourself Teenie." Don said with a chuckle, as Dorine swatted at his arm.

"Well, of course we wanted to cheer for your boy, Donnie," Teenie added quickly.

"He was the star quarterback," Mavis explained as she leaned around Teenie, who stubbornly returned to the subject of Tammy.

"Well, you've got to admit a talent such as hers doesn't come along every day," he said with a flutter of his hands. "After jumping around doing all those cheering stunts and dance routines, Tammy would run back to the girl's locker room as the football players left the field at the halftime. Mavis and Pauline would be waiting for her there to help her change into her majorette regalia. The only time she ran into some difficulties was when she was the homecoming queen. Whew! We were just nervous wrecks for that one!"

"Where did Tammy go to college?" Mary Lynn wondered aloud. She assumed higher education was very important to Doll, after hearing about the Washington family.

"Well, Hon, Tammy never went to college," Dorine explained delicately. "She wasn't very interested in what you could learn out of a book, you see. All she cared about was dancing, baton-twirling, and cheerleading, and after the extra classes she had to enroll in to be able to stay in high school for an extra year, she'd had enough of school."

"That's when Rhonelle and I thought up the idea of a dance academy!" Teenie inserted brightly. "Tammy's best friend, Amber, wasn't going to college either. She had been the head cheerleader and she really wanted to teach cheerleading. So Doll used the money she had set aside for a college education and used it to get Tammy and Amber set up with their dance studio."

"They had wanted to call it the 'T and A House of Dance'," Mavis said dryly. "But Rhonelle convinced the girls that title might give people the wrong impression." Everybody at the table got a good laugh over that one.

Mary Lynn looked across the room and saw Tammy laughing and talking with a table full of "Tappers" and their parents. She was a beautiful young woman. She looked very fit, although a bit full in the bust for a dancer.

Marv had followed Mary Lynn's gaze. "Tammy's a real knockout, ain't she!" he said with a smile which bordered on being a leer.

"Isn't she though!" sighed Teenie, also watching Tammy as she walked over to Pauline, who was headed back to their table.

"Oh! I think Pauline is bringing her over! Yoo-hoo. Tammy, honey! " Teenie was about to climb onto his chair to wave, until Mavis put a restraining hand on his arm and shook her head.

"She's coming over here," Dorine said as she squinted across the room. "Lordee, Teenie, settle yourself down!"

Tammy was still clutching her enormous bouquet of flowers as she walked gracefully toward them. When she caught sight of Teenie waving madly and Marv flashing his wide grin, she broke into a high-heeled tiptoe run and jiggled gleefully towards them. Her bountiful breasts bounced and strained against the low-cut, sequined blue dress. "Teenie Pop!" she squealed before leaning over to give the little man a one-armed hug and a kiss on his forehead. "Unkie Marv!" After Teenie let go of her, Tammy leaned over to Marv and planted a big "mmwaak" kiss on his cheek before he could stand up. "How did ya'll like my girls?" she asked breathlessly.

"Oh we loved it!" they all said at once.

Dorine took Tammy's hand and gave it a squeeze. "Here, Honey, I want you to meet Mary Lynn. She's come along as our guest tonight. She's all the way down from Missouri."

"I'm so pleased to meet you," Tammy said as she beamed blankly at Mary Lynn.

"It's a real treat to meet you, Tammy. Your dance program was spectacular. I've never seen anything quite like it!"

Dorine explained to Tammy that Mary Lynn was driving through Peavine and had decided to spend the night so she could come to the party.

"Oh, that is so great," gushed Tammy. "You are so GREAT to do that!" She flung her arm around Mary Lynn and gave her a hug. "My Granny just loved that sort of thing." When she straightened back up, Tammy wiped a fresh tear from the corner of her eye. This has been so much fun! We'll all get a chance to dance as soon as the band starts playing some better music."

Mary Lynn felt deeply touched by the genuine sweetness and open-hearted acceptance this young woman had shown her.

"I'd better go get some of your pie now, Uncle Don, so I can keep my energy up. Cecil is waiting on me." Tammy waved happily, then tip-toe-ran over to a table where a red-faced stout young man stood watching and smiling at her.

"Well, I just hope Cecil appreciates our sweet girl," Teenie said as he looked suspiciously toward the object of Tammy's affection.

"Oh, I'm sure he does," Marv said with a sly grin. "What that girl lacks in brains she makes up for with her two special assets."

Before Mary Lynn could ask Marv what he meant by that remark, Dorine looked over her glasses and asked sternly, "By assets, I'm sure you are referring to her talents for Dance and Baton right, Marv?"

"Right," said Marv with a quick wink toward Don who stifled his snickering when Dorine elbowed him sharply.

Fortunately Teenie was absorbed in adjusting his poodle's tutu at that moment and was totally oblivious to Marv's frank appraisal of Tammy's generously endowed "assets."

CHAPTER TWENTY-ONE

And a Good Time Was Had By All

Doll watched as her beautiful granddaughter bounced over and enthusiastically threw her arms around her boyfriend, in a prolonged hug. The shy young man blushed to an even deeper shade of red.

"He will be good for Tammy," she thought. *"A plain-looking man who is kind and faithful beats a selfish, handsome one any day, and it's obvious how much he loves her."*

Ah, yes, there was so much love all over that room. Doll was so filled with it; she could only experience the wonder of it all. It was flowing into her just as she felt it radiating outwards from her. She realized she was floating up to the ceiling and looking out over the large gathering of her family and dearest friends.

Each soul glowed with a different color, like a string of bulbs on a Christmas tree, yet a much more glorious sight. She began to see her whole life spread out before her as if it were one of Mavis' embroidered quilts. Golden threads connected each beloved life light. A pattern she had never comprehended or understood before this moment began to emerge and become clear to her.

Her awareness zoomed in on the light that was Mary Lynn. She saw many threads leading to and from this woman. Johnny was standing right beside Mary Lynn, glowing with his own special light. He and Laurite were watching Doll and smiling up at her.

"From the looks of things," said Johnny to Laurite as Doll slowly descended to stand beside them, *"someone has just had her first Come-to-Jesus moment."*

Laurite nodded in agreement as she pointed to the pink glow emanating from Doll. *"I think she be just about ready to tell her story to Mary Lynn."*

"Granny Doh, did you like my dancing?" Dora Lee came prissily clacking up to Dorine.

"Oh, honey, you were the greatest ever!" Dorine said as she squeezed her granddaughter in a hug. "How did you ever learn to dance so good?"

"I guess I just got talent," said Dora Lee in all honesty. "And I practice all the time," she added rolling her eyes.

The poodles, Dolly and Pitty Too came scampering up to Dora Lee. They had been visiting with another poodle across the room until they spied Dora Lee. Dolly did a tottering pirouette on her hind legs, and both dogs yipped and pawed happily at Dora Lee. They seemed to be entranced by her sparkling dance costume.

"Get OFF me! You're gonna TEAR my TUTU!" Dora Lee scolded sharply, causing both dogs to slink under the table with their stubby little tails tucked down.

"Dora Lee, please don't be so rude to Dolly and Pitty," Dorine said as she bent down under the table to console the quivering poodles.

"They'll get over it," said Mavis calmly. "You done good up there, Dora Lee," she added with a smile.

"Your cartwheels were flawless. Bravo, honey!" Teenie clapped his hands at Dora Lee.

"Thanks, Miz Mavis, Mr. Teenie. I've been working on those real hard all winter."

"Have you had your dessert yet? Poppy's gone out to the kitchen to get us some coconut cream pie, you want any?" Dorine asked Dora Lee.

"No thank you, Granny Doh, I'm not hungry. Momma's gonna take me home, so I can change into my new poodle skirt that Aunt Vaudine got for me in Memphis!" Dora Lee was dancing a jig with excitement.

"The boys will be lining up to get a dance with you, sweetie!" said Pauline.

"Well I'd better get going, Momma's waiting for me. Nice seeing ya'll." Dora Lee gleefully tap-danced back across the room.

"I'm gonna go refresh my drink." Marv stretched and stood up. "Can I get anybody else something while I'm at the bar?"

Everyone declined, except for Mavis, who, to Mary Lynn's surprise, ordered a Manhattan.

Don arrived carrying a whole coconut cream pie, with a spatula and extra plates under his arm.

"Here ya go, Mavis," he said as he dug out the first slice and handed it to her. "I just talked to Lucille, and she said to save her a piece, too. She'll come over here to set a spell as soon as she gets a cup of coffee."

Pitty Two had jumped up into Mavis' lap and was sneaking little licks of coconut cream pie from under her arm flab.

Pauline looked over Mary Lynn's head and pointed at someone across the room. "Look ya'll, here comes Lucille. And Shirleen is with her. Hey ya'll! Over here!" Pauline's bracelets sparkled and jingled as she waved her arms until Lucille spotted their table.

The woman walking beside Lucille had an astonishingly large hairdo, blonde of course. She and Lucille were so deep into a serious conversation; they'd almost walked past the table before Pauline was able to get their attention.

"You remember me telling you about Shirleen Naither don't you, Mary Lynn?" Dorine whispered. "That's her right there."

"How on earth does she get her hair to do that?" Mary Lynn hadn't seen a bouffant like that in years, and this one seemed to defy the laws of gravity.

"Her phenomenal hair-styling skills have improved even more since the Curl Up and Dye days." Dorine broke into a wide smile when Lucille and Shirleen arrived at their table. "Hey girls, what have ya'll been up to?"

"Hey Miz Dorine, I've been dying to see you!" Shirleen leaned over to give her a hug. "Luci-girl has been keeping me so busy I haven't had a chance to come by the Diner and get my cheeseburger and French fries fix." Shirleen took a step back, cocking her head to one side as she studied Dorine' frizzy gray hair. "Good Lord, Doh, I'm gonna have to give you a deep conditioning treatment before I leave town."

Far from taking this as an insult, Dorine seemed delighted. "That better be a promise, Shirleen. I'll be expecting you after breakfast in the morning."

"I think you ought to dye her hair blonde while you're at it," Lucille said chuckling at them. "That'd make Don sit up and take notice!"

"I just might have her do that!" Dorine said. "How do ya think I'd look as a blonde, Don?"

"Well, you'd look different, that's fer sure." Don replied carefully as he pulled up extra chairs for Lucille and Shirleen. "Have a seat, ladies. I've got you some pie."

"Whew, I can finally rest my dawgs!" Lucille flopped heavily into her chair and set her "Too-Tite-Tavern" coffee mug on the table.

"This is a relief!" Shirleen sat a bit more daintily before she kicked off her high-heeled pink pumps. "Gettin' all those little girls corralled plum wore me out! I'm not used to kids."

Dorine reached over and patted Lucille on the arm. "Honey, you've done a wonderful job with the Memorial Bash. This is exactly what your mamma would have wanted: everybody sure seems to be having a good time."

"It's a lovely party, Miss Lepanto." Mary Lynn wanted to be a properly polite guest. "Please accept my sincere condolences on the loss of your mother."

"Thank you." Lucille looked quizzically at Mary Lynn, and then seemed to recall something. "You must be the 'Mystery Guest' Don was telling me about. I'm real glad you decided to join us. I don't think I caught your name?"

"I'm sorry. I'm Mary Lynn Stanton, from Missouri."

"I'm pleased to meet ya, Mary Lynn from Missouri. This here is my childhood partner in crime, Shirleen Naither."

"Smedly is my last name now. Pleased to meet you too, Mary Lynn." Shirleen shook hands with Mary Lynn and glanced up at her hair. "Nice color you got there. Auburn is very becoming on you and your ends look good too, a lot better than Doh's."

"Uh, thank you, I try to take good care of them," Mary Lynn patted her hair self-consciously.

"Yeah, well go easy on those spiral-wrap perms. They're murder on your ends, you know."

"Gawd, Shirleen. You just met the woman and you're already talkin' about her 'ends'! Where's your sense of decency?" Lucille followed this with a slap on Mary Lynn's back and deep lung-rattling laughter. "Shirleen is obsessed with people's ends!"

Shirleen cackled over that remark. "I'm not even goin' to tell you what Luci-girl is obsessed with." To Mary Lynn's embarrassment both Shirleen and Lucille began to laugh even harder.

"You girls straighten up now. What will Mary Lynn think of us?" Dorine said with mock sternness.

"Ooookay . . . sorry 'bout that." Lucille took a swig of coffee to clear her throat. "Hey Don, hand over a slice of that pie, will ya? I'm starving."

"I'll bet Mary Lynn ain't too shocked by me and Shirleen," she added with a wink in her direction. "Dorine must have told her all about us by now."

"Uh, well," Mary Lynn blushed as she tried to think of how to respond. "Dorine has told me about so many of the people from around here . . . she ought to be the official Peavine historian. I have been especially interested in her stories about your mother and the many people she has helped out over the years." Mary Lynn realized this was her true reaction to all she had learned that day, not just the polite thing to say.

"Doll sure saved my butt, that's for sure!" Shirleen's eyes were getting a bit dewy at the thought. "I don't see as how I'd ever gotten back home except for her."

Pauline leaned forward earnestly. "Shirleen, you did a great job of fixing up Doll for the funeral today. She looked beautiful."

"Yes, she did," agreed Teenie, "and so peaceful." He sighed as everyone around the table nodded in agreement, except for Dorine, who squirmed around in her chair and squinted toward the bar.

"Where's Marv?" she asked Don. "I could use another drink about now."

"I'll go get you one," offered Pauline, springing out of her chair. "Can I get anybody else anything?"

"I'm sticking with coffee," said Lucille, raising her mug.

"I'll have a martini!" said Teenie gleefully.

"I don't think you will," said Mavis

"Okay then, a wine spritzer, please," Teenie said with an attempt at sounding sophisticated.

"Get me another whiskey sour, Pauline," said Dorine. "And bring another for Mary Lynn. I insist."

"Oh no, I haven't quite finished this one," Mary Lynn protested.

"Bring her one anyway," Lucille directed. "The night is young!"

"I'll take another beer," said Don.

"Bring me whatever you're having, Pauline," said Shirleen.

"This is great having somebody else takin' orders fer once," Lucille said as she propped her cowgirl-boots up on Pauline's chair.

"You deserve it, sweetie," Pauline said before sashaying quickly off towards the bar.

"Lucille, when does the band start to play?" asked Teenie excitedly.

"It'll be pretty soon from the looks of it." Lucille nodded toward the stage where the Gay Caballeros were setting up their drums, speakers, and guitars.

"Oh, goody!" Teenie was bouncing in his chair and clapping his hands excitedly. He turned and clasped Mary Lynn's arm. "You have got to promise me a dance, Mary Lynn. Mavis hates dancin' and I'm wearin' my new dancin' shoes tonight, so I won't be setting here like a lump on a log if that band is as good as I hear they are."

"You better take him up on it, Mary Lynn," Dorine said, smiling. "I'm saving my energy for the Mexican Hat Dance, and Pauline will want to dance some of the time with Marv."

"Hey, I'll do the two-step with ya, Teenie," said Shirleen. "When Bo plays some of those country albums I brought I'll teach you how to do the 'Cotton-Eyed Joe' line dance, words and all."

"You will?" Teenie squealed.

"Sure!" said Shirleen. "But Mary Lynn will have to do the honors on what the band is gonna play. I never could boogie to that kind of music."

Mavis leaned forward. "I really think you'll enjoy it Mary Lynn. Teenie is a lovely dancer."

"A regular little Fred Astaire, aren't ya, Teenie?" Marv said grinning as he and Pauline returned to the table with a tray laden with fresh drinks. "You'll never know what you're missing if you don't give him a spin, Mary Lynn."

Everyone was watching as Mary Lynn sat frozen and wide-eyed for a moment. She did not consider herself to be much of a dancer and wondered how she would manage being partnered with a man that was at least five inches shorter than she was. She drained the last of her watery cocktail and set down her plastic cup with resolution.

"I'd be delighted to dance with you Teenie," Mary Lynn said, to her own surprise.

The band began to play not long after that. Mary Lynn was impressed with Teenie's ability to maneuver her gracefully through the exotic blend of disco and Mexican-style dance music, a specialty of the Gay Caballeros.

She was having a wonderful time. This was certainly the most fun she'd had in years, and on those rare occasions when she did "cut the rug," it was never with anyone other than Leroy. She wondered what he would think of her partying like this without him.

When it came time for the Mexican Hat Dance, everybody . . . including Dorine and Mavis, got up to join hands and form a large circle. The men moved the tables and chairs out of the way to make room for people of all sizes and ages to fit in.

When everybody finally got into their place and Louise Dolesanger started the music, Mary Lynn found herself between David, the floral designer, on her left and of all people, Rhonelle Dubois on her right. Rhonelle laughed at the startled expression on Mary Lynn's face as she took her by the hand, leading her around the circle and showing her the proper steps.

Everyone cheered when the music stopped, but Rhonelle held fast to Mary Lynn's hand and turned to face her as she spoke quietly. "I want to apologize for being so weird earlier when we first met. I didn't mean to frighten you. It's just . . ." Rhonelle hesitated before continuing. "It's just that my old Granny Laurite was carrying on so, I wasn't able to speak properly."

"She was?" Mary Lynn's eyes widened at this.

"Yeah, that happens sometimes when I meet someone new," Rhonelle said with a laugh.

Mary Lynn's heart began to pound, but she had to ask, "What was she telling you? Was it something to do with me?"

Rhonelle narrowed her eyes and studied Mary Lynn a moment before she spoke, choosing her words carefully.

"Granny told me it was a really good thing you did, coming here to Peavine."

Mary Lynn exhaled with relief. "Well I agree with that. This is just about the best party I've ever been to and I've had a grand time!" It didn't take a psychic to come up with that observation, thought Mary Lynn.

Dorine was shuffling toward them, supported by Don on one side and Pauline on the other. A sleepy Dolly was packed in her bunting once again.

"Hey, Mary Lynn, we're ready to go home now," Dorine's speech was slightly slurred and her bow of curly ribbon had just about slipped off of her head. "Marv's gone to bring up the car for us."

Mary Lynn quickly disengaged her hand from Rhonelle's grasp and sang back, "I'm coming! Well, goodnight Rhonelle, thank you for helping me with those dance steps."

Mary Lynn was turning away when Rhonelle caught her by the arm. "One more thing," she said as her dark eyes looked intensely into Mary Lynn's face. "Granny wanted me to tell you something else: to expect the unexpected . . . and no matter what happens, don't be afraid."

CHAPTER TWENTY-TWO

A Midnight Visitor at Cottage Number Five

It was eleven o'clock when Mary Lynn closed and locked the door of her Cottage, after a last "nighty-night!" called out to Marv and Pauline. It had been very thoughtful of them to drive her right up to her cottage and see to it she got inside safely. This was after depositing Don and a very unsteady Dorine at the doorstep of the Dew Drop Inn office.

Mary Lynn's long day of driving, followed by drinking and dancing all evening had caught up with her at last. It took all the energy she could muster just to get undressed and ready for bed.

As she was brushing her teeth, she heard the crunch of gravel as a car pulled up to the cottage next to hers. Squeals of laughter and slamming doors were followed by shouts, hoots, and even more laughter. Kristy and Misty had plenty of party left in them and unfortunately for Mary Lynn, they were staying right next door.

Another car pulled onto the gravel, more car doors slammed. Mary Lynn turned off the light and peeked out the window. "Oh no, it's the Gay Caballeros band!" She jerked the curtains closed in exasperation. "I'm sure they'll want to stay up till all hours."

Mary Lynn dragged a small ladder-back chair over to the door and propped it up under the door knob. She always took this extra safety precaution on the rare occasions that she found herself sleeping alone in a strange place.

The laughter and voices next door got louder as Mary Lynn pulled back the pink and white coverlet and slid into bed. As soon as she lay down, dance music began to play and the thump-thumping of the base notes vibrated through the wall behind her head. The Gay Caballeros had brought over one of the eight-track cassettes they'd been promoting at the party, along with a really powerful boom-box.

"Oh, this is just great!" Mary Lynn was too tired to do anything more than stuff the two rubbery pillows against her ears and hope that her state of exhaustion would soon win out over all the noise. That seemed to muffle the noise a little. Kristy's screams of laughter didn't sound quite so shrill now. The music even began to sound quite pleasant. A quieter guitar ballad had replaced the dance hits.

"Ah, that's better!" Mary Lynn sighed deeply and closed her eyes. Scenes of the party kept flashing in her mind. She had especially enjoyed the dancing. As Mary Lynn drifted off to sleep she replayed the evening in her head. "That old gal Rhonelle still moved with a special rhythm and grace, I guess you would say. She didn't seem so crazy either, once she talked to you like a normal person would . . . Now what was it she'd told me? There was something she had said as we were getting ready to leave. Expect something . . . and don't be afraid . . . Be afraid of what? Oh, well, she didn't look too worried when she said that, only kind of sad, or . . . it doesn't really matter . . ."

Suddenly, everything went quiet. All the music and laughter from next door stopped. Mary Lynn's eyes flew open. She sat bolt upright in her bed with the distinct feeling that she was not alone. She could have sworn she heard someone clear their throat and there was a hint of cigarette smoke in the air.

"That's silly of me," she said as she glanced over toward the door. She was reassured to see the chair still propped up under the doorknob, exactly as she had left it. "I must have heard somebody outside." Mary Lynn was just about to sink back into her pillows when she heard a wavering voice speak from the opposite corner of her room.

"No, honey, it's me . . . I'm over here."

Mary Lynn felt the hairs on her arms and neck stand on end as she slowly turned her head toward the voice. Someone was sitting in the recliner chair in the corner of the room! She could see a woman silhouetted by the soft pink glow of a night light plugged into the wall behind her. The lit end of a cigarette flared and was reflected in a pair of rhinestone-set, cat-eye glasses.

Mary Lynn stared in astonishment as the pink glow from the night light began to grow until it illuminated the woman, head to toe. Her hair was jet black and piled high into a beehive. She was wearing brightly colored clothing and flashy jewelry. Copious amounts of rouge colored her wrinkled cheeks. It was a very familiar face that sat there smiling at Mary Lynn.

Now where had she just seen this person? Of course . . . the life-sized poster of Doll Dumas! She remembered seeing it at the party that night. "Well, this is some kind of a crazy dream now, isn't it," Mary Lynn said aloud, laughing at herself.

"Sure, honey, if you need to see it that way, it's alright by me." The ghost grinned back at her. "I'm just a vision generated by Ozelle's spicy bar-b-q sauce, and Kristy and Misty's teenie weenies."

They both laughed over that, and Mary Lynn felt like it was completely normal to be conversing with this friendly apparition. She thought it best that she not wake herself up. She had a busy day planned tomorrow and needed the sleep.

There was a pause and a sudden change in the demeanor of the woman who sat gazing at Mary Lynn. The ghost, who appeared to be none other than Doll Dumas, started to speak . . . hesitated, and took a long pull on her cigarette, blowing the smoke out the side of her mouth. "I sure am obliged to you for coming to Peavine, honey." Doll said in a shaking voice. "We spirits have been working pretty hard to get you here."

"Why would you do that?" Mary Lynn was flustered by Doll's sudden serious tone and began to giggle nervously. "Whatever could have made you want to get little ole me down here? What have I got to do with Peavine, or you, or anybody else around here?"

Mary Lynn could feel her face begin to turn red as sweat trickled down her back. She kicked back the covers and picked up a magazine from beside the bed to fan herself. Hearing that unseen forces were conspiring to manipulate her into arriving and then spending the night in Peavine was unsettling, to say the least. She wanted the focus to be off her so she changed the subject.

"From the stories I've heard about you from Dorine and the others you've got to be some kind of a saint or guardian angel or something!" Mary Lynn flushed even more as she realized her faux pas. "I don't mean because you're deceased and all but while you were alive, if there ever was a 'Saint of Peavine,' it would be you!"

Doll was smiling and shaking her head as she watched Mary Lynn struggle. "Darlin, you shouldn't have believed everything they said. You only heard one side of it."She took a long pull on her cigarette, exhaling a trail of smoke as she spoke. "Sure, I was able to help a lot of folks. I'll be forever grateful to Hermie that I was able to use his money to do some good works, but it's become clear to me now that none of that could have happened if one special person hadn't come to Peavine."Doll paused again and looked directly into Mary Lynn's eyes, as if she expected a response from her.

"How's that? That doesn't make sense." Mary Lynn was getting really confused now, but dreams were like that, she reminded herself.

Doll went on in a tremulous voice. "I'm talking about when that person showed up here thirty-seven years ago . . . with my sweet Hermie as his bride!"

"What do you mean, and why are you looking at me like that?" Mary Lynn's heart began to beat rapidly. "I believe you must have me confused with someone else." Against her will, Mary Lynn's hot flash went into overdrive. What if this spirit was here for revenge, and had decided to take it out on her!

"It's alright, honey. I'm not here to do you any harm." Doll's voice was gentle as a tear ran unchecked down her cheek, leaving a streak in the powder. "Please, just hear me out. You've been so kind to listen to everybody else's stories. I cain't Move On to Glory with Hermie until I tell you what really happened with Madge back then . . . my version

Doll Dumas in her prime

of it anyway."

"I'm just Mary Lynn . . . Mary Lynn Stanton . . . and I'm not so sure I like this dream anymore!" She didn't know how to wake herself up though. She began to flutter the front of her nightgown in an attempt to cool off as a rivulet of perspiration ran from below her breasts.

Doll looked past Mary Lynn at something unseen. "I'm not doing so well here," she said to the wall behind the bed. "Isn't there anything you can do to help me out?" She cocked her head to one side as if listening. "Okay, okay, thanks, Hon."

Mary Lynn whipped her head to look behind her then back at Doll. What in the world? Who else is in here, she wondered fearfully.

Doll reached out her hand towards Mary Lynn and smiled again. "Remember, this is only a dream. You probably won't even remember much of it come morning. You have nothing to fear from me."

The words that Rhonelle had spoken to Mary Lynn at the end of the party suddenly came back to her: "Expect the unexpected and whatever happens, don't be afraid."

Mary Lynn had no idea why, but she began to feel relaxation spread throughout her body. The hot, prickly panic melted away. For some odd reason, she felt completely safe and somehow protected. With a deep sigh of contentment she leaned back against the pillows and let the peaceful calm surround her. What harm would there be in listening to one more story she thought, and this one could prove to be the most interesting of all.

"Okay, well, uhmm, Miss Doll, I would be honored to hear what you have to tell me." Mary Lynn said, trying not to dwell on the fact that she was speaking to a woman who had died two days ago. "I don't have anywhere to go until morning. Looks like I'm all yours. Heh, heh."

CHAPTER TWENTY-THREE

The True Confession of Loretta Lepanto

Y*ou can go ahead and call me Loretta. That's the name I went by back then, Loretta Lepanto.*" Doll seemed immensely relieved that she had succeeded in getting Mary Lynn to calm down and listen to her. She cheerfully lit up a fresh cigarette before continuing. She used the pause to glance at an area to the right of Mary Lynn's shoulder and give a quick wink and a nod.

"*It was Hermie that got everybody to calling me Doll. He'd say, 'Hey Doll, come on over here and bring me a drink.' That was back when I was working at the Too Tite, but I'm gettin ahead of myself here.*" She leaned back in the recliner, took a long drag on her cigarette and puffed out a series of smoke rings. One of them hung above her beehive like a halo.

"*I'd had the biggest crush on Hermie, ever since I was a young girl. My mamma used to clean house out at the Dumas Mansion. She started working for them several years before the war . . . that was right after Old Man Dumas discovered his oil wells. I'd come to help out whenever there was a special event or holiday dinner.*

"*I was completely star-struck by Hermie! I thought he was the cutest thing on two legs, always joking around. He wasn't bad-looking back when he was a young man, before the whiskey had its effects on him. Being rich and living in a big, beautiful house seemed very glamorous to me. You see, I was infatuated by the perfect life I thought I saw out at the Mansion.*" Doll sighed and tapped the ash off the end of her cigarette.

"*Of course, Hermie never even looked in my direction back then. I was nothing but a no-count, white-trash girl to his family, and Hermie was all caught up in drinkin' and carousing with those old college buddies of his. Not that I blamed him or anything. He just wasn't ready to settle down quite yet.*

"*Reality finally hit me when I turned twenty-one. I knew I'd never have a chance with the likes of him, so I took up with the first feller who'd have me, Roy Lee Lepanto. Good Lord, what a low down rascal he was! Once again, I was going by what I saw on the surface of things. Roy was handsome, much better looking than Hermie, so I felt like I was making a good choice. I married Roy pretty fast because little Lucille was on the way. I'm surprised he stuck around as long as he did.*

"*Two and a half years to the day after we got married, Roy run off and left me and my baby, high and dry. He'd gambled and drunk up every dime of the money he'd earned working on the Dumas Oil rig, before he got fired for fighting on the job.*

"*Lucille and I had to move in with my mamma. I was able to start helping out again at the Dumas Mansion to earn some money. Dumas Oil Company had started to become very prosperous before the war and they had lots of big parties out there. Eventually I took over for Mamma and was out at the 'Big House' most every day.*

"*I saw Hermie, for the first time since my ill-fated marriage to Roy Lee right after the war started. He'd come home for a month's leave before being shipped out overseas.*"

"*Lordee mercy! When I laid my eyes on him again I fell harder than ever. I decided I would do whatever I could to be near him and if he made it back from the war alive I'd find some way to get him to notice me. I would finally muster up the courage to let him know how I'd felt about him all those years.*

"*Then, after all that time worrying and waiting for him to return from war, he came back home safe and sound but married to somebody else!*"

Mary Lynn swallowed hard, but stayed quiet.

Doll shook her head and stared at the floor. "*It was a huge shock that Hermie would marry a woman like her. Sorry to say this, but that's the way I felt. Madge was a woman lower than me! I just couldn't believe he could have done such a thing. Been fool enough to have fallen for such a . . . it just wasn't fair! Something inside me broke that day, much more than just my heart. From that moment on I was a changed woman.*

"*On the outside I seemed the same. Everybody still thought I was as sweet and nice as ever but I knew on the inside I had become as mean as a snake. At least Madge had the honesty to not even try to act like she cared about any of us, not even Hermie. But I acted nice to her, like I was her best and only friend. Meanwhile I spent every waking moment thinking about the best way to get rid of her.*"

When she heard Mary Lynn's gasp, Doll looked up at her.

"*Oh I didn't want to do any real harm to her or nuthin, I just wanted to do whatever I could to make the situation even worse than it was.*"

"*What kind of things did you do?*" Mary Lynn asked softly.

Doll gave a little snort of laughter and took a long draw on her cigarette. "*Well, it sounds pretty darn silly now. I started with pranks like a little kid would play on somebody.*"

She winked at Mary Lynn and leaned forward, with her elbows resting on her knees. "*For starters, I wanted to make Madge as unattractive as possible. So, when I was cleaning her room, I'd pour vinegar into that fancy cologne Hermie bought for her in Memphis. And then I kept adding Clorox bleach, just a few drops at a time, to her shampoo.*

"*She didn't trust the local beauty shop to fix her hair and always did her own at home. She never could understand what was happening to her platinum blonde when it began to turn green on her. Meanwhile, I went over to Dee Dee's Dos at least once a week to dish out the latest dirt on Madge, knowing full well Dee Dee would have the gossip spread over half the population of Peavine by the next day. If you think Dorine is a talker, her sister Dee Dee is even better at it, especially the real juicy stuff. I gave her plenty of that, even if I had to make some of it up.*

"Whenever Mrs. Dumas Senior had some company over I'd invent some reason for Madge to make an entrance and embarrass everybody. I'd tell her those old ladies were talking bad about her and it worked." Doll's smile faded and she stared down at the floor again, shifting uncomfortably before continuing. "But, I wasn't no kid anymore, and neither was Hermie." Doll chewed at her lip and seemed to be choosing her words carefully. "I betrayed Madge in other, more serious ways too."

Mary Lynn tensed up a little, wondering what Doll would say next.

"I never dreamed I would end up carrying on with a married man but it was just too easy."

Mary Lynn certainly had not expected to hear this. She was surprised yet had an urge to giggle and was barely able to stifle it. She was glad she did, because Doll was really struggling with this subject. She fiddled with the large diamond ring on her finger and kept her eyes on her hands while she talked.

"Madge had been playing poor Hermie along, like a big ole bass on a hook, ever since their wedding night. He had been so drunk then he couldn't remember anything about it. He told me all this later, after we got married. As far as he could tell, he and Madge never consummated their vows."

Doll glanced up at Mary Lynn to see her reaction. Mary Lynn attempted to smile in a way she hoped would convey nothing more than her sympathy. Doll turned her attention to the window and continued her uncomfortable confession.

"Like I said, Hermie and I, well we both had our needs. It all just

sort of exploded one day about three months after he'd arrived home with
Madge. I didn't plan it. I just happened to be upstairs that afternoon making
the bed in his room when Hermie walked in. He was angry because of
another fight with Madge and of course he'd been drinking. Everybody else
was either gone or in another part of the house. I had no idea he was even
home.

"He startled me, coming in so sudden like that, slamming the door
behind him. He was surprised to see me too. He stood there staring at me
for a minute. He wasn't angry anymore. I guess there was something funny
about the way I was standing there, wide-eyed and flustered. All he said
was 'Well, well, what have we here?' Then he started to laugh and I was
blushing and giggling like a school girl. It just seemed natural that he would
cross the room and take me into his arms.

"Before I knew it, we started going after each other like we was crazy.
Then there was that big bed conveniently right behind me and it was like
all my dreams had come true. I sure wasn't gonna try to discourage him."
Doll grinned sheepishly and peered through her sparkling glasses right
into Mary Lynn's eyes. She was reassured to see that no judgment lay
there.

Actually, Mary Lynn understood better than Doll would ever
guess how quickly a situation like that could get out of control. She
actually began to blush when she remembered how she had felt with
Johnny. Doll didn't seem to notice, as she went back to examining her
polished fingernails before she began to talk.

"Madge had just announced that she was pregnant and wanted to
have her own bedroom. The timing for that couldn't have been better.
For the next several weeks Hermie and I played a dangerous and exciting
game. We'd sneak off to Hermie's room every chance we got. We'd meet
each other at the Too-Tite Tavern on my days off and he'd take me out of
town to a cheap motel for the evening. I even considered letting myself get

pregnant again just to get my own hold on him. Thank God I had sense enough not to bring another unwanted child into the world." Doll heaved a great sigh and folded her hands on her lap.

"The night came when Madge had that terrible fall. Oh my Lord! We thought she was gonna die from it, she lost so much blood!

"It was an awful way to lose a baby. Even though I wasn't there, I felt like somehow I'd wished it on her."

Doll raised her mascara stained face toward Mary Lynn.

"I swear I never would have wanted her to go through something that bad."

"Of course you wouldn't have," Mary Lynn said consolingly, hoping that the tears welling up in her own eyes would go unnoticed. *"There is no way you could have caused her to fall down those stairs."*

Doll sighed shakily. *"No, I didn't cause that accident but I hate to tell you, it did raise a little bit of hope in me that without the baby to keep 'em together maybe that marriage would be over soon.*

"Later on when Madge came home from the hospital she was a pale thin shadow of the girl we had come to know. Hermie felt sorry for her, we all did. We both felt guilty and tried our best to be nice to her."

Doll shook her head and looked over at the window as she spoke, unable to meet Mary Lynn's eyes.

"But, sad to say, my feelings of remorse didn't last long. Hermie and I stopped our affair after the night of the accident. He had been over at the Too-Tite Tavern meeting up with me when it happened. I understood why he cut me off. Our relationship had been mainly about sex for him. He had no idea how much I still loved and wanted him.

"That mean ole snake I had wrapped 'round my heart began to choke off all my good intentions when Hermie fixed up the old trailer park for Madge to run. I was so jealous I could hardly see straight! I should have been running it! He and I had talked a few times about giving that job to

me, not her. So I bided my time. Sooner or later I'd get my chance. All I had to do was keep on acting sweet and nice and make like I was the only friend in world that poor girl had."

The ash on Doll's cigarette lengthened until it dropped and fell onto the arm of the recliner. She brushed it off hurriedly and lit up another. She fortified herself for more of what was becoming an increasingly difficult narrative.

"I got my chance in April of 1948 when I came across Madge in her room crying her eyes out. That's when she confessed everything to me, I mean all of it. She told me how she had tricked Hermie into marrying her because she was already pregnant and she'd faked not only her age but her name on the marriage certificate. She'd been skimming off some of the money she collected for rent at the trailer park so she could run away.

"Hot Dog, I thought! Now I got her! But I just kept on acting like I felt so sorry for her so I could get her to tell me more . . . and she did. The reason she was so tore up that night was that all the money she'd been tucking away had been stolen from her by that cowboy feller from over at the trailer park. She'd been working on him for over a month hoping she could sweet-talk him into helping her to escape from Peavine and he took her for a fool.

"Ha! I thought she'd got just what she deserved. I told her not to worry . . . I'd do what I could to help her out." Doll swallowed hard and crushed out her cigarette in the ashtray beside her. She looked directly into Mary Lynn's shocked face and remained quiet, as if something had just dawned upon her.

"You know what, I wasn't lying. I did help her out. I just had some mixed-up motives at the time." Doll began to smile as she twitched her earring. *"It's all so much clearer to me now. I can see everything in a whole different light since I crossed over to the Other Side. What I done back then and was so ashamed of all worked out in the Big Plan, eventually."*

"Why? What did you do?" Mary Lynn urgently wanted to know.

"I went directly to Miz Adelaide and tattled on Madge!" Doll said looking very pleased. "I told Old Lady Dumas about the fake name and age on the marriage certificate and said now was her chance to get this unholy union over and done with. If she was to pay Madge enough money, say around two thousand dollars, she'd never have to see her around Peavine again."

Mary Lynn was a bit taken aback by that statement, but Doll rushed on to explain herself.

"Don't you see? This was Madge's best chance to start over in her life. Everybody had a chance for a fresh start after that!"

"Well, I guess I see what you mean." Mary Lynn was not quite convinced about everybody else having a chance at a 'fresh start.'

"I didn't feel so good about it back then, especially the day after Madge left. I overheard Miz Adelaide having a great big laugh over it with Herman Senior. They were so proud of how they'd scared the living daylights out of that girl by telling her that they had connections with some mafia thugs who was gonna stay on her trail. They'd convinced Madge that if she ever came back near Peavine or Junior, or any of them, she'd be killed outright. Nobody would ever find the body after the mafia got done with her."

Mary Lynn's hands flew to her mouth. "Did they really have private eyes and mafia thugs watching her to keep her from coming back?"

"No. I found out later it was all lies. They just wanted to be sure Madge was too scared to ever bother them for money again." Doll sighed and shook her head, looking at the floor. "But I understand they made some pretty serious threats." Doll raised her face up and looked steadily at Mary Lynn. "Madge may have acted like she was real tough and mean but she was only a lonely, desperate young girl when she snared Hermie. I found out all that when she confessed everything that night, but I let them scare her anyway. I quit working at the Mansion that very day. I went out and got a job over at the Too-Tite Tavern. Me and Lucille moved into the little apartment out back of it.

"Meanwhile things got worse at the Dumas Mansion. Adelaide and Herman Senior was in really bad health and most of the Company business had to be handled by Ozelle. Hermie got in the habit of coming to the Tavern so's to get away from it all and, of to drown his sorrows in a bottle of Jim Beam. He was there about every night. I was so happy to see him it didn't matter that I was only making his drinkin' worse. I think I was hoping he would see me as more than the housemaid he'd used for sex. Serving him as a bartender made me feel a bit more powerful.

"I did a lot of listening those nights. Quite a few times I ended up letting him sleep it off at my place. Ozelle had to come get him most nights, but I . . . well, I wanted him to get to know me so I'd take him home with me sometimes. The sex started up again but it wasn't fun like before. I decided that wasn't what I really wanted, Hermie needing me just because he was drunk and lonesome. I wanted him to like me when he was sober. So I tried to figure out a way to wean him off that whiskey.

"I'd talk and laugh with him and make him get up and dance with me to the jukebox music. Then I would put in a call to Ozelle before he got too far gone. All the while I was watering down his drinks a little bit at a time. But none of that worked. I was only fooling myself. One night after Herman had passed out and Ozelle had to carry him to the car like a big old baby. Jim Bob Teeter (he was the owner of the Too-Tite) came up to me as I was watching the car drive off. He put his arm around me and led me back inside to his office. That's when he set me straight on Hermie and all his drinking. He told me it was time for me to let Hermie go. He knew I'd tried my best but I wasn't the one to sober him up. I got all huffy at first. Truth was, I knew in my heart he was right. He said Junior was a sick man and he and Ozelle was going to take him to a special hospital in Memphis the next morning. To get him dried out.

"I'll have to admit, I was pretty relieved. I didn't hear from Hermie until he called me two months later. He was back in Peavine and wanted to take me out to supper at Don and Dorine's new diner. It was our first real date. From that point on Herman and I had a proper courtship.

"We got to know each other all over again. He took me out to eat and to the movies. He even took me over to the Mansion for Sunday dinners, although his parents didn't quite know how to react to that. For the first time, I felt like he was not ashamed to be seen with me and was proud to have me as his girl. I never saw him take a drink after that. His new buddies were the ones he met at the AA meetings Jim Bob had brought him to. I had no idea Jim Bob Teeter had once been a drunk."

Doll smiled and sighed deeply. "He was the real 'saint' to work there at that bar. He told me it was the best place to find the people that needed help. He also suggested I find another job or I'd be having some real problems with my daughter. That's when I started working at Don's Diner."

"You worked at Don's Diner?" This was news to Mary Lynn. "Dorine never told me about that."

Doll laughed at the idea that Dorine would leave out any details when telling a story. "Maybe she feared you'd think less of me if you knew I'd worked for her and lived free in one of the old cottages. Anyways, we didn't live there very long, less than a year. It seemed the most natural thing in the world when Hermie asked me to marry him. There wasn't anybody left to stand in our way because by then both his parents had passed away.

"Only one person was suffering, my own daughter, Lucille. While I had been lavishing all my attentions on Hermie, I'd completely ignored her. She and her pal, Shirleen, was growing up wild as weeds! I didn't care. I just wanted Hermie and all that went with him. I thought surely things would work out after we got married. I was wrong about that. Lucille acted worse than ever. I felt so guilty that I just kept on letting her have her way. When she ran off I felt like I was getting what I deserved.

"Poor ole Hermie tried his best but for a year there I was about as low as could be, and he was at his wit's end. Ozelle and Sally helped out. Them and their kids helped to cheer me up a little and I still had Hermie."

"Then Hermie died, and all I wanted was to die too." Doll buried her face in her hands.

Mary Lynn edged a bit closer to the spirit, wishing she could find the right words to say to her. *"I know what that's like,"* she found herself saying. *"I was . . . once there was someone that I was so in love with and he died in a car accident. I wanted to die with him, but . . ."*

"You kept on living though, didn't you, Hon?" Doll raised her head to face Mary Lynn. She wiped away her tears and smiled kindly at her. *"I'm sure he has watched over you ever since then and is mighty proud of how you turned out."*

Mary Lynn wondered if Doll was just making a general statement, or . . . Did she dare even ask if maybe she had run across Johnny? It was just too weird a thing to ask, even in a dream.

Doll seemed about to say something else when she hesitated, as if listening. She glanced to her right and nodded slowly. She straightened her tall hairdo a bit, cleared her throat and purposely continued her narrative.

"I didn't have anything to live for except the hope that maybe Lucille would come back home and I could make things up with her. It occurred to me that I was suddenly a very wealthy widow. Ozelle laid out all the Dumas estate papers for me to ponder over. I knew Hermie was rich, but I never realized he was that rich! It didn't make me any happier though, I only felt guiltier. I thought I didn't deserve any of it after what I'd done to get it. I just wanted to give everything away. Thank goodness Ozelle and Sally sat me down and helped me get a plan. They didn't really want to own the Mansion, but look what good use they made of the place. I didn't want all that money, but look at all I was able to do to help out people because of it."

A smile spread across Doll's face as she began to nod her head slowly. *"Now that I'm . . . Over Here, I understand it all so much better."* She cleared her throat and leaned forward in her chair before continuing. *"None of those good things would have happened if skinny little Madge hadn't showed up and turned Peavine on its tail!"*

Mary Lynn furrowed her brow in confusion, and was about to say she disagreed, but Doll cut her off.

"Now bear with me here a minute, Mary Lynn. Before Madge arrived most people around here was kept held down to know their 'place' and never cross the line. The colored folks all kept to themselves and the rich folks looked down on them and all us white trash. Well, look at Peavine now!" Doll began to laugh and slap her knee.

"The richest man, in a town full of Southern Arkansas whites, is a black man. Who would've thunk it back in 1946? And me, a tacky, old, white-trash, bartending, trailer park manager became Peavine's most revered benefactor."

Mary Lynn found herself laughing along as tears flowed down her cheeks. She was filled with an odd sense of relief. They began to regain control of themselves as the light in the room grew. An old Creole woman had silently appeared at the foot of the bed. This sight only made Mary Lynn begin to giggle helplessly all over again. She knew who this ghost had to be.

"You must be Rhonelle's Granny, right?" Mary Lynn pointed and fell back onto her pillows in gales of laughter.

The little old woman nodded as if nothing was out of the ordinary, then motioned to Doll and pointed to the door. Doll rose lightly from the recliner, smoothed out her purple slacks and straightened her beehive a little. *"Okay, Laurite. I'm ready to go."* As she walked over beside Granny Laurite to stand at the foot of Mary Lynn's bed, the glow in the room grew brighter.

"*Thank you, Mary Lynn, for listening to me. I'll be forever grateful to you!*"

Just as Doll and Granny Laurite began to fade away, Mary Lynn caught a glimpse of a handsome, young Air Force lieutenant standing between them.

"*Johnny?*"

Then they were gone and the room was filled with the pink light of sunrise.

CHAPTER TWENTY-FOUR

On the Road Again . . .

The next morning dawned bright and beautiful. At seven o'clock Mary Lynn stretched and sat up in her bed feeling fully rested and refreshed. A vague recollection of a rather odd, yet meaningful dream was drifting around somewhere on the tip of her mind. Whatever it had been about must have been pleasant because it had left her feeling uncommonly cheerful.

She dressed and packed quickly, in order to have time to enjoy her "complementary full country breakfast" at the diner. Don was manning the griddle while his daughter filled in as waitress. They had decided that after all of Dorine's celebrating the night before she would need to sleep in for once. Don served Mary Lynn a larruping good breakfast: two fried eggs, grits, sausage, and biscuits with gravy.

She made a call to her cousin Lizzie from the Dew Drop Office to let her know she would be on her way shortly. Lizzie told Mary Lynn that Leroy had called the night before looking for her. Lizzie explained to him their plan for a New Years Eve celebration in New Orleans and that sounded like a grand idea to him. He was able to book a nice room at a motel in Baton Rouge where he and Mary Lynn would spend the weekend. He was riding down to Monroe with one of his duck buddies tomorrow.

It sounded so romantic for them to spend a weekend in the city where they had met and fallen in love. To top it off, Lizzie's husband had gotten them all dinner reservations at The Rib Room in New Orleans for New Years Eve. This excursion was all turning out to be better than Mary Lynn could ever have imagined only forty-eight hours ago. She would always be appreciative of Don and Dorine's hospitality. It was especially nice of them to include her in the celebration of their dear friend, Doll Dumas.

What a life-changing experience this had turned out to be. She found it hard to believe that she had been so frightened and upset about getting lost and ending up in Peavine. There wasn't anything to be afraid of after all. Don gave her a map and directions on the best route from Peavine to Monroe. She only had about a two-hour drive ahead of her. He recommended she make a fuel stop at the Gas-n-Git, down the road to the right, on her way out of town. He said she wouldn't find gas prices cheaper anywhere else because of the local Dumas Oil Company discount.

As Mary Lynn started down the highway the first billboard she saw was:

IF YOUR LIFE STINKS, WE HAVE A PEW FOR YOU! KPEW AM RADIO 1011

Mary Lynn let out a guffaw. "That has got to be Little Bo's idea of the perfect advertisement." She switched on her car radio and tuned into KPEW. Little Bo was playing some of the hits from the Gay Caballeros' album and conducting an interview with Louise Dolesanger's grandson, Kyle.

Listening until the signal faded to static, Mary Lynn smiled to think of all the new people she had met on her little adventure. Her new-found confidence swelled. She felt like an explorer and for the first time in many years she felt lighthearted and free of regret. She could not quite pinpoint what had happened to change her outlook so dramatically. She hummed one of the tunes from the Gay Caballeros repertoire and casually noted the large oak trees on either side of the narrow highway. One of them was split in half with a large branch hanging precariously over the roadside. It looked to be a casualty of last spring's heavy thunderstorms. Mary Lynn remembered how frightening those intense storms could be in this area of the south.

Suddenly the memory of her dream from last night flashed before her as clearly as a replay of a movie. She experienced such an intense emotional response she had to pull off the road in order to collect herself. "Doll was in my room last night and she knew who I was!" Mary Lynn believed with all her being that the experience had been something much more tangible than an ordinary dream. "I'm positive that she not only knew who I was, but she knows what I've done and it's alright. Things did work out for the best after all."

Mary Lynn began to sob, not because she was afraid - but because she felt as if she could finally forgive Johnny and everyone else she'd blamed for her troubles. Most importantly she was able to forgive herself. She had stopped her car beneath the lightning struck tree. Looking up at it through the blur of tears another scene from her past began to bubble up into her awareness.

CHAPTER TWENTY-FIVE

The Last Picture Show

South Arkansas . . . A Stormy Night in April 1948

A fireball exploded splitting the oak tree in half, bringing it down with a thunderous crash! Ozelle slipped in the mud and blindly rolled toward the roadside.

The Cadillac jerked and swerved along the road until it finally sputtered to a halt. The car door flung opened. Madge jumped out and ran back down the road toward the flaming tree. The wind had died down and the steady rain was beginning to slacken a little.

"**Hey, Mo! Where are you?** Oh sweet Jesus! I've killed him!" Madge was crying and screaming his name when she spotted him lying on his back beside the road. A huge tree branch had fallen several feet away from him but the flames were beginning to die down.

She fell to her knees beside Ozelle, lying in the gravel and mud. "Oooooh me!" she sobbed. "Mo, I'm so sorry. I didn't never drive a car all by myself before."

"What have I done to you? **Speak to me!** You just gotta be alive!" She grabbed his overall suspenders and began to shake him, in hopes of reviving him.

Ozelle's hands slowly rose to his mud spattered eyeglasses. He took them off and smiled up at Madge. "I'm alright, I'm alright." He began to chuckle. "I was jus' lyin here bein' grateful to be alive and wondering how I was gonna explain to Ole Man Dumas how I let you go and run off with his favorite car."

He sat up and guffawed in his deep-throated, rich laughter. He raised his face up to the cleansing rain and began to bellow, "***Praise the Lord, Sweet Jesus, Praise the Lord!***"

Madge was so amazed that she fell right back into the mud on her behind and began to giggle uncontrollably.

There they both sat in the pouring rain. A huge black man and a skinny, young white woman laughing and shouting, "Praise the Lord!"

By the time Ozelle and Madge got back into the car and onto the highway again, the storm had rumbled off to the north, and the sky was beginning to clear. A line of pale gold to the east made them realize dawn was approaching.

Ozelle glanced at the clock on the dash. It was five-thirty already and they had a long way to go to get to the train station in El Dorado.

"Miz Madge, it looks like we're gonna miss that six-o-clock train." Ozelle had hoped to deposit her there before daylight. It wasn't a good idea to be seen traveling alone with a young white woman without his chauffeur uniform on. Having been awakened at midnight and ordered to dispense with Madge, he had hurriedly thrown a pair of overalls on over his pajamas. "We don't look too presentable all covered in mud like dis. Do you have any place I could take you? You got any family you could go to?"

Madge looked down at the mud-stained knees of her dungarees. All she had to her name were the ruined clothes she was wearing and the contents of her handbag. Hidden at the bottom of that bag were the twenty one-hundred-dollar bills that Mrs. Adelaide Dumas had shoved into her hands when she ordered her out of the mansion. How could she start her new life looking like a tramp?

However, there was someone she should have called long before now.

"I have my aunt and cousin who live in Monroe. They might take me in, if you could take me there."

"Sure I could! That's not too far from here and the road won't be so bad that way." Ozelle was relieved to hear she had someplace to go. He was beginning to worry what would happen to the girl. Three hours later the large, mud-spattered Cadillac pulled up to a row of small neat houses on a street in Monroe, Louisiana.

"Dis must be it, five-o-three, the number is right there on the mailbox," Ozelle said as he stifled a yawn. He turned and smiled sheepishly at Madge in the back seat. "I think it'd be best if I stayed in the car . . . you know lookin like dis, it wouldn't be fittin."

She sat quietly a moment, staring out the window, then opened the car door and got out, holding the red handbag tightly under her arm. She stopped at the driver side window and bent down to look Ozelle directly in the face. "Mo, if anybody ever asks, you tell them Madge is dead," she said with calm determination. "No, I mean it. I ain't . . . I'm not Madge anymore. I just made up that name anyway. Now she's gone, and I'm back to myself again. "I can't ever thank you enough for helping me." She pulled her purse open, fished out a crumpled one-hundred-dollar bill and held it out to Ozelle. "Here, take this for your trouble."

He waved it away. "Naw, I don't want no money. You gonna be needing it more than me. Now put that back," he said gently.

Reluctantly, yet gratefully, she stuffed it back into her handbag. "I'm not worth your kindness you know, not after all I've done."

"Well, Miz . . . whoever you are," said Ozelle. "You can best thank me by promising to make somethin' good out of your life. How 'bout that?" He extended his hand to her. "Shake on it?"

She hesitated momentarily before grasping his large warm, brown hand with both of hers; small, pale and cold, because she was so nervous. "I will. I promise. I'm gonna be good from now on. And thank you, Mo."

Never in her young life had she ever touched a colored person. She was relieved to discover that there was no sense of revulsion, only deep gratitude. As she watched the Cadillac drive off down the street and disappear around the corner, she pulled Ozelle's white cotton handkerchief out of her shirt pocket. She scrubbed the remnants of lipstick and mascara off her face, and stuffed the stained hankie into the bottom of her purse.

Then she took a deep breath, straightened up her clothes as much as possible and patted at her matt of frizzy platinum hair. She marched herself down the sidewalk to the front door of the small, stucco house. Without hesitation, she rang the doorbell. She rang it three more times before she heard a familiar voice yelling from inside.

"I'm coming, I'm coming! I don't know who it is, Mamma. How the heck do I know who would be here at this hour on a Sunday morning?" A sleepy-eyed, teen-aged girl in her pajamas appeared and looked out suspiciously through the locked screen door.

"Who are you?" she asked the frowzy-headed young woman standing before her with dried mud covering her clothes and shoes.

"Hey there, Lizzie . . . don't you know your own cousin when you see her?"

Lizzie threw open the door and stared with her mouth open. Slowly recognition dawned on her and she threw her arms around her long-lost cousin as both girls burst into tears.

"**MARY LYNN!!** I cain't believe it's really you!" Lizzie squealed. "We all thought you must be dead or worse when we couldn't find out where you'd gone off to."

"I guess you could say I was more 'worse' than dead," Mary Lynn said sniffing and wiping her face on her shirt sleeve.

Lizzie stepped back to take a good look at her cousin, making a face as she stared at the top of Mary Lynn's head. "Jeepers, cuz, what on earth have you done to your hair? You look terrible as a blonde!"

Blytheville, Arkansas in a small trailer park, 1946

Strands of auburn hair lay strewn on the tiny bathroom floor. Mary Lynn stared at them before slowly walking into the kitchen to fetch a broom and dustpan. After cutting her beautiful long auburn hair, she had bleached it to the palest shade of peroxide blonde available at the drugstore. She wrapped her head in a towel and carefully turned away before she could see herself in the medicine cabinet mirror.

With the dustpan piled high, she started to dump the hair into the trash, but changed her mind. She opened the back door to the trailer, and tossed it out into the yard.

A gust of an early spring wind whisked the hair off the ground and out into the field beyond the fence. The suddenness of the wind and almost lifelike movements of her shorn locks, as they flew away, startled Mary Lynn. A small cry escaped her pale lips, and tears abruptly sprang to her eyes.

This was the first sign of emotion she had allowed to escape her since that awful night two weeks ago. It was the night of the terrible storm, which caused the tragic car accident that had killed Johnny. That was the moment her only chance of happiness had been cruelly snatched away. She wasn't even allowed an opportunity to say goodbye to Johnny. His body was shipped home to his family, and they never even knew she existed. Tears streamed down her cheeks as she squinted into the early rising sun, trying to find where those last scraps and pieces of her old self had flown off to, but they were gone for good. She wiped the tears angrily from her face.

That was that. No more Mary Lynn, and no more tears. Nothing was left of her former softness. Only a hard knot of determination remained where her tender heart had once been. She had to survive not only for herself but for the sake of the baby she carried. She had to change who she was and do whatever it was going to take to protect this tiny treasured bit of Johnny, left growing inside her.

She had done a lot of thinking over the past two weeks and had come to the conclusion that she could no longer survive as Mary Lynn. Their baby would need someone tougher and stronger rather than a weak, innocent, foolish Mary Lynn. She had been busy making plans and preparations to improve the odds of a decent life for her child.

Two hours later she sat staring at the stranger reflected in the mirror of her dressing table. Her short newly blonde hair was dried and curled around her ears. Severely plucked eyebrows and the makeup she'd bought the day before completed her transformation, covering any vestiges of youth and clean innocence. The deep red lipstick gave her a hardened look and matched the red dress she was wearing. The blue traveling suit was long gone.

Her attire was as new and alien to her as the mascara, powder, and lip rouge. Mary Lynn would never have worn red before because it was considered a sign of loose morals. However, it wasn't just the color that would have prevented Mary Lynn from wearing a frock such as this. The figure-hugging style made her look downright dangerous!

She stood up and backed away to examine the full effect. So far her indelicate condition was unnoticeable. The fact that she could hardly manage to keep any food down lately had caused her to actually lose weight. Her breasts were all that had gotten larger and the neckline of the dress played up that fact. She had known when she saw the mannequin wearing the whole ensemble of dress, hat and shoes in the window of the department store that it would be exactly what she needed.

"Yeah, this ought to work just fine!" she sneered as she turned to check the seams in her stockings and slip into her matching red pumps. "This is just perfect." She patted at her short blonde curls before donning the new hat she had laid out on the bed. "I'll pretend like I'm in a movie, act tough like Jean Harlow and smart like Barbara Stanwyck. I know I can do that." The thought of pretending to be one of her favorite movie stars sounded almost fun until she realized just how good an actress she would have to be to pull off her plan.

Fear clutched at her stomach, and for the third time in the past hour, she compulsively snatched up the remains of her honeymoon cash that was neatly stacked on the dressing table. For the past month their friends had been stuffing tip money and donations into a jar down at the diner where she worked. Over eight hundred dollars had accumulated by the day before what should have been their wedding night. Some of that money recently had been spent on her new clothes and cosmetics.

She carefully counted it again before rolling it up with a rubber band and stuffing it down into the bottom of her handbag. She delicately picked up the blank marriage certificate from the dresser. Attached to the certificate with a paper clip was a slip of paper with the name of Johnny's friend, a Justice of the Peace who worked as the night manager at the Peabody Hotel. Her hands trembled as she folded the document and slipped it into her purse beside the money.

With grim determination she jammed on her new gloves, picked up her small suitcase and turned once more to face the mirror. She shook her shoulders a little, took a deep breath and stood up straighter. In a voice that was strange even to her own ears she announced forcefully, "Now I am Madge . . . Madge Du Claire and I'll be damned if I'm gonna raise my baby poor and alone like my mamma did me!" She turned away from her reflection, walked out of the trailer and down the road toward the bus stop, away from all that remained of her old life and she never looked back.

Back at the Moving Theater

"*It's hard to believe the Mary Lynn I just met could have done such a thing.*" Doll sighed out a puff of smoke as she crushed the stub of her cigarette on the conveniently placed ashtray on the arm of her blue velvet theater chair.

Johnny slouched in the seat beside her, watching the image on the screen blur and fade to black. His face was wet with tears which he unashamedly wiped away with a handkerchief. The engraved silver lighter was clutched tightly in his other hand.

"*Yeah, it tears me up every time I see it.*" He blew his nose and sat up straight. "*I tried so hard to stop her, but I couldn't get through. She had no idea I was so close to her, practically screaming into her ear, but she never even heard me.*"

"*Dat's because you was not supposed to stop her.*" Laurite had appeared on the other side of Johnny. Doll was beginning to get used to having the old Creole pop up suddenly like that, yet she wondered how she'd become so accomplished at it.

"*You're right, Laurite.*" Johnny leaned back and put an arm around Doll's shoulder and gave it a squeeze. "*Now that I've had the honor of Mrs. Doll Dumas' presence here on the Other Side I realize Mary Lynn's crazy stunt ended up being a crucial part of the Big Plan. She has responded to a few of my 'nudges' from time to time. There was the day she met Leroy at that drugstore and several other occasions. I think she has been aware of me even before I helped to get her back to Peavine."*

"I sure am glad it's all worked out so well for both of us." Doll patted Johnny's arm. *"I could never have gotten her to sit still and listen to me if you hadn't calmed her down. Thanks again, Hon."* She leaned out toward Laurite intending to thank her also for all her guidance in the Afterlife but found the chair empty.

A quiet buzzing of many voices talking all at once began to emanate from behind the darkened movie screen where a small point of light had appeared. As the sound grew louder the light swelled to a magnificent brightness.

Laurite reappeared behind Doll and Johnny, firmly grasping each one by a shoulder.

"It's time you both got on about it now," she said in the kindest voice Doll had yet heard the old spirit use.

The blue velvet armchairs vanished as Laurite, Johnny, and Doll stood up and walked toward the intensely bright rectangle of light where the movie screen had been.

Doll took the first step up onto the stage, paused and turned to her companions.

"I know I'm about to Move On," she shouted over all the noise. *"What about you two?"* She had the feeling they weren't going to be following her.

"I'm gonna go back, to be with Mary Lynn!" Johnny shouted happily.

"How's that possible?" Doll wanted to know.

"You know the girlfriend Mary Lynn's son told her about, the girl whose family he went to meet over Christmas, in Memphis?" Johnny was grinning wide as ever.

"I don't think I remember that being mentioned," Doll answered bemused.

"There's a grandson on the way, and I think I might be named Jonathon

this time around, too." Johnny gave a wink. *"The other grandmother just happens to be my little sister!"*

"Well, I'll be," was all that Doll could think to say before Johnny crushed her to him in a big hug.

"Bless you Doll," he said in a voice choked with emotion. He let her go and turned to Laurite standing there, hands on hips and grinning so widely that all of her gold teeth shone.

"Come here, you!" To Doll's astonishment, Johnny grabbed hold of Laurite, leaned her back and planted a big, long kiss on her mouth. When he let her back up, it was the first time either of them had seen her look flustered.

She let out a peal of laughter as she straightened the red kerchief on her head and smoothed at her skirt where a red petticoat was showing. *"Oooooh Johnny, you a pretty good kisser! No wonder you get so many girls in trouble!"* A little of her composure returned as she put both her small brown hands on his chest and gave him a gentle shove. *"Get on wid you now."*

Johnny threw back his head and blissfully opened his arms wide. He dissolved into a million tiny sparks of light spinning round and round until they coalesced into an intensely bright, pea-sized sphere, bobbing between Doll and Laurite.

They heard a gleeful, *"Wheeeeeeeeee!"* as it soared upwards into the darkness and disappeared.

The engraved silver lighter clattered to the floor. Laurite picked it up and slipped it into a pouch on a string around her neck, giving it a gentle pat as she dropped it back inside her blouse. *"Dis will come in handy later on,"* she said to Doll with a mysterious smile.

The sound of a familiar, beloved voice turned Doll's attention back to the brightly glowing movie screen. *"Come on Doll,"* the voice happily called out. *"What are you waiting for?"* In the midst of all the light, Doll could make out the form of Herman Junior. His image grew clearer and clearer as she saw him for the first time as his True Self. All the love she had ever wanted flowed out toward her.

With unrestrained joy, Loretta Doll Dumas kicked off her shoes, ran up the steps and dove right into the light. The screen went dark as she vanished. All was quiet again.

Granny Laurite smiled contentedly and turned toward the EXIT sign at the back of the theater. She was going to stay In Between a while longer to keep an eye on things for Rhonelle. She would wait and be here for her granddaughter's Crossing Over. She had promised Rhonelle and was glad to stay true to her word. Laurite walked out the door.

The Moving Theater was now closed.

How Road Signs Became Sculptures that Begat a Novel by Jane F. Hankins

"Fannie Flagg, you have no idea what you have started!" Those were the first words I blurted out when I met the talented actress and author at an event in Blytheville, Arkansas the fall of 2003. I wanted to tell her that reading her novel back in 1987; Fried Green Tomatoes at the Whistle Stop Café had inspired a whole series of sculptures of elderly southern ladies.

In 1992 I entered some of those pieces in a juried show for the National Museum of Women in the Arts and was one of ten artists chosen to represent Arkansas in an exhibit in Washington, DC. The juror, Grace Glueck, art critic for the New York Times, ended up purchasing one of the sculptures because it reminded her of her neighbor's mother. She wisely told me that, "it can be funny and it's still art!" Thus I became serious about making art with a sense of humor.

I proceeded to babble on to Ms Flagg about my latest creations; sculptures of characters inspired by road side signs, and making up little stories about them. Bless her heart, she was very kind – even had a photo taken with me, but I probably came across as a bit much.

I relate this story because there is something about Fannie Flagg that seems to nudge my creativity into totally new territory.

Foremost of all, I am a visual artist working with sculpture and paintings. I have also been at various times an actress, TV pitch person and singer, but never thought I'd be a writer. I can't tell you how many times people have looked at my fantasy paintings and said, "You ought to write a children's book." However, it turned out that my inner Muse had other plans: a full length novel about a group of people living in a south Arkansas trailer park!

In 2000 I did a one woman sculpture show of characters inspired by homemade road signs I saw on car trips between Little Rock and New Orleans.

The first characters that came to mind were Teenie and Mavis Brice when I saw "AKC Toy Poodles and Dog Outfits". (I offer my sincere apologies to the actual persons who put out that sign. No offense intended.). A Curl up and Dye sign begat Shirleen Naither the beautician, and so on. Once I invented the town where they all moved into a local trailer park, the possibilities were limitless. If there can be a Lake Woebegone, Wisconsin and a Tuna, Texas there can be my imaginary town, Peavine Arkansas.

Each of the sculptures came with a one page story about what they did, their connection to the town of Peavine, and a drawing of their trailer. The manager of the park, Loretta Doll Dumas, was the widow of the richest man in town who had moved from her mansion to a lavender doublewide and became friend and benefactor to her community of quirky residents. I gave her a tall dyed black beehive up-do, cat eye glasses, holding a cigarette in one hand and a cold PBR beer in the other.

The art show was a success, especially the refreshments served at the opening reception. I had a table full of junk food delights "catered" by two of the characters – Kristy and Misty, the Party Girls. There wasn't a single Vienna sausage left by the end of the evening!

Over the next three years I kept adding characters to the collection of People of Peavine, and each had their own story. Doll Dumas had become my Muse, riding on my shoulder, whispering tales of her pals. By 2003 I had a collection of short stories, but no idea what to do with them.

Then I met Fannie Flagg.

Three days after Christmas following the Blytheville event, I figured out a way to connect all my character's stories through a single narrative. Doll Dumas was the connector and I now had developed a beginning, middle and end for a plot. I began to build upon that structure much as I would build a sculpture over an armature. My husband was out of town, so I sat in my writing chair for the next four days hand writing an outline, opening and ending to "The Mavens of Madge's Mobile Home Park".

On New Year's Eve, my husband and I attended a party at the local Repertory Theatre. We were talking with the director, Bob Hupp when my husband announced, "Jane's writing a book."

Bob said, "Wonderful! Let's do a reading." He wanted to plan it for the following spring, but fortunately we could wait until later in summer after my daughter's wedding. As if I would have finished it by then... sure I could!

I guess my brave ignorance was a blessing, because I doubt I would ever have had the will or perseverance to write this novel had it not been for committing myself to getting a script ready for the reader's theater production. My gifted talented husband, daughter and son joined me in three sold out performances. Once again, Kristy and Misty's junk food buffet that preceded each show was served and gleefully devoured.

At the time of the reader's theater production I had completed writing the first seven chapters. Hearing the voices of my characters and seeing the positive reactions of the audience gave me the confidence to keep writing.

For the next year, I would take breaks from my studio and go on writer's dates several times a week at Barnes and Noble. I would order my latte and take a seat in the café, careful to position myself facing the New Releases book shelf. I would start writing by hand nonstop for the next hour. Later would come the painstaking chore of transferring what I'd written to typed text documents on my new laptop computer. I must add here that I never took typing in high school preferring drama and choir as electives.

My family joined me again in performing the reader's theater script a year later at my church as a fundraiser for Habitat for Humanity, again to a sellout crowd. By then I had written and typed most of the original novel. So why did it take me six more years to get it published?

For one thing this project was the proverbial red-headed-step-child of my creative endeavors (and I'm not a real redhead by the way). My income is from my visual art, and that's where most of my time and energy was spent. Yet every time I talked about my novel, I'd get so excited I'd get goose bumps. I loved my characters and felt like I was writing down what they told me just as fast as I could.

Doll Dumas was patient as well as persistent. I kept coming back and finally after four versions the novel had grown from a "stranger comes to town" theme to that plus "hero's journey". I also have more than enough characters for a trilogy at the very least!

I decided I needed to find some way to share this story of Doll Dumas and Madge DuClaire and their redemption. After some kind and constructive reject letters from publishers, I decided to post the novel in serial form on my business Face Book page, one chapter at a time. The response was wonderful with close to 900 readers following the story at one point. I was getting close to the last third of the novel, when I got a call from Ted Parkhurst as I was driving my granddaughter home from nursery school. He said a little birdie had told him that I needed a publisher. I sure am glad I took that call, and didn't wreck the car!

So after a summer of more rewrites, I have the fifth and final version of the story of Madge's Mobile Home Park. It's a little different and better than the version I had on Face Book which I had promptly removed after getting my publisher. I also spent my summer working on illustrations and cover art.

One form of art feeds another in my creative world. I listen to music and see an image which tells a story, and it becomes a painting. I see a play or read a book and am compelled to create a sculpture of how I see a character. All my visual artwork is a form of storytelling, so it's not that much of a stretch for my sculpture to tell me so much of a story that I began to write it down. Eventually I ran out of room to write on the back of my sculptures.

That's how Jane the sculptor and painter wrote herself a novel.

As Dorine the waitress in Don's Diner located across from the mobile home park would say," Lordeee Hon, it's about time!"

Q & A with Author
Jane F. Hankins

From an interview with the author by Bo Astor
of KPEW radio station (Peavine, AR 1003.5 AM)

1. **Bo** Why did you choose Peavine and south central Arkansas as the location for your story?

    Jane I needed the Dumas family to have a large enough fortune to attract a gold digger like Madge, and for Doll to inherit enough money to give so much away. Cotton land wasn't enough so I chose an area with oil wells, yet still in Arkansas.

2. **Bo** There is a lot of comedy in this novel. Are you making fun of us?

    Jane No, not at all! I'm not laughing at these people, just laughing near them.

3. **Bo** Do you have family down in this area?

    Jane No, but I do have friends in Pine Bluff who've been great sources of information. Then there's Doll Dumas who feels like family now that I've gotten to know her so well.

4. **Bo** I hear your husband was in radio for 35 years and now does TV news. Can you introduce me to him?

    Jane I'd be delighted to. I think you would find you have a lot in common with him.

5. **Bo** How did you find out all this stuff you wrote about? I've lived here all my life and I never knew those secrets.

    Jane Doll told me most of it, and Teenie Brice was very helpful.

6. **Bo** What do you want people to take away from reading your book?

Jane That redemption can come in the most unexpected ways.

7. **Bo** Well that sounds deep. Do you really believe in ghosts?

 Jane I believe in something beyond this life, but I'm not sure what form it would take. Ghosts are so much fun to write about!

8. **Bo** How does an artist like you become a writer?

 Jane To make a long story short; all my sculptures have their own stories and I ran out of room to write them on the backs of them.

9. **Bo** You mentioned Mr. Brice earlier. If his wife Mavis were to design an outfit for your dog, what would you like it to be?

 Jane I would like a Doll Dumas outfit complete with beehive wig and glasses, but I don't think my fat old doggie would wear it for more than five minutes.

10. **Bo** Have you considered making this book into a stage play or a movie?

 Jane Yes I have! When I was first working on the book, I did a staged reading with my husband and grown children who are all talented actors. It was great fun and the audience seemed to really enjoy it. I can see it as a movie too. (I am very visual.)

11. **Bo** If you made a movie, who would you cast as Doll Dumas?

 Jane If I could have anybody in the world, I would love to see Mary Steenburgen play that role!